Marguerite Kaye writes hot historical romances from her home in cold and usually rainy Scotland, featuring Regency rakes, Highlanders and sheikhs. She has published almost fifty books and novellas. When she's not writing she enjoys walking, cycling (but only on the level), gardening (but only what she can eat) and cooking. She also likes to knit and occasionally drink martinis (though not at the same time). Find out more on her website: margueritekaye.com.

FROM COURTESAN TO CONVENIENT WIFE

Marguerite Kaye

MILLS & BOON

First published in Great Britain 2018 by Mills & Boon, an imprint of HarperCollins*Publishers* 1 London Bridge Street, London, SE1 9GF

Large Print edition 2018

© 2018 Marguerite Kaye

ISBN: 978-0-263-07488-8

MIX
Paper from
responsible sources
FSC® C007454

This book is produced from independently certified FSC™ paper to ensure responsible forest management. For more information visit www.harpercollins.co.uk/green.

Printed and bound in Great Britain by CPI Group (UK) Ltd, Croydon, CR0 4YY

For Paris, City of Light, city of romance, and my favourite city in the world.

Je t'adore.

Prologue

London—May 1818

The house that was her destination was located on Upper Wimpole Street, on the very edge of what was considered to be respectable London. The woman known as The Procurer stepped down lightly from her barouche, ordering her coachman to wait until she had successfully secured entry, then to return for her in an hour. An hour, The Procurer knew from experience, was more than sufficient time to conclude her unique business. One way or another.

Number Fourteen was situated at the far end of the terrace. A shallow flight of steps led to the front door, but the entrance to the basement she sought was around the corner, on Devonshire Street. The Procurer descended the steep stairs cautiously. Despite the bright sunshine of the late spring morning, it was cool down here, dank and gloomy. The curtains were pulled tight over the single, dirty window. A fleck of paint fell from the door when she let the rusty knocker fall.

There was no reply. She rapped again, her eyes on the window, and was rewarded with the ripple of a curtain as the person behind it tried to peer out at her unobserved. She stood calmly, allowing herself to be surveyed, sadly accustomed to the reticence of the women she sought out to welcome unsolicited visitors. The reasons were manifold, but fear lay at the root of all of them.

The Procurer offered an escape route from their tribulations to those women whose particular skills or traits suited her current requirements. The exclusive temporary contracts she offered provided those who satisfied her criteria with the funds to make a fresh start, though what form that would take was always entirely up to them. The unique business she had established was very lucrative and satisfying too, on the whole, though there were occasions when The Procurer despaired of the tiny impact her altruism had, when set against the myriad injustices the world perpetrated against women. Today, however, she was in a positive mood. A new client, another extraordinary request to test her reputation for making the impossible possible. She had heard of Lady Sophia Acton's spectacular fall from grace and had wondered, at the time, what had been the cause of it. Now, thanks to her spider's web of contacts, she understood only too well. Her heart was touched—as much as that frozen organ could be, that is.

The Procurer gave a little nod to herself. She could not, she thought wryly, have designed a more appropriate task for the woman if she tried. Who had by now, she judged, had more than sufficient time to decide that her visitor was neither her landlady come to evict her, nor a lady of another sort come to harass her. It was time for Lady Sophia Acton to come out of hiding and return to the world. Albeit a very different one from that which she had previously inhabited.

The Procurer rapped on the door again, and this time her patience was rewarded, as she had known it would be. The woman who answered was tall and willowy, dressed in an outmoded gown of faded worsted which might originally have been either grey, blue or brown, and which was far too warm for the season. Her silver-blonde hair was fixed in a careless knot on top of her head from which long, wispy tendrils had escaped, framing her heart-shaped face. The wide-spaced eyes under her perfectly arched brows were extraordinary: almond-shaped, dark-lashed, the colour of lapis lazuli. There were dark shadows beneath them, and her skin had the fragility of one who slept little, but none the less Lady Sophia Acton was one of the most beautiful women The Procurer had ever encountered. It was an ethereal beauty, the type which would bring out the protective nature in some men, though more often than not, she thought darkly, the fine line between protection and exploitation would easily be crossed. Men would assume that Lady Sophia Acton's fragile appearance equated to a fragile mind. Meeting the woman's steady gaze, The Procurer thought very much otherwise.

'Who are you? What do you want?'

The questions were perfunctory, the tone brusque. Lady Sophia had no time for social niceties, which suited The Procurer very well.

She insinuated herself through the narrow opening, closing the door firmly behind her. 'They call me The Procurer,' she said. 'And I want to put a business proposition to you.'

Sophia stared at the intruder in astonishment. *This* elegant, sophisticated woman was the elusive Procurer?

'You are thinking that I look nothing like the creature of your imagination,' her uninvited guest said. 'Or perhaps I flatter myself. Perhaps you have not heard of me?'

'I doubt there is anyone in London who has not heard of you, though how many have had the honour of making your acquaintance is a another matter. Your reputation for clandestine dealings goes before you.'

'More of the great and the good use my services than you might imagine, or they would care to admit. Discretion, however, is what I insist upon above all. Whatever the outcome of our meeting today, Lady Sophia, I must have your promise that you will never talk of it.'

Sophia laughed at this. 'Madam, you must be aware, for since you know my name you must also know of my notoriety, that there is no one who would listen even if I did. Those with a reputation to guard will cross the street to avoid me, while those who wish to further tarnish my reputation have no interest in my opinions on any subject.'

As she spoke, she led her visitor into the single room which had been her home for the last three weeks. The fourth home she had occupied in the months since her return from France, each one smaller, dingier and less genteel than the preceding one. It was only a matter of time before she was expelled from her current abode, for London, despite being a big city was in reality a small place, and London's respectable landladies were even smaller-minded.

'I am afraid that my accommodation does not run to a parlour,' Sophia said, drawing out one of her two wooden chairs. 'A woman in my position, it seems, has no right to comfort.'

'No.' The Procurer took the seat, pulling off her kid gloves and untying the ribbon of her poke bonnet. 'A woman in your position, Lady Sophia, has very few options. I take it, from your humble surroundings, that you have decided against the obvious solution to your penury?'

'You do not mince your words,' Sophia replied, irked to feel her cheeks heating.

'I find that it is better to be blunt, when conducting my business,' The Procurer replied with a slight smile. 'That way there is no room for misconceptions.'

Sophia took her own seat opposite. 'Very well then, I will tell you that your assumption is correct. I have decided—I am determined—not to avail myself of the many lucrative offers I have received since my return to London. I was forced into that particular occupation for one very important reason. That reason…'

Despite herself, her throat constricted. Under the table, she curled her hands into fists. She swallowed hard. 'That reason no longer exists. Therefore I will never—*never*—demean myself in that manner again, no matter how straitened my circumstances. So if you have come here in order to plead some man's cause, then I'm afraid your journey has been a wasted one.'

Tears burned in her eyes, yet Sophia met her visitor's gaze, defying her to offer sympathy.

The Procurer merely nodded, looking thoughtful. 'I have come here to plead on behalf of a man, but my proposal is not what you imagine. The services he requires of you are not of that nature. To be clear, you would be required to put on a performance, but quite explicitly not in the bedchamber. The role is a taxing one, but I think you will be perfect for it.'

Sophia laughed bitterly. 'I am certainly adept at acting. The entire duration of my last— engagement—was a performance, nothing more.'

'Something we have in common. I too have earned a living from performing. The Procurer you see before you is a façade, a persona I have been forced to adopt.'

Which remark begged any number of questions. Sophia, however, hesitated. There was empathy in the woman's expression—but also a clear warning that some things were better left unspoken. Locking such things away in the dark recesses of memory, never to be exposed to scrutiny, was the best way to deal with them, as she knew only too well. Sophia uncurled her fists, clasping her hands together on the table. 'I will be honest with you, Madam, and trust that your reputation for discretion is well earned. A woman in my position has, as you have pointed out, very few options, and even fewer resources. I do not know in what capacity I can be of service to you, but if I can do so without compromising what is left of my honour, then I will gladly consider your offer.'

Once again, The Procurer gave a little nod, though whether it was because she was satisfied with Sophia's answer, or because Sophia had answered as she expected, there could be no telling. 'What I can tell you is that the monetary reward for the fulfilment of your contract, should you choose to accept the commission, would be more than sufficient to secure your future, whatever form that might take.'

'Frankly, I have no idea. At present, my only future plans are to survive day to day.' But oh, Sophia thought, how much she would like to be able to discover for herself what the future might hold. Six months ago, bereft and utterly alone, raw with grief, she had been so low that she had no thought at all for the future. But life went on, and as it proceeded and her meagre funds dwindled, Sophia had not been able to look beyond the next month, the next week, the next day. Now, it seemed that a miracle might just be about to happen. The Procurer, that patroness of fallen women, was sitting opposite her and offering her a chance of redemption. 'I have no idea what the future holds,' Sophia repeated, with a slow smile, 'but I do know that I want it, and that whatever it is, I want it to belong to me, and to no one else.'

'Something else we have in common, then, Lady Sophia.' This time The Procurer's smile was warm. She reached over to touch Sophia's hand. 'I am aware of your circumstances, my dear, including the reason you were compelled to act as you did. You do not deserve to have paid such a high price, but sadly that is the way of our world. I cannot change that, but I do believe we can be of mutual benefit to each other. You do understand,' she added, resuming her business-like tone, 'that I am not offering you charity?'

'And I am certain that you understand, for you seem to have investigated my background thoroughly, that I would not accept charity even if it was offered,' Sophia retorted.

'Then indeed, we understand each other very well.'

'Not quite *that* well, Madam. I am as yet completely in the dark regarding this role you think me so perfectly suited for. What is it that you require me to do?'

But The Procurer held up her hand. 'A few non-negotiable ground rules first, Lady Sophia. I will guarantee you complete anonymity. My client has no right to know your personal history other than that which is pertinent to the assignment or which you yourself choose to divulge. In return, you will give him your unswerving loyalty. We will discuss your terms shortly, but you must know that you will be paid only upon successful completion of your assignment. Half-measures will not be rewarded. If you leave before the task is completed, you will return to England without remuneration.'

'Return to England?' Sophia repeated, somewhat dazed. 'You require me to travel abroad?'

'All in good time. I must have your word, Lady Sophia.'

'You have it, Madam, rest assured. Now, will

you put me out of my misery and explain what it is that is required of me and who this mysterious client of yours is.'

Chapter One

Paris—ten days later

The carriage which had transported Sophia all the way from Calais drew to a halt in front of a stone portal surmounted by a pediment on which carved lions' heads roared imperiously. The gateway's huge double doors were closed. Was this her final destination? They had passed through one of the entrance gates to the city some time ago, following the course of the bustling River Seine, which allowed her to catch a glimpse of the imposing edifice which she assumed was Notre Dame cathedral. Despite this, Sophia still couldn't quite believe she was actually here, in Paris.

The days since her momentous meeting with The Procurer had passed in a blur of activity as her papers were organised, her travel arrangements confirmed, and her packing completed. Not that she'd had much packing to do. The costumes required for her to carry out her new duties would be provided by the man who presumably awaited her on the other side of those doors. The man to whom she was bound for the duration of the contract. The shudder of revulsion was instinctive and quickly repressed. This contract was a world away from the last, less formal and much more distasteful, one she had reluctantly entered into to, she reminded herself. The Procurer had promised her that her stipulated terms would be honoured. Though she must do his bidding in public, this man had no right to any part of her, mind or body, in private. So it was not the same. This man was not Sir Richard Hopkins. The services he was paying for were radically different in nature. And when it was over, she would be truly free for the first time in her life.

The butterflies which had been slowly building in her stomach from early this morning, when she had quit the last of the posting houses to embark on the final leg of her journey, began to flutter wildly as Sophia saw the huge doors swing inward and one of the grooms opened the carriage door and folded down the steps. Gathering up the folds of her travelling gown she descended, glad of his steadying hand, for her nervous anticipation was palpable.

'*Monsieur* awaits you, *madame*,' the servant informed her.

'*Merci,*' Sophia replied, summoning up what she hoped was an appropriately eager smile, thanking the man in his own language for taking care of her during the journey. The servant bowed. She heard the carriage door slam, the clop of the horses' hooves on the cobblestones as it headed for the stables.

Bracing herself, Sophia prepared to make her entrance. The *hôtel particulier* which she assumed was to be her temporary home was beautiful. Built around the courtyard in which she now stood, there were three wings, each with the steeply pitched roof and tall windows in the French baroque style, the walls softened with a cladding of ivy. The courtyard was laid out with two parterres of box hedging cut into an elaborate swirling design which, seen from above, she suspected, would form some sort of crest. The main entrance to the *hôtel* was on her left-hand side. At the top of a set of shallow steps, the open doorway was guarded by a winged marble statue. And standing beside the statue, a man.

Late afternoon sunlight glinted down, dazzling her eyes. She had the absurd idea that as long as she stood rooted to the spot, time would stand still. Just long enough for her to quell her fears, which were hardly unjustified, given her experience. Men wanted but one thing from her. Despite The Procurer's promises and reassurances, until she could determine for herself that this man was different and posed no threat to her, she would, quite rightly, be on her guard.

Though she must not appear so. Sophia steeled herself. The future, as she had discovered to her cost, did not take care of itself. This was her chance to forge her own. Though she had assumed her new persona in Calais, now she must play it in earnest. She had coped with much worse, performed a far more taxing role. She could do this! Fixing a demure smile on her face for the benefit of anyone watching from the myriad of windows, she made her way across the paved courtyard.

The man she approached was tall, sombrely dressed, the plain clothes drawing attention to an impressive physique. Black hair. Very tanned skin. Younger than she had anticipated for a man so ostentatiously wealthy, no more than thirty-five, perhaps less. As she reached the bottom of the steps, he smiled, and Sophia faltered. He was a veritable Adonis. She felt her skin prickle with heat, an unfamiliar sensation which she attributed to nerves, as he descended to greet her.

Jean-Luc Bauduin, The Procurer's client and the reason she was here, took her hand, making a show of raising it to his lips, though he kissed the air above her fingertips. 'You have arrived at last,' he said in softly accented English. 'You can have no idea how eagerly I have been anticipating your arrival. Welcome to Paris, Madame Bauduin. It is a relief beyond words to finally meet my new wife.'

Jean-Luc led the Englishwoman through the tall doors opening on to the terrace, straight into the privacy of the morning room. 'We may speak freely here,' he informed her. 'Tomorrow, we will play out the charade of formal introductions to the household. For now, I think it would be prudent for us to become a little better acquainted, given that you are supposed to be my beloved wife.' Thinking that it would take a while to accustom himself to this bizarre notion, he motioned for her to take a seat. 'You must be tired after your long journey. Will you take some tea?'

Though he spoke in English, she answered him in perfect French. 'Thank you, it has indeed been a long day, that would be delightful.'

'Your command of our language is an unexpected bonus,' Jean-Luc said, 'but when we are alone, I am happy to converse in yours.'

'You certainly speak it fluently, if I may return the compliment,' she said, removing her bonnet and gloves.

'I am required to visit London frequently on matters of business.'

The service was already set out on the table before her, the silver kettle boiling on the spirit stove. His wife—*mon Dieu*, the woman who was to play his wife!—set about the ritual which the

English were so fond of with alacrity, clearly eager to imbibe. In this one assumption, at least, he had been correct.

Jean-Luc took his seat opposite, studying her as she busied herself making tea. Despite the flurry of communications he'd had with The Procurer, there was a part of him that had not believed the woman would be able to deliver someone who perfectly matched his precise requirements, yet here was the living, breathing proof that she had. In fact, in appearance at least, the candidate she had selected had wildly exceeded his expectations. Not that her allure was the salient factor. Finally, after all these weeks of uncertainty and creeping doubt, he could act. Recent events had threatened to turn his world upside down. Now, he could set it to rights again, and the arrival of this woman, his faux wife, was the first significant step in his plan.

Her name was Sophia, one of the few facts The Procurer had shared with him. Of her origins, her life, past or present, he knew nothing. His request had been for a woman whom the society in which he moved would accept as his wife without question, a woman he could credibly have fallen deeply in love with, enough to cast caution to the winds and marry post-haste. His request had been more than satisfied. The woman The Procurer had sent him was the answer to prayers he hadn't even said.

He had assumed she would be an actress, but looking at her he found it difficult to believe, though he could not say why. Her beauty was quite dazzling, but it was fragile, sylph-like, ethereal, with none of the overblown showiness required to tread the boards. She was slim as a wand, and looked as if she could slip through rain, as the saying went. Her hair seemed almost silver in the glare of the sunlight behind her, her skin almost translucent, her lips soft pink. But it was her eyes which drew the attention, an extraordinary shade of blue, like the Mediterranean in the south, though he would not call it turquoise or cornflower or even azure. He had never seen such a colour.

To his embarrassment, Jean-Luc felt the first stirrings of desire. It had not occurred to him that he would find the woman he had come to think of as his shield attractive. Her stipulation that there should be absolutely no physical intimacy between them had surprised him. His expectations of the role his wife would play most certainly did not extend to his bed, but on reflection, he thought it wise of her to clarify a matter which could easily be open to misinterpretation, and had agreed without hesitation. Though he did not doubt his ability to honour his promise, he wished that The Procurer had not sent him a woman who was the perfect embodiment of desire—or of his desires, at any rate. He did not wish to be sidetracked by passion, even if it was destined to remain utterly unrequited. He could only hope that the amount of time they would be forced to spend in one another's company would cure him of such inopportune thoughts. What mattered was not what she was, or what effect she had on him, but what she appeared to be to everyone else.

Accepting the Sèvres cup of tea reluctantly, Jean-Luc's fingers brushed hers. She was icy cold. She had flinched, out there in the courtyard, when he had affected to kiss her hand, though she had tried to conceal it. She was nervous, he expected. Well, so too was he. There was a great deal riding on her arrival.

On her wedding finger, she wore the simple gold band he had asked The Procurer to purchase on his behalf. She sipped her tea delicately. There was a poised refinement in her manner, that made him wonder if her birth was numerous rungs up the pedigree ladder from his own. But why would a gently born and raised female agree to play a French wine merchant's wife? An intriguing question, though one he had no time to pursue. Whatever her origins, what mattered was that she was here, allowing him to establish his own. The Procurer had chosen well, as he would expect, given her reputation and the large fee she had demanded. A fee he'd happily pay twice, thrice over, if this masquerade of theirs proved effective.

Unthinking, Jean-Luc took a sip of the dishwater so beloved of the English, and immediately set the cup down with an exclamation of distaste. 'So, *madame*,' he said, 'to business. Perhaps we could begin with what it is you know of the task which lies ahead of you?'

Sophia set the delicate Sèvres cup down carefully. Despite the tea, her mouth was dry, her heart thudding. To business, he had said, the identical cold phrase that Hopkins had used. But this time she was no ingénue. She cleared her throat. 'Before we start, Monsieur Bauduin...'

'Before we start, *madame*, I think we should agree to address one another less formally. We are, in the eyes of the world at least, married. My name is Jean-Luc. I would ask that you use it.'

'Jean-Luc. Yes, I am aware. And I am Sophia.'

'Of that I am also aware, though I know no more.'

He waited, one brow slightly raised. His eyes were a very dark brown, the lashes long, thick and black. One could not describe a man's eyes as beautiful, and in any case, this man was too— too masculine. His jaw was very square. There was a permanent furrow between his brows. Not an Adonis, she had been mistaken to label him that, and not handsome either, if one took Lord Byron's classic perfection as an example. This man who was to be her husband for the time being was not at all like Byron or Adonis or any other model of perfection, but in another mould altogether. Memorable. A vibrant presence one could not ignore. If one was inclined to find a man attractive, then this was undoubtedly such a man. But she was not so inclined. Nor was she about to satisfy his curiosity about her surname either, especially since he was a regular visitor to London. So she met his gaze blankly and said nothing. She was good at that.

'Simply Sophia it is, then,' he said eventually, with a casual shrug that might have been defeat, or more likely indifference. 'Will you at least deign to tell me, Simply Sophia, what The Procurer told you of this assignment?'

Was he teasing her or mocking her? She couldn't decide, and so decided not to care, which was always the safest thing to do. 'I was told very little,' Sophia replied stiffly. 'Merely that you require me to play the part of your wife, and that I must convince everyone that it has been a love match. The reasons for my presence here, and my duties, she said would be explained by your good self, as would be the terms upon which our contract is to be deemed complete. In short, she was not forthcoming at all, though she assured me that you had disclosed all to her, and that she believed me to be an excellent match for your requirements.'

'Her reputation for discretion appears to be well founded.' Jean-Luc twisted the heavy signet ring he wore on his right hand around his finger. 'It is ironic, that I must explain myself to you, while you are not obliged to tell me anything about yourself. Not even your surname.'

Ironic, and very convenient for her, but, judging by the tension around his mouth, extremely inconvenient for him. Why did a man like this— rich, confident, successful and, yes, Sophia could admit it to herself, extremely attractive—need to *pay* a complete stranger to act as his wife?

He was still eyeing her expectantly, waiting for her to fill the silence with the answer to his implied question. Sophia kept her expression carefully neutral. 'If I am to fulfil my role convincingly, then, painful as it may be to explain yourself to a complete stranger, it seems you must.' And painful as it might be, she must first ensure that her own terms were clearly understood. 'Though before we proceed, I would like to discuss the conditions which I stipulated.'

'I am not sure what there is to discuss,' Jean-Luc answered. 'I accepted them, as you must know, else you would not be here.'

Sophia smiled tightly. 'In principle, yes. But I find it is best to be crystal-clear about the detail.'

His brows shot up. 'You find? You have entered into contracts such as this previously?'

'I have never before entered into an arrangement such as this one,' she said stiffly, which was after all the truth, but he need not know the precise nature of her previous *arrangements.* 'What I meant was, that I find it is—I think it would be best for us both to be absolutely clear, before we start, as to the extent of our—our intimacies.' Sophia squirmed inwardly. She sounded like a prude. 'If I am to play your wife, I presume it is for the benefit of an audience, and that therefore there will be some displays of affection required? I would be obliged if you could explain in plain terms what form you anticipate those taking.'

'I confess, I had not thought so specifically— but you are right, it is best to be clear.' Jean-Luc stared down at his signet ring. 'Very well, in plain terms then, our marriage will be for public consumption only. In private, you have my word of honour that I will make no physical demands upon you of any sort. For the sake of appearances, in public and in front of my servants, our "intimacies", as you refer to them, will be confined to only those acts which can be performed in public with propriety. Do you wish me to be any plainer or is that sufficient?'

'It is more than sufficient.' And an enormous relief. Some of the tension in her shoulders eased. Her instincts told her that she could trust him to keep his word, though her instincts had proven to be fallible in the past. Disastrously so. 'You understand that any breach of these terms would render our contract null and void? Not only would I leave immediately, but you…'

'I would be obliged to recompense you with the full amount. I am aware. I have already given you my word that I will not breach the terms, Sophia, I'm not sure what else I can do to reassure you, save to tell you that my reasons for bringing you here in the first place are, *en effet*, life-changing. This charade of ours must succeed. I have no intentions of doing anything to endanger it. You understand?'

'I do.' A little more of the tension eased. She allowed herself a small smile. 'And I can assure you, *monsieur*—Jean-Luc—that I will also do all I can to ensure that our charade does succeed.'

'*Eh, bien*, then I trust that is an end to the matter?'

'Thank you, yes.'

He returned her smile, but only in a perfunctory way. 'You must understand though, Sophia, that it is vital that we are convincing? I do not expect you to make love to me, but I do expect you to appear as if you wish to, or better still as if you just have.'

'Of course.' She could feel the slashes of colour stain her cheeks. It was mortifying to discover that even after all she had been forced to endure, her sensibilities could still be so obviously inflamed. It would be considerably easier than she had expected to spend time in his company. It might even be—no, it was too much of an exaggeration to say enjoyable, but it would be no hardship. 'Though I'm still not at all clear,' Sophia said, flustered by her thoughts, 'as to why you need a wife? And why must it be a love match?'

'Oh, as to that, it is quite simple. Love,' Jean-Luc said with a wry smile, 'is the only credible explanation for the suddenness of our union, and the suddenness of our union will come as a great surprise to all who know me.' He frowned, choosing his words with care. 'It is not that I am against marriage. It is an institution I have always planned to embrace at some point in the future, but for the time being, it is well known that I am effectively married to my business. Ironically, my passion for my business has largely been responsible for my success, which in turn means that I am rather inconveniently considered a much sought-after marital prize.'

His tone made his thoughts on this state of affairs clear. 'Yet you have so far evaded capture,' Sophia said. 'I cannot believe that you have employed me in order to ensure that you continue to do so. You do not strike me as a man who could be persuaded to do anything against his will.'

'Not so Simple Sophia after all,' Jean-Luc said, smiling. 'You are quite right. It is precisely because I will not have my hand forced that you are here.'

'Good heavens,' she exclaimed, startled, for she had spoken mostly in jest. 'You can't possibly mean that you are being forced to marry someone against your will?'

His smile became a sneer. 'There is indeed a woman attempting to do exactly that. Whether she is a charlatan or simply deluded I cannot decide, but whichever it is, she is doomed to failure. I intend to prove to her that her various claims are utterly without foundation. Producing you as proof that I am already married is just my first salvo across her bows.'

Sophia was gazing up at him, her extraordinary blue eyes wide with astonishment. 'I don't understand. One cannot be *forced* into marriage, not even when—not ever,' she said, hastily amending whatever it was she had been about to disclose. 'This woman, she can hardly hold a gun to your head and force you to take her hand in marriage.'

'But she does have a gun, and she has been holding it at my head since April.' Jean-Luc laughed grimly. 'It is loaded, she thinks, with a silver bullet which will be the answer to all her problems. You are the armour I need to deflect that bullet'

Sophia shook her head in þewilderment. 'I still don't understand. Why not simply tell her that you won't marry her?'

'Because it is not that simple. I'm sorry, I have been living and breathing this farce for so long, and now you are here, I am so eager to put my plans into action that I forget you know nothing of them.'

She smiled, her first genuine smile, and it quite dazzled him. 'Let me reassure you, I am just as eager as you are to begin. So why don't you tell me more about this woman who wishes to be your wife. Starting with her name, perhaps?'

'Haven't I told you?' Jean-Luc rolled his eyes. 'Juliette de Cressy is her name, and she turned up, quite unannounced on my doorstep six weeks ago. Until that point I had never heard of her.'

Sophia wrinkled her brow. 'But if she was a complete stranger, why did you grant her an audience?'

'One of the many things which makes me ambivalent about Mademoiselle de Cressy is that she appears, on first inspection, to be eminently respectable. She called with a maid in tow. She had a visiting card. I have an enquiring mind and was intrigued enough to hear what she had to say. When I did, my immediate reaction was simply to dismiss her tale out of hand. In a bid to take the wind out of her sails I told her that she was wasting her time, as I was already married.'

'I take it she didn't believe you? Hardly surprising, considering what you have more or less confessed to being known as a dedicated bachelor.'

'Yes, but it was more than disbelief. She was—I don't know, it is difficult to explain. At first she was quite distraught, but she very quickly recovered. That is when she produced the legal documents—her silver bullet—which she believed would substantiate her claim. And that is when I realised she was not, as I had assumed, simply a brazen and audacious opportunist who would be put off by the threat of an invisible wife. It wasn't only that she didn't believe I was married, you see, it was that she was extremely convincing in the strength of her own case. Of course, the chances were still high that she was an extremely convincing charlatan, but…'

'It occurred to you that she might simply be, as you said, deluded.'

'Yes, that is it. Either way, it was clear that she was not going to go away.'

'And you were faced with the problem of admitting that you had lied when you said you were already married, or coming up with the evidence to back up your fiction.'

'Precisely, though I did not immediately rush to The Procurer for help. My next step was to test her resolve by telling her that I wished my lawyer to examine the papers she had to support her claim. She handed them over willingly, informing me that she had expected no less. It was clear she had faith in their authenticity, and equally clear that it had not occurred to her that I might simply destroy them.'

'Any more than it would have occurred to you, I assume?'

'You assume correctly.'

'That is reassuring,' Sophia said, with an odd little smile. 'So, Mademoiselle de Cressy's seemingly innocent trust in you was, then, another point in her favour?'

'It was.'

'And the documents, whatever they are?'

Jean-Luc rolled his eyes. 'Most likely genuine.'

'So you hired me to prove to Mademoiselle de Cressy that regardless of these documents she has, she is, as we say in England, barking up the wrong tree? You cannot marry her, because you are already married?' Sophia frowned down at her hands. 'You have gone to a great deal of trouble and expense to call this woman's bluff. Couldn't you simply have paid her off?'

'I offered to do just that, to make the problem go away, but she refused. She said she wanted what was rightfully hers, not blood money. As you will have realised by now,' Jean-Luc continued, 'the matter is complicated, and I am aware that you have only just arrived. You have not even seen your room.'

He sat at an angle to her, his long legs tucked under the sofa, which had the effect of stretching his pantaloons tight over his muscled thighs. He might not look like an Adonis, but his build was reminiscent of one. His physical proximity made Sophia uncomfortable. Not unsafe, she was surprised to notice, but—odd. Her pulses were fluttering. It was because he was so close, a warning sign, she supposed, though she felt no inclination to move. 'All in good time. I take it your plan is to introduce me to Mademoiselle de Cressy sooner rather than later?'

'All in good time,' he answered, smiling. 'My plan for what remains of today is to allow you time to rest and recover from your journey. There is a good deal more to this tale, but it can wait.'

Jean-Luc took her hands between his, a light clasp from which she could easily escape, which meant she had no need to. 'I will have them bring you dinner in your room, and water for a hot bath, if you wish?'

Sophia couldn't imagine anything nicer. His thoughtfulness touched her. It had been so long since anyone had thought of her comfort, for in the end even Felicity...

'That would be perfect,' she said, desperately trying not to let fall the tears which suddenly stung her eyes. 'I think I am a little fatigued after all. *Merci*, Jean-Luc.'

'It is my pleasure, Sophia.' He pressed her hands. Then he let her go.

Chapter Two

Jean-Luc was in his working in his office the next morning when his new wife appeared, looking much refreshed.

'May I come in?' Sophia asked. 'The footman told me that you don't like to be disturbed, but I thought...'

He jumped to his feet to pull out a chair for her. 'Remember that you are my wife, as far as the footman and every other servant is concerned. This is your household to command. In any event, you are not disturbing me. I am far too distracted to work, thanks to you. Are you rested?'

'Fully.' She took the seat he indicated, opposite him, but moved it forward, so that she could rest her hands on the desk which separated them.

'Before you relate the rest of your story, I think it only fair that I reassure you, since you were so patient in reassuring me yesterday.'

'Reassure me about what?'

She smiled at him faintly. 'You said that your reasons for bringing me here were life-changing. I should tell you that my reasons for agreeing to come are also life-changing. Coming to Paris, taking on this role, contract, commission, I'm not sure what to call it—this false marriage of ours, if I make a success of it, and I am determined to do just that, the money I will earn will allow me to quite literally change my life.' She bit her lip, considering her words carefully. 'I will be free. Free to make my own way in the world, on my own terms. For the first time in my twenty-six years I will be able to live only to suit myself, to finally discover what it is I like, what I want, what makes me happy. So you see, the stakes are too high for me to fail. You can have no idea how much that means to me. I won't let you down.'

There was a sparkle in her eyes, a tinge of colour that was not embarrassment in her cheeks, giving him a tantalising glimpse of the woman she could be, or would be, if she achieved her goal. He had thought her beautiful before, but seeing her like this, she positively glowed. 'I can see for myself how much it means,' Jean-Luc said, quite beguiled. 'Thank you. May I say that I can think of no one I would rather pretend to be married to than you.'

She laughed. 'We have not even been married two days. I will be more flattered if you still think so in a week's time.'

'Actually, as far as the world is concerned, we have been married since March. But I get ahead of myself. Are you comfortable? Because the tale I'm about to relay is long and convoluted.'

'I don't know what to say,' Sophia said some time later. 'I am utterly confounded. Juliette de Cressy not only claims that you are contracted to marry her, but that you are a duke!'

'Of all the preposterous things this woman alleges, the lunatic notion that I might be the long-lost son of an aristocrat who went to the guillotine—' Jean-Luc broke off, shaking his head. 'Me! It is simply ridiculous.'

'You know, most men would be both delighted

and flattered to be informed they were of noble birth.'

'Even if it means disowning the parents who raised them, who loved them and who tried to give them the best life possible in difficult circumstances? No.' His mouth firmed. 'I know who I am. My father—yes there were times when we did not agree, when I thought that he did not care for me, that he—he somehow resented me, but that is normal, for a father and a son, as one grows older, and the other stronger.'

'I can imagine it would have been normal for you. I expect you were very sure of yourself, even as a boy.'

Jean-Luc laughed. 'What was your upbringing like? No, you need not answer,' he added hurriedly, 'I did not mean to pry.'

Sophia hesitated. She was under no obligation to tell him anything, but it seemed wrong to shut him out completely when he had just confided so much to her. 'My relationship with my father was difficult. He wanted a son. As a female, I was of limited use to him.'

'But you knew he cared for you?'

She knew he had not. 'I never doubted he was my father,' Sophia said, unwilling to lie.

'You refer to him in the past tense.'

'He died four years ago. My mother many years earlier. To return to the matter in hand,' she said hurriedly, 'are you saying that, thanks to Mademoiselle de Cressy, you are doubting your own parentage?'

'*Mon Dieu,* no! The difficulties I spoke of were a long time ago. My father was very proud of my success. He told me not long before he died, ten years ago, just nine months after Maman, that he could not have asked for a better son.' Jean-Luc's hand tightened around the quill he had been fidgeting with. 'For my father, that was quite an admission, believe me.'

'More than I ever got,' Sophia said with feeling. 'My father never missed an opportunity to tell me that he had never wished for a daughter of any sort, never mind...' *Two.* The pain took her by surprise, making her catch her breath. All too aware of Jean-Luc's perceptive gaze on her, she took a firm grip of herself. 'Never mind my father,' she amended lamely. 'We were talking of yours.'

He waited, just long enough to make it clear he knew she was changing the subject, then set down his quill. 'My father, Robert Bauduin, you mean, and not the Duc de Montendre.'

'Indeed. May I ask how you plan to prove your heritage? I'm assuming that you doubt a simple introduction to me will send Mademoiselle de Cressy running for the hills. That you require me to be by your side to maintain the façade, in order to buy yourself the time you need to gather the evidence to quash her claim completely?'

'Ah, you do understand.'

'But of course. If a wife does not understand her husband, then she is a poor spouse indeed,' Sophia quipped.

Jean-Luc smiled, albeit faintly. 'I must confess, I'm concerned as to how she will react when she does meet you. To date, she has quite simply re-fused to accept that I have a wife.'

'Then we must hope that she does not try to eliminate me—an outcome not at all unlikely in the context of this tale, which is worthy of Shakespeare himself.'

'Or perhaps more appropriately, Molière,' Jean-Luc said drily, 'for it has all the hallmarks of a farce. It is, to say the least, inconvenient that the agent which Maxime—Maxime Sainte-Juste, my lawyer, that is—sent to Cognac to retrieve documentary evidence of my birth, came back empty-handed.'

Sophia wrinkled her nose. 'You don't find it odd that he couldn't locate the certificate of your baptism?'

Jean-Luc shrugged. 'I was surprised, I had assumed that I was born in Cognac, and my parents had always lived there but they must have moved to that town when I was very young. I was born in 1788. It was a time when there was much unrest in the country, crops failing, the conditions which resulted in the Revolution. There could have been any number of reasons for my parents to have relocated.'

'What about your grandparents then? You must know where they lived.'

'I don't. I never knew them, and have always assumed they died before I was born, or when I was too young to remember them.'

'But there must have been other relatives, surely? Cousins, aunts, uncles?'

'No one.' Jean-Luc twisted his signet ring

around his finger, looking deeply uncomfortable. 'When you put it like that, it sounds odd that I never questioned my parents when they were alive, never even noticed my lack of any relatives at all when I was growing up.'

'But why would you? Your parents are your parents, your family is your family.'

'Yes, but most people *have* a family,' he said ruefully. 'It seems I did not, though of course I must have relatives somewhere. Unfortunately, I have no idea where I would even begin to look in order to locate them.'

'What about family friends, then?'

But once more, Jean-Luc shook his head. 'None who knew my parents before I was born. You're thinking that is ridiculous, aren't you? You are thinking, there must be someone!'

'I am thinking that it is extremely awkward for you that there is no one.'

'Extremely awkward, and a little embarrassing, and very frustrating,' he confessed. 'I cannot prove who I am. More to the point,' he added, his expression hardening, 'I cannot prove to Mademoiselle de Cressy who I am, which means that…'

'You must prove that you are not who she says you are, the long-lost son of the fourth Duc de Montendre.'

'*Exactement.*' Jean-Luc grimaced. 'Unfortunately, not as straightforward a task as you might imagine. I have, however, made a start on testing the veracity of Mademoiselle de Cressy's documents. Unlike me, she does have a baptism certificate. Maxime's agent has been despatched to Switzerland to check it against the relevant parish records. If it proves to be legitimate, then his next task will be to attempt to obtain a description of Juliette de Cressy. As the only child of the recently deceased Comte de Cressy, there must be someone in the neighbourhood where she says she lived for all her twenty-two years who can shed some light on her.'

'So she was born after her parents left Paris?'

'If her parents were the Comte and Comtesse de Cressy—who were, incidentally, real people, that too I have established—then she was born six years after they arrived in Switzerland, fleeing Paris in the days when it was still possible to do so, before The Terror.'

'And the marriage contract, it was written when?'

'It is dated 1789, the year of the Revolution, and one year after I was born—not that that has anything to do with it.' With an exclamation of impatience, Jean-Luc got to his feet, prowling restlessly over to the window to perch on the narrow seat in the embrasure, his long legs stretched in front of him. 'The marriage contract appears to be signed by the sixth Comte de Cressy and the fourth Duc de Montendre. It stipulates a match between the Duc de Montendre's eldest son, whose long list of names does not include mine, and any future first-born daughter of the Comte de Cressy.'

'And this fourth Duc de Montendre was killed during the Terror?'

'As was the Duchess, some time in 1794. This much Maxime has been able to discover, though the circumstances—there are so few records remaining, so much has been destroyed. It may be that the witnesses to the contract also—if they were loyal servants...'

'They too may have gone to the guillotine?'

'Like so many others. The final months of

the Terror following the Revolution saw mass slaughter, so many heads lost for no reason. Maxime thinks that trying to prove Mademoiselle de Cressy wrong could turn into a wild goose chase.'

'A whole flock of geese, by the sound of it. It sounds daunting in the extreme.'

Jean-Luc grinned. 'There is no finer lawyer than Maxime, and no better friend, but the reason he is so successful in his chosen profession is because he is a cautious man, and the reason I am so successful in my chosen profession—or one of them—is that I recognise when it is necessary to cast caution to the wind.'

He returned to his seat behind the desk, picking up his quill again. 'Maxime is right, though, it will not be a simple matter to prove I am not this Duke's son. There have been many cases in France over the last few years, of returning *émigrés* or their apparent heirs, claiming long-lost titles and estates. With so many of the nobility and their dependents dead, so many papers lost, estates ransacked, it is very difficult to prove—or to disprove—such claims. And even if they prove to be true, in most cases, the reward is nothing, or less than nothing, you know? What money existed has long gone, along with anything of value which could be sold or stolen. No one really cares, you see, if Monsieur le Brun turns out to be the Comte de Whatever, if only the name is at stake.'

'So it would be, ironically, easier for you to accept the title than to reject it?'

'Equally ironically, acquiring a title, especially such a prestigious one, would, in the eyes of some, be of value to my business. It would,' Jean-Luc said with a mocking smile, 'be more prestigious to buy wine from the Duc de Montendre that from Monsieur Bauduin.'

'But it is not a mere title which *mademoiselle* would have you claim, but a wife. And another family. Another history.'

'None of which I desire.'

'No, but Mademoiselle de Cressy does. Which begs the question, if she is the real Juliette de Cressy, and the contract is valid, if her father really was the Comte, then why didn't *he* pursue it when he was alive?'

Jean-Luc nodded approvingly. 'A good question, and one which you can be assured I asked her. She told me that her parents vowed never to return to France. For them, the country was tainted for ever by the Revolution, which is perfectly understandable—Paris must for them have been a city redolent with terrible memories. Her betrothal to the son of the Duke who was the Comte's best friend, was a sort of family myth, she said, a story that she was told, and that she believed to be just that—a story. It was only when her father died, and she discovered the marriage contract in his papers, that she realised it was true. His death, she openly admits, left her penniless, for his pension died with him.'

'So she came here, to Paris, to claim her only inheritance, which is you.'

He shook his head. 'According to her family tale, as Mademoiselle de Cressy tells it, the Duke sent his son to Cognac in the very early days of the Revolution, to keep him safe, to be raised in secret by a couple named Bauduin, until such a time as he could safely reclaim him. Only his best friend, the Comte de Cressy, was aware of the ruse, and the Comte and his wife fled France around about the same time as their daughter now claims I was sent to live in Cognac. And so it was to Cognac Mademoiselle de Cressy went first, when her father died. And from there, she claims, traced me to Paris—not a difficult thing to do, since my business originated in that town and the office which I keep there today bears my name. This element of her story is, obviously, the most dubious, and equally obviously, impossible to either prove or disprove.'

Sophia frowned, struggling to assimilate the tangle of implications. 'You think she had the contract and the baptism certificate in her possession, and that she targeted you to play the long-lost heir?'

Jean-Luc spread his hands on the blotter. 'I am one of the wealthiest men in France. My parents are dead. I have no siblings. And she believed me to be single.'

Sophia couldn't help thinking that when Jean-Luc himself was added to the equation, it was not surprising that Mademoiselle de Cressy had elected him. 'Do you think she has taken account of the risk that the real son of the Duc de Montendre might turn up in Paris?'

'It is fifteen years since Napoleon allowed the first of the *émigrés* to return, and almost four since the Restoration. If the fourth Duc and Duchess of Montendre had a son—something which is still not verified—and if he is still alive, I think he would have surfaced before now.'

Sophia shook her head. 'If it is a scheme, it is very ingenious, and Mademoiselle de Cressy must be very bold to attempt to carry it off.'

'Or very greedy.'

'Or very desperate.' As she had been. Desperate almost beyond reason, and utterly heedless of the consequences. Sophia's stomach churned at the memory, that constant feeling of panic as she searched for a solution, any solution to her own dilemma.

'Sophia?' Jean-Luc lifted his hand from hers as soon as she opened her eyes. 'You look as if you are about to faint. Can I get you some water?'

'No.' She clasped her hands tightly together, trying to disguise the deep, calming breaths she was being forced to take. Never again. That was why she was here, wasn't it? Never again. She could not afford to draw parallels between herself and this Juliette de Cressy, must not allow herself to imagine that they had anything in common. More than anything, she must not allow any sympathy for the woman to jeopardise her own future. 'I'm fine,' she said thinly. 'Perfectly fine. So, where do we go from here?'

He looked unconvinced by her smile, but to her relief, he did not question her further. 'Establish you as my wife, first and foremost. Introduce you to Mademoiselle de Cressy, which will be in in the presence of Maxime. Try to verify the existence of the lost heir. Try to verify the marriage contract. I have a very long list of tasks, which I will not bore you with.'

'I won't be bored. I'd like to help.'

He looked startled. 'Your role is to play my wife.'

'Doesn't a wife help her husband? What do you envisage me doing, if not that?'

Jean-Luc shrugged in a peculiarly Gallic manner. 'What does a wife do? I have never been married, perhaps you can tell me.'

Almost, she fell for the trap he had laid, but she caught herself just in time, and smiled blandly. 'Why don't you let me think about that, come up with a plan of my own, which we can discuss.'

He laughed, holding up his hands in surrender.

'Very well. I have made arrangements for you to visit the modiste to select your trousseau tomorrow. There will be time before that for me to introduce you to the household. The day after that, a tour of the *hôtel*. And after that, I am happy to hear your ideas. I do have a very competent housekeeper though, I'm not expecting you to burden yourself with household matters.'

'At the very least she will expect to take her instructions from me.'

'Do you know enough of such things to instruct her?'

'I would not offer if I did not.'

He leaned forward, resting his head on his hand to study her. 'I was expecting The Procurer to send me an actress.'

'I'm sure that there are some actresses capable of managing a household.'

'You are not an actress.'

She rested her chin on her hand, meeting his gaze, reflecting the half-smile that played on his lips. 'A better one than you, Jean-Luc, for your motives are quite transparent.'

'But I'm right, am I not? You are not an actress?'

'I have never been on the stage.'

'No, I thought this morning, when I first caught sight of you, that your beauty was too ethereal for the stage.'

She could feel herself blushing. She ought to change the subject, to break eye contact, but she didn't want to. 'I'm tougher than I look.'

'Of that I have no doubt. To come all the way to France, alone, even with the assurance of The Procurer's contract, demonstrates that you are made of stern stuff. And now you offer to help me with my search for the truth, too.' He reached over to cover her free hand with his. 'Beautiful, strong and brave, and clever too. I am very glad to have you on my side, Sophia.'

For some reason she was finding it difficult to breathe. 'We are both on the same side, Jean-Luc.'

'I like the sound of that. I am not so arrogant as to imagine that I and only I can resolve this mess, Sophia. It's true, I am accustomed to making all my own decisions, but one of the reasons they are sound is that I take account of other opinions. I would very much appreciate your help. Thank you.'

'Thank you.' No man had been interested in her opinions before. No man had been interested in her mind at all. That's why she was feeling this strange way, light-headed, drawn to him, even enjoying the touch of his hand on hers. Until he withdrew it, broke eye contact, and sat up straight.

'We are agreed then. However, before we begin the difficult task of proving that Mademoiselle de Cressy's story is without foundation, there is the small matter of convincing Mademoiselle de Cressy that we are married.'

'Can we do that? We don't have any paperwork. What if she tries to verify our story while you are trying to prove her story wrong?'

'My lawyer has informed her that we were married in England. As to paperwork, it hasn't occurred to her to ask, perhaps because she doesn't believe you exist.'

'So, when do you plan to produce me as evidence?'

'As soon as we can prove to ourselves that we can be convincing.'

Sophia pursed her lips. 'You think we need some sort of dress rehearsal?'

He smiled at that. He really did have a very nice smile. It was easy to return it. 'Tonight,' Jean-Luc replied. 'We will have dinner, just the two of us, with the attendant servants looking on. It will be a gentle introduction.'

'You think so? In my experience, servants are the group most difficult to fool.'

'Then we will know, after tonight, that if we can fool my household we can fool Paris society, and more importantly, Juliette de Cressy, yes?'

'Yes.' Was there a chance that Paris society would contain any visiting English society likely to recognise her? She could not possibly enquire, for to do so would be to betray herself. But The Procurer would not have sent her here if she had considered it a possibility, would she, for then she would have failed in meeting Jean-Luc's terms, and The Procurer was reputedly infallible. She had to take confidence from that.

'What is worrying you, Sophia?'

She gave herself a little shake. 'Nothing. Save that we must concoct a love story, mustn't we? People will ask how we met, won't they, and how our whirlwind romance developed.'

'Whirlwind romance,' Jean-Luc repeated

slowly. 'I am not familiar with that phrase, but it is—yes, I like it. We will come up with a love story tonight worthy of your Lord Byron,' he said, his eyes alight with mischief. 'We dine at seven. I took the liberty of sending your maid out for an evening gown. I had no idea whether you would have anything suitable with you. I hope you don't mind.'

'There was no need. I do possess an evening gown, you know.' Albeit a very shabby and venerable evening gown.

'Don't be offended, Sophia. Think of it as your stage costume,' Jean-Luc said. 'When you put it on, and not your own clothes, then it will help you, will it not, to play your part?'

How on earth had he guessed she had used that trick before? She had left her previous costumes behind in that house in Half Moon Street, but when she'd worn them—yes, it had been easier to pretend. 'Thank you,' Sophia said.

Jean-Luc got to his feet, holding out his hand. She took it. He bowed over it, kissing the air just above her fingertips. '*À bientôt.* I look forward to meeting my wife properly, for the first time.'

Chapter Three

The evening dress that Jean-Luc had thought-
fully provided was deceptively simple in its construction, consisting of a cream-silk underdress,
and over it a very fine cream muslin cut in the
latest fashion, the waist very high, the sleeves
puffed, the skirts fuller than had been worn a
few Seasons before. Gold-figured lace in a leafy
design formed a panel in the centre of the skirt
at the front and the back, with twisted gold and
cream lace on the décolleté, and a matching trim
on the hem.

'*Ça vous plaît, madame?*' the dresser asked
Sophia, fussing with the bandeau which was tied
around her hair.

'*C'est parfait,*' Sophia replied in her softly
modulated French, twisting around in front of
the mirror to take in the back view.

It was indeed perfect. The most expensive gown she had ever worn as well as the most chic. Madeleine, the dresser recently employed by Jean-Luc for his new wife, had excellent taste. She would have Madeleine accompany her, Sophia decided, when she visited the modiste tomorrow to select the remainder of her outfits. Or trousseau, as Jean-Luc had referred to it. She was extremely relieved that he was taking no hand in proceedings, though it was ludicrous to compare his taste with Hopkins's, and even more ludicrous to compare the costumes, or their purpose.

And even more ludicrous again to compare the two men, Sophia chided herself. She must not allow the past to influence her present behaviour. Tonight, she had to prove to Jean-Luc that she could play as his loving bride. Sophia rolled her eyes at her reflection in the mirror, as she held out her wrists to allow Madeleine to button her long evening gloves. Playing the bride was one thing. It was the loving part that was more problematic.

They might be dining *à deux*, but when the footman threw open the double doors and announced her, Sophia felt as if she was walking on to a stage set. The room was quite magnificent, the pale green walls extravagantly adorned with plasterwork and cornicing gilded with gold. Two mirrors, hung opposite each other at either end of the long room, endlessly reflected the huge dining table and its array of silver and gold epergnes in the form of galleons sailing along the polished mahogany surface like an armada. A magnificent chandelier cast flickering shadows through two tall windows and out into the now dark courtyard.

Two place settings were laid at the far end of the table. A fire roared in the white marble hearth. Jean-Luc, austere in his black evening coat and breeches, set down the glass he had been drinking from, and came towards her. His hair was still damp from his bath, combed back from his forehead, almost blue-black in the candlelight. He was freshly shaved, his pristine shirt and cravat gleaming white against his skin. His waistcoat was also plain black, though the buttons were gold. He wore no other adornment, save his diamond pin, a gold fob, and the gold signet ring, but the very plainness of his attire let the man speak for himself, Sophia thought fancifully. A man with no need of ostentation. A man without pretension. A man who exuded confidence in himself. Looking at him, refusing to acknowledge the flicker of attraction which she determinedly attributed to nerves, Sophia concentrated on the other, much more important thing about Jean-Luc. He was a powerful and influential man, but he was not a man who would abuse that power. Her instincts told her so. She decided that in his case, she could trust them.

'Ma chère.' He took her hand, bowing over it, his kiss as it had been earlier, bestowed on the air above her fingers. 'You look ravishing.'

He was waiting, Sophia realised, to take his cue from her. She smiled up at him, the practised smile of one dazzled. 'Jean-Luc, *chéri,*' she said breathlessly, 'as ever, you flatter me.' Catching his hand between hers, she allowed her lips to brush his fingertips in the most featherlight of kisses. It was entirely for the benefit of the three—no, she counted four footmen, and the butler, who were standing sentinel around the room, but the touch, voluntarily given, seemed to take Jean-Luc by surprise. He recovered quickly enough, enfolding her hands in his, pulling her towards him, smiling down at her besottedly in a manner she thought must be every bit as practised as her own.

'I could not flatter you, no matter how hard I tried. The reality exceeds any compliment,' he said. And then more softly, for her ears only: 'Bravo, Sophia!'

He ushered her towards the table, releasing her hand only when the footman pulled her chair out for her. She thanked the man, though she knew it was the custom in such large households to pretend that servants were invisible, but this was one habit of her own she would not break, and so she thanked the butler too, when he poured her a flute of champagne, receiving a small, startled nod of acknowledgement.

The food began to arrive in a procession of silver salvers, each set down by a footman, the domed lid removed with a flourish by the butler, and the contents solemnly announced. *Artichauts à la Grecque; rillettes; saumon fumé; escargot Dijonnaise; homard à la bordelaise; côtes de veau basilic; lapin Allemande;*

daube Avignonnaise; asperge gratin; salade Beaucaire...

Sophia's mouth watered. 'How did you know to order all my favourite foods?' she teased.

Jean-Luc laughed, shaking his head. 'The credit must go to my housekeeper.'

'*My* housekeeper.' Sophia laid her hand over his. 'I look forward to meeting her tomorrow. From the little I have seen of my beautiful new home, I can tell she is most efficient, but there are certain aspects that I wish to attend to myself, to ensure your maximum comfort, *chéri*,' Sophia simpered. 'I intend to make you proud to have me as a wife.'

'My love.' Jean-Luc lifted her hand to his mouth, pressing a theatrical kiss to her palm, his eyes dancing with laughter. 'I have all the proof I need that you will be a perfect wife, now that you are here.' He raised his champagne glass, touching it to hers. 'To us.'

'To us.' The champagne was icy cold. The food looked absolutely delicious, her mouth was already watering. 'I would like to start by sampling some artichoke, if you please, they look delicious. Are they from Brittany?'

Handing her the dish, Jean-Luc casting an enquiring look at his butler, who bowed and informed him that Madame Bauduin was quite correct, that these were the first of the season.

'I had no idea you were a horticulturist, my little cabbage,' Jean-Luc said.

Sophia sighed theatrically. 'You have forgotten my passion for the culinary arts.'

'In my passion for you,' he replied fervently, 'I forget everything else.'

He was almost as accomplished an actor as she. If she did not know better, she would think the heavy-lidded, heated look he gave her was genuine. She could feel her own cheeks flushing, and reminded herself that she did know better. 'Have a care, my love,' she chastised, 'we are not alone.'

Jean-Luc responded by raising his glass. 'I am counting the moments until we are.'

'Then it would be prudent to have some sustenance first,' Sophia said, completely flustered. 'May I have some snails please. I find them a great delicacy.'

He laughed at that, a low rumble of genuine amusement as he handed her the platter. 'An

English woman who likes snails. I truly have captured a prize.'

'These are not just any old snails, these are *escargot Dijonnaise*.' Sophia inhaled the delicate aroma with her eyes closed. 'A red-wine reduction, with shallots and bone marrow, garlic and truffles. You are very fortunate to have such an accomplished chef.'

Jean-Luc helped himself to the remainder of the snails, popping one into his mouth. '*We* are fortunate,' he corrected.

'We are. Please pass on our compliments to...?'

'Monsieur le Blanc,' the butler informed her graciously. 'I will indeed, *madame*.'

'So it seems I have married a gourmand,' Jean-Luc said. 'Would you like to sample some of this veal?'

'I'd prefer the rabbit, please. I would not describe myself as a gourmand, but I am very fond of cooking. Though of late I have not—not had the opportunity to indulge my passion.' The truth was, she had more or less lived on air since her return to England. She looked up to find Jean-Luc studying her once more. She wished he wouldn't do that. She returned her attention to her plate, absentmindedly sipping on the dry white wine which had seamlessly replaced her champagne.

'Paris has some excellent restaurants these days. We will sample some of them, if you wish?' Jean-Luc smiled at her eager expression. 'In my view, the best places to eat are the cafes, but the type of women who frequent them are not the sort I would wish my wife to mingle with. There is a place near Les Halles, where the oysters...'

Sophia continued to smile, but she no longer heard what he was saying. What would he think if he knew his faux wife was, in her previous life, exactly the sort of woman he would not wish her to mingle with? A cruel paradox. She cursed under her breath. Hadn't she decided to leave that other life behind!

'...a great many new restaurants opened in the last ten years,' Jean-Luc was saying. 'Run by chefs who once ruled the kitchens of the grandest houses, and who lost their livelihoods when their former employers lost their heads. Chez Noudet in the Palais Royal, for example.'

'I had not thought—but I suppose many people

depended for their livelihoods on the aristocrats who went to the guillotine.'

'*Absolument.* My own—*our* own chef, Monsieur le Blanc, is one such case I am afraid. And this town house too is a *victim* of the Revolution, in a way. I purchased it four years ago, from the heirs of the noble owners. It had, like most of the abandoned *hôtels particuliers* here in St Germain and more especially across the river in Le Marais, been looted. Tomorrow, when I show you round properly, you will see there are still bullet marks in the walls of the courtyard. It may have been almost thirty years since the Bastille fell, but the scars of the Revolution are still there, if you know where to look.'

'But now King Louis is back on the throne, surely things have changed?'

Jean-Luc shrugged. 'Superficially, perhaps, but it is *plus ça change, plus c'est la même chose*, I think. Some of us, like me, roll our sleeves up and get on with the business of trading, in an effort to restore our country's finances—and in the process, the fine buildings of our city such as this one. And others, many of our so-called nobility, sit complacently on their rears and expect others to spoon feed them.'

Sophia was somewhat taken aback by this. Would her own heritage place her in the opposite camp to him? Or would her determination to make her own way in life on her own merits be her saving grace? It didn't matter, she told herself, what Jean-Luc thought of her, provided she fulfilled her contract. But the assertion didn't ring true. Despite herself, she found him intriguing, his opinions interesting, his determination to be only himself admirable. 'Are they all so idle, these returning exiles?' she asked. 'Can none redeem themselves in your eyes?'

'Oh, they do. A large part of my business depends upon their custom and patronage. The heirs of the *ancien régime are* some of my best customers and a valuable source of contacts and new clients throughout Europe. Unlike them, I do not distinguish between old money and new. I can be very *charmant* when I wish to be. As you know, *mon amour.*'

This last was said with a smouldering look, and accompanied by another kiss pressed to her palm. Sophia wanted to laugh, only she felt that she couldn't breathe. Though she still wore her evening gloves, though his lips did not touch her skin, his kiss sent a *frisson* up her arm. The alarmingly visceral attraction made her feel all tangled up inside. It made her forget that she was playing a part. She looked down at her empty plate, at her full wine glass, with dismay. Lost in their conversation, she didn't recall what she had eaten, after the rabbit. She didn't recall the wine changing from white to red. She didn't recall the footmen clearing the table, bringing in a second course of fruit and ices and mousse.

'Will you be so very *charmant*, as to serve me some of that lemon sorbet?' Sophia asked, extricating her hand. 'And perhaps you should have some too?'

'But yes, you are right, something cooling is what is required. In your presence...' Jean-Luc placed his hand over his heart. 'I burn like a moth drawn inexorably to the flame.'

Sophia bit back her laughter. 'Then perhaps you should not come any nearer. I have no desire to cause you pain.'

'Indeed, that I do believe. For when you agreed

to marry me, *ma chère*, did you not prevent my heart from breaking?'

The soulful look he gave her was too much. Sophia chuckled. 'Enough,' she exclaimed in English. 'I am not sure whether you are aping Lord Byron or one of his creations, but…'

'You think this is a performance! *Madame*, you stab me to the heart.'

'I will, with this cake slice, if you do not stop. It is the most lamentable—oh!' Sophia covered her mouth, casting a horrified glance over her shoulder, where the butler was making a show of arranging several decanters on a tray. 'I'm so sorry,' she mouthed, 'I quite forgot.'

He smiled at her warmly, his voice too low for any of the servants to hear. 'And so made your performance all the more believable. You have a most infectious laugh, though you do not have call to use it very often, *hein?* And now I have made you sad, by saying so. I'm sorry.'

Sophia tried to shrug. 'It doesn't matter.' With years of practice of shielding her emotions, both from those she loathed and the person she loved most, she found it unsettling that this man, almost a stranger, seemed able to read her thoughts. She ate a spoonful of lemon sorbet. 'This is delicious.'

'And so the performance resumes,' Jean-Luc said under his breath, before turning to dismiss the servants, telling the butler to leave the clearing up until the morning. 'Now,' he said, as the door closed behind the last footman, 'you may relax. If that is possible, in my company. I merely made a comment, based on a supposition. I was not attempting to pry into your affairs.'

Sophia pushed her sorbet aside. 'I am perfectly relaxed. It is better that you know nothing of me or my past. Then you will not confuse me with the creature you have brought me here to play.'

'Sophistry, Sophia?'

Which it was. 'Talking of which,' she said, ignoring him, 'we said we would agree our cover story. How we came to meet, I mean, and fall headlong in love.'

'Our whirlwind romance.' A cursory glance at her, Jean-Luc thought, getting up to pour himself a brandy, would be sufficient for any man to understand perfectly why he would wish to marry her. In her travelling dress, he had thought her slender, but her figure, revealed by the flimsy fabric of the evening gown, was certainly not lacking in curves. She was the kind of enigma that unwittingly brought out the most primal instincts in men: innocent yet sensual; fragile yet resilient; a woman who yearned to be protected, and one who desired nothing but to be left entirely alone. Was it unwitting? Impossible, surely, for any woman to be so accomplished an actress.

'Would you care to join me?' he asked, holding the decanter aloft, unsurprised when she shook her head. A woman who liked to keep a clear head. And who was, he told himself, simply doing the job she had been brought here to do. It was not her fault that he was distracted by her. Though one would have to be made of stone not to be.

Jean-Luc set his brandy impatiently aside and resumed his seat. He had his faults, but woolly thinking was not one of them. 'Let us plot the arc of our romance. Obviously, we met in England,' he said. 'Fortunately, I was there on business in February for a few weeks. It was not long after I returned, at the beginning of April, that Juliette de Cressy found her way to my doorstep.'

'So we met and married in the space of a few weeks,' Sophia said.

'We met and fell deeply in love and married,' Jean-Luc corrected her. 'It was a *coup de foudre*, for both of us. One look was enough.'

'You don't really believe that can happen? That one would decide to bind oneself for ever to a complete stranger, on the basis of a—a heated glance, without knowing anything of them, or of their intentions?'

It was, in fact, a notion he had always derided, but the scorn in her voice made Jean-Luc contrary. 'Doesn't love triumph over all?'

'Love does not put food on the table, any more than it puts a roof over one's head. In fact, in my opinion, love is the flimsiest possible reason for anyone to marry.'

'What would you consider more sound reasons?'

'It is a matter of quid pro quo, isn't it?' Sophia answered, as if this was perfectly obvious. 'Pedigree, wealth, position, influence, these are the bulwarks of marriage contracts. Where there is a fair exchange, then affection may flourish, but there are so very few fair exchanges, aren't there, and in most cases, it is the women who has least to offer, and so must sacrifice the most.'

She was staring off into the distance, having almost forgotten that he was there. 'And even then,' she continued coldly, 'it is often not enough. Lies are offered in exchange for promises. Could any such marriage flourish? No,' she concluded firmly. 'No. It is best that it does not even begin. No matter what the consequences.'

Could she be referring to herself? Fascinated, Jean-Luc had a hundred questions he was burning to ask and frustratingly, he could not ask any of them. 'Fortunately, we do not have to concern ourselves with that, since our marriage is entirely fictitious,' he pointed out instead.

Sophia blinked. 'You're right. It is just that, a figment of our imagination. They say everyone loves a romance, don't they? Why should they question ours?' She pursed her lips. 'So, we met in England. I expect you bumped into me when you were shopping for some shirts, and I was looking to match some ribbons for a new hat. I dropped my packages. You picked them up. Our eyes met, and we knew, yes?'

Her smile was as brittle as the spun sugar which decorated the honey cake. Jean-Luc returned it, like for like. 'I took you to tea,' he said, 'and then the next day for a carriage ride in Hyde Park, and we met every day after that. A week before I was due to return to Paris, I realised that I could not return without you, and so I proposed on the spot.'

'And I accepted with alacrity, and we were married by special licence—that is something one can easily accomplish, if you have sufficient funds,' Sophia added, her smile turning bitter. 'But I could not travel with you immediately, because I had...' She faltered. 'Why could I not come with you?'

'Perhaps you had family, loose ends to tie up?'

'No, none. Recently I have lived alone.' She blushed. 'Oh, you meant did the Sophia who married you live alone. No, she wouldn't have, would she, a genteel unmarried woman like that? She would have had a companion of some sort.'

Which made him wonder what sort of woman that made Sophia, if not a woman like that? She had been completely confident with his servants, and quite at home taking this long, elaborate dinner. Her manners, her general air of refinement, were completely natural, the product of good breeding and habit. His butler had taken to her at once, and like his chef, Fournier was another of the aristocracy's old retainers. Who was she? He itched to ask, but it would be futile. Subtlety was the key to extracting any information from the real Sophia. For now, he must concentrate on the fictional one. 'So, this companion of yours, she has to be settled elsewhere, then?'

'In the country,' Sophia said, nodding. 'In a cottage of her own, in the village where she grew up. I could do that for her. As the wife of a wealthy man, it would be the least I could do. And I'd want to make sure she was comfortable too, wouldn't I, since she had been my companion for so long? So I remained in England, counting the days until we were reunited.'

'And I waited here in Paris, counting the days until you came.'

Sophia frowned. 'Why didn't you tell anyone though?'

'I did, I told Maxime, my oldest friend. It

would have been he who drew up the settlements. I wanted to keep you a secret, to unveil you in person, knowing that when they saw you, everyone would understand in a moment why I fell so madly in love with you.'

'And your servants?'

'Our servants,' he reminded her. 'Have known of your arrival from the day after I received confirmation of your appointment, from The Procurer, but they won't have talked.'

'You are very confident of that.'

'I have every reason to be. I pay very well, and I do not suffer insubordination.'

'So your intention then, is to present me to Mademoiselle de Cressy...'

'As soon as possible, now that we have our story straight.'

She smiled tentatively. 'Do you ever shop for your own shirts?'

He laughed, as much with relief that their story had lifted her mood, as at her acumen. 'Never, if I can avoid it. What if I had business with Berry Brothers, the wine merchants in St James's Street—a company I do have dealings with, as it happens. Walking back to my town house, I'd go along Bond Street, wouldn't I, and that was when I bumped into you. There, does that work?'

'I think so. Will you relate it?'

'We shall tell it together, just as we did there.' Jean-Luc grinned. 'Although we'll have to add in a few loving glances.'

She clasped her hands together at her breast and fluttered her lashes at him. 'Cornflower blue, the ribbons I was trying to match. You said they were the colour of my eyes.'

He smiled. 'Ah no, I would not have said that, for your eyes are no such colour. I was wondering to myself only this morning, what colour are they, those beautiful eyes of my beautiful wife, for I would not call it turquoise or cornflower or even azure.'

'What then would you call it, my love?'

She was not laughing, but there was laughter in her eyes, just as there had been before, when she had forgotten to act. Heat prickled down his back and his belly contracted as desire caught him in its grip. 'I have no name for the colour, but it is the blue of the Mediterranean in the south on one of those perfect days, when the sun is almost white in the sky, and the sea glitters, and the heat makes your skin tingle.'

Sophia nodded. 'I know,' she said softly.

He leaned closer. She smelled of flowers, like an English springtime after the rain, but at the same time he could swear there was an intoxicating heat emanating from her. 'You want to dive in,' he said, 'to feel the cool lap of the waves soothe your burning skin.'

'Yes.' She smiled. 'Like gossamer, that is how I always imagined it would be.'

Their knees were touching. He could sense the rise and fall of her breasts, only inches away from him, but he couldn't take his eyes off her mouth. 'Gossamer,' Jean-Luc repeated. 'No, it is like silk. Like your hair,' he said, his fingers brushing one long strand which had escaped her coiffure, then trailing down her cheek, her neck, to rest on her shoulder.

He heard her sharp intake of breath and waited, but she did not move. 'Jean-Luc, is this still— are we acting?'

He could lie, but that would be a big mistake. No matter how beguiled he was by her, her scent, her curves, the allure of her mouth, he could not pretend in order to take advantage. 'I am not,' he said, releasing her. 'Not any more. I forgot myself. Forgive me.'

'There is nothing to forgive,' Sophia said, shaking out her skirts as she rose. 'We immersed ourselves in our roles rather too enthusiastically, that is all.'

He chose not to contradict her. 'You play yours to perfection. No one will doubt you. But it is very late, and we have a very full day tomorrow. Come, I will escort you to your chamber.'

He knew he wouldn't be able to sleep, with her so tantalisingly close on the other side of the locked door. But at least tonight, it would be this astonishing creature who was to play his wife who would keep him awake, and not that other, deluded creature, the reason Sophia was here in the first place.

Chapter Four

The next morning Sophia joined Jean-Luc in the breakfast room, attended by Fournier the butler, who seemed to have taken a shine to her, and two footmen. Afterwards, Jean-Luc introduced his wife to the rest of the household, who were lined up in serried ranks in the entrance hall. She lost count of how many there were, but her determination to speak to everyone, down to the youngest scullery maid, met with Madame Lambert the housekeeper's approval, as well as Jean-Luc's.

The remainder of the day was spent acquiring her trousseau. Clothes had never held much interest for Sophia—a happy circumstance since, for most of her life, there had been little money to spend on them. She had refused to spend any of their meagre allowance on her previous trousseau, telling Felicity afterwards, in an attempt to make light of the situation, that she'd shown remarkably foresight. As to the silks lavished on her by Hopkins, she never considered those anything but garish costumes for the performance she was required to put on.

This latest, and hopefully last, part she would have to play required costumes too, but of a very different kind. Seated in the plush receiving room of one of Paris's most exclusive modistes, aided and abetted with enthusiasm by Madeleine, her dresser, Sophia momentarily abandoned herself to the seductive delights of high fashion. Morning dresses, carriage dresses, promenade dresses, evening dresses and ball gowns were paraded in front of her, in a flutter of silk and satin and lace, crape and gauze, figured muslin, plain muslin, zephyr and sarcenet. There were under-dresses and over-dresses. There were nightgowns and peignoirs, chemises and petticoats of the finest cambric, silk stockings, corsets trimmed with satin and that latest fashion in undergarments, pantaloons. There were pelisses and coats and tippets and cloaks, boots and half-boots, sandals and shoes.

There were pairs of gloves of every colour to suit every occasion, and so many bonnets that Sophia quite lost track of their various appellations and purposes.

'No, I've seen a plethora,' she said after several dizzying hours. 'I require only a few dresses, perhaps one evening gown, certainly no ball gowns. There is no point—' She broke off abruptly. Neither the modiste nor the dresser must suspect that her role as Jean-Luc's wife was temporary. 'What I mean is,' she amended, 'I would like time to consider my future needs, and will purchase today only what I require to see me through the next few weeks.'

'But of course, a most sensible approach,' the modiste said, smiling approvingly. 'Might I suggest Madame Bauduin leaves it to her dresser and I to make the initial selection? *Madame* is very fortunate that she has the figure to carry off any garment.'

'Yes. Thank you—though please, only the bare minimum for now,' Sophia said, already wincing inwardly at the expense which Jean-Luc would be put to, despite the fact that he had insisted, before she set out this morning, that she considered only her requirements to dress as befitted his wife, and not the expense.

Entrusting Madeleine with the task, Sophia returned in the carriage to the *hôtel*, a brief and uncomfortable journey through the narrow streets, the view from the mud-spattered window giving her frustratingly little sense of the city she longed to explore. This would be her only chance to see Paris. Under the terms of their contract, she had agreed to disappear from both Jean-Luc's life and his country when her task was completed. How would he explain his short-lived marriage? It was not her problem, she told herself as the carriage halted outside the gates of the town house and the footman folded down the steps. But she was curious none the less, and finding her husband waiting for her on the terrace, took the opportunity to ask him.

'I will say that you have returned to England to nurse your former companion. Is that not a plausible explanation?'

'Very plausible.'

'Good! Then, when time has passed, I will say that you had come to the conclusion that you could not settle in France and wished to remain in England. It would mean painting you in an unfavourable light, though.'

'Tell people whatever you wish. It cannot be any worse than—'

She broke off abruptly. *What they say already.* So obvious a conclusion to that sentence that there could be no possible alternative. But Jean-Luc did not finish it for her. Instead he pressed her hand, and there was something in those dark brown eyes, sympathy or pity or—whatever it was, it made her feel uncomfortable, so she looked away, fussing with the strings of her reticule.

'Did you have successful shopping trip, *ma mie*?'

A finger under her chin gently forced her to meet his gaze. 'It depends how you define successful. I suspect I have spent a great deal of your money.' Which, she thought sardonically, was the goal of every woman in her former situation, though it was one she had never shared. One of the things, she suspected, that had kept her under Hopkins's protection for so long, and had made him most reluctant to give her up. She had a much more precious use for his largesse.

'Welcome back.' Jean-Luc was eyeing her quizzically. 'Do you realise you do that? Something I say, or some remark you make, sends you to a place far away. Not a very pleasant place, either, judging from your expression.'

And he had done it again, Sophia thought, irked with herself. The man saw far too much. She really must be more on her guard with him. She pinned on her brightest smile. 'I can think of no place more pleasant to be now, however, than Paris.'

A tour of the town house had been the plan for the next morning, but Jean-Luc had a change of plan. 'I thought you would prefer a tour of my city instead,' he said to Sophia over breakfast.

'Oh! I was thinking only yesterday that I would like nothing better,' she exclaimed, clasping her hands together. 'But...' Her face fell. 'As your wife, surely my priority should be to explore my new home?'

'Paris is your new home. And though I am undoubtedly biased, for me, Paris is the most bewitching and beautiful city in the world. I wish to introduce you to it.'

His thoughtfulness touched her. She executed a deep curtsy. 'Then your wish is my command, Husband.'

'To be perfectly honest,' Jean-Luc said, as he tooled the small, open one-horse carriage out of the stables and on to the main road, 'the best way to see Paris is on foot. Our streets are very narrow, for the best part, but I wanted you to get a sense of the layout of our city. This is the Rue de Grenelle, in the Faubourg St Germain district. As you can see, there are a number of *hôtels particuliers* here. Some of them have been abandoned since the Revolution, but the Restoration has seen many reclaimed and restored to their former glory.'

'What happened to the family who previously owned your *hôtel*?'

'The are domiciled in England, with no plans to return—they left long before the Terror. *Naturellement*, I know them because they buy my wine.'

'*Naturellement,*' Sophia said, with one of her genuine smiles. 'I presume your wine has an excellent reputation then?'

'Premier Cru, of course,' Jean-Luc said. 'This is the Rue du Bac, which is the main route from the Left Bank to the Tuileries. Many carriages with insignia travel down this street every day, as the King's nobles make their way to the palace to pay court.'

'What makes your wine the best?'

'Just between us, I would not claim that it is absolutely the best. Many of the châteaux keep their finest vintages for their own consumption. People buy my wine and cognac and port and madeira because they know they are buying quality, and that they will get the same quality every time. The Bauduin name is one of the most prestigious in the wine trade, not only in France but in all of Europe. I do not adulterate wine, pass off poor quality spirit for cognac, or put new wine in old barrels. Those who do business with me do so because they trust me.'

'A man of principle. I can see why you are so successful. Do you have offices here? Or warehouses? Perhaps you could tell me a little of your business? A wife should not be entirely ignorant of her husband's activities.'

'I thought women were not interested in commerce. Maman actively disapproved of my taking up the wine trade.'

'But why? You had to earn your living.'

'She would have preferred me to continue my education for a few more years. I attended a monastery school, which meant living away from home during term time.'

'Goodness, those kind of establishments don't come cheap.'

'Which explains why my education was terminated at the age of twelve. Maman's ambitions for me were beyond her means.'

'And that's when you went into the wine business?'

'And broke Maman's heart, though I loved the business from the start, the almost magical alchemy of turning grapes into fine wines. I was industrious and had a good head for figures. My employer took me under his wing. I became his protégé and it grew from there. The fact that I was so successful relatively early allowed me to look after my parents. With hindsight, it was clear to me that they had lived beyond their means when I was younger, spending money they didn't have on my education, for a start. At least I managed to ensure that their later years were spent living in comfort.'

'No wonder your father was proud of you.'

'Unfortunately Maman, to her dying day, saw it differently. She lamented the fact that I was involved in business and not some loftier endeavour. If she had lived to see me settled in the *hôtel*, then perhaps she would have finally come to terms with my choice of career.'

'She clearly loved you very much,' Sophia said, surprising him by laying her hand on his arm. 'Is your place of business near here?'

'No, it is on the river, much further downstream. I will take you, one day, on a tour of the *halle aux vins*. It is a new building, one of the more practical improvements which Napoleon managed to complete, along with the quays and the water supply.'

'So he was not wholly a monster, then?'

'That is how the English would like us to view him—or more particularly, your Duke of Wellington,' Jean-Luc said wryly. 'Here, they say he was a man whom no one liked but everyone preferred. He was certainly better for France than those he replaced and, I think, better than the

King who has replaced him, over there in the Tuileries, which you'll see in a moment, when we cross the Pont Royal. But if you look to the right you will see…'

'Notre Dame?' Sophia exclaimed as he pulled over from the traffic to allow her a better view. 'I thought so. It is one of the few landmarks I recognised when I arrived.' She gazed around her wide-eyed as they crossed the grey choppy channels of the Seine. 'It is a beautiful city, I can see why you love it. There is something about a river running through a city, isn't there—and all those bridges. So much life. So many people bustling about, from a myriad of different walks of life.'

There was that rare sparkle in her eyes, her real smile curving her mouth. 'You are not someone who prefers the pastoral serenity of the countryside then?'

'I've had very little experience of it.'

'So you have spent most of your life in London?'

'Yes.'

The smile was still there, but there was an immediate wariness in her eyes. Jean-Luc turned the subject. 'During the Revolution, when the churches were deconsecrated, Notre Dame was used as a vast wine cellar.'

'Really? It must have held a positive lake of wine. It would have been quite a sight. Did you ever see it?'

'I wish I had, but the church was restored to its proper use long before I came to Paris.'

'When was that?'

'The first time, I think I would have been about sixteen, so 1804. By then, my employer was becoming very frail, and was not fit to travel on business.'

'That is very young, to have to shoulder so much responsibility.'

'I relished it, and when he died, he left it all to me.'

And you turned wine into gold.'

Jean-Luc laughed. 'You could say that. Many people claim that a fine Sauterne, from Graves, near Bordeaux is like drinking liquid gold.'

'Bordeaux is not far from Cognac, I think?'

'You know that region?'

'I have passed through the city.'

'You have friends there, acquaintances? Is that how you come to speak French so well?'

'No.'

And just like that, she was lost again, though it was not bitterness this time he saw in her beautiful eyes, but sadness, a yearning that squeezed his heart with compassion. 'Sophia?'

She blinked, and it was gone, as if she had raised a stage curtain, to reveal a new backdrop. 'I—I spent some months in the south last year. Do you like art, Jean-Luc? Is it true that the walls of the Louvre hang empty, now that many of the works that Napoleon appropriated have been returned to their rightful owners?'

And that, he understood, was the end of the matter. Sophia was the mistress, he was coming to learn, of the carefully crafted answer, followed by the carefully crafted deflection. So he turned the carriage on to the bridge, and he let the vista divert her thoughts. Which, not surprisingly, it did. She leaned forward, throwing questions at him and pointing, her eyes once again alight with interest.

Laughing, Jean-Luc pulled over on the other side of the Seine, to give her a view of both palaces. 'That is the Tuileries on the left. What you see in front of us is the Pavillon de Flore, the part of the Louvre which joins the Tuileries. The main entrance, which is the Arc de Triomphe du Carrousel is behind there. We can drive round to take a look, or we can go for a stroll in the gardens. Which would you prefer?'

'Oh, the gardens, if you please.'

'So you do like to walk, even though you are not a country maid?' Jean-Luc asked, making a show of finding a safe spot to leave the carriage. He helped her down, handing the reins and a coin over to an eager urchin. 'I know London pretty well. I have a *pied-à-terre* in Jermyn Street.' She smiled blandly. 'Near St James's Park,' Jean-Luc continued doggedly, 'and Green Park, which I prefer since it is less manicured and more open. What about you?'

'I am more interested in this park—these gardens,' Sophia said, and he gave up, offering her his arm, which she duly took after hesitating for only a moment. 'Are we likely to encounter any of your friends or acquaintances?'

'The chances are slim, at this hour, but in the evening, these pathways are full of people taking a constitutional. You will have noticed the air is considerably fresher here.'

'I confess I have,' Sophia said. 'Paris is not the sweetest smelling of cities,' she added, wrinkling her nose.

'That is putting it very politely, though in the years since I first made it my home, considerable improvements have been made, believe me.'

'And how long is that?'

'Ten years, since my father died.'

'Though you acquired your town house only four years ago.'

'I lived in lodgings before that, in a much less salubrious location down by the docks. My house was very far from grand when I bought it. You'll see when I show you around, that there's still a deal of work to be done. One wing is still almost entirely derelict. I'd be interested to know what you think should be done with it.'

'You wish my advice? For all you know, I might have execrable taste.'

'On the contrary, I know you have impeccable taste. You married me, did you not?'

Sophia smiled up at him uncertainly. 'I hadn't realised we were playing our allotted parts, but you're right, when we are in public, it is best we make a habit of it.'

'I was not acting, I was simply making a joke. I'm sorry if it was ill judged.' Jean-Luc urged her over to a wooden bench set off the main path, covering both her hands in his. 'You are supposed to be my wife. My much-loved wife. Whose opinions matter to me.'

'I know. It is just that Paris is so very beautiful, and you have been so kind as to show it to me. I suppose in my excitement I forgot that it was actually your notional wife Sophia you were sharing with and not me.' She managed a very feeble smile. 'I won't forget again.'

'But I want you to forget,' he said. 'When you forget, when you relax and are yourself, that is when you are most convincing because your true nature shines through. I prefer you when you are yourself, Sophia.'

'Oh. Do you really?'

'Why wouldn't I?'

'I don't know. I'm here to play your wife, you didn't hire me to be myself. I'm not even sure that I know how—' She broke off, biting her lip.

'To be yourself?' She did not answer, but

she did not contradict him. She looked so very lovely, and so very vulnerable, on the verge of tears yet determined not to give way to them. What had happened to her? What dark secret was she hiding?

'Who is Sophia?' he asked, gently teasing. 'I will start with the obvious. You are a breathtakingly beautiful woman. When you arrived on my doorstep the other day, I thought, this Procurer, she is a sorceress, for she has conjured up the woman of my dreams.'

She blushed. 'That's ridiculous.'

Jean-Luc shook his head, smiling. 'It is the truth, but it is the formidable person behind that captivating face who truly interests me.'

'There is nothing remotely formidable about me.'

'I'm afraid I'm going to have to disagree with you. You are intelligent. You are perceptive. You are a most excellent listener. You are brave— no, don't interrupt me when I'm complimenting you. Consider this, Sophia—how many women would have the courage to do as you have done, to come to France alone, to take on this role—'

'A great many, if they were offered such a large fee,' she interrupted drily.

'Though very few I think, would be up to the part while you—not only have you embraced it, you have offered to do more, to help me. So that is another thing about you—you like to be useful. You have an enquiring mind. There—that is a good many things I know about you already, after only a brief acquaintance. But enough to state with certainty that I do indeed like you, Sophia.'

Her fingers tightened around his. 'I, on the other hand, don't know what on earth to make of you, but I find I like you too, Jean-Luc, and can say so with equal certainty. It seems such an odd thing to say to a man I barely know, but I do.'

They had drawn closer to each other on the bench. Her knee was brushing his. Her smile lit her eyes. Her skin was flushed with the late spring sunshine. Around them, people strolled, the trees rustled softly in the breeze, the birds sang, and yet for this one perfect moment they were entirely alone. 'If you really were my wife,' Jean-Luc said, 'if you were my heart's desire, just arrived from England, I would kiss you right now.'

Her eyes widened. Her lips parted. 'Here? In a public park?'

'This is Paris. Public parks are designed expressly for the purpose of kissing.'

'Then it is a pity that we are unable to put this unique design feature to the test.'

Dear heavens, was there anything so tempting. But she could not possibly be inviting him to—though she was leaning towards him, and when he dipped his head towards her, she did not pull away, and her lips were so tempting. With a supreme effort of will, Jean-Luc pulled himself back, cursing under his breath. She was only just beginning to trust him. He pressed a very poor substitute of a kiss to the back of her gloved hand. 'I think we'd better resume our walk.'

They strolled the length of the Tuileries Gardens and back, Jean-Luc describing the many changes he had witnessed in the last ten years. He was talking to set her at ease, she knew that, requiring only that she nod and smile occasionally, for which Sophia was extremely grateful. She couldn't fathom her contrary reaction. Jean-Luc was kind and thoughtful and understanding. He *liked* her, for goodness sake. She should be happy, not tearful. She was in Paris, living in the most luxurious of town houses, with a charming man who made no demands on her save that she cling to his arm and act the besotted wife. When set against what had been expected of her before, this was—well, there was simply no comparison. So why was she so emotional? Why couldn't she draw a clear line between herself and the performance he expected of her? Why, indeed, had she volunteered to cross that line, and to play significantly more of a role in his life than he expected?

Because he *liked* her! Because she *liked* him. Because he didn't expect or demand more than she was prepared to give. Because he seemed genuinely interested in her, her thoughts, her ideas, her opinions. Because, in essence, he was quite utterly different from any other man she had ever met. Would it be so wrong of her to do as he bid her, to be herself with him? If the result was that she was a more convincing, then that was to be welcomed. Of course she could never confide in him, her shameful history would revolt him, but if she could find a way to do as he asked, and be more herself—yes, it was a very attractive proposition.

'What have I said to make you smile?'

And Jean-Luc, Sophia thought, allowing her smile to broaden, was a *very* attractive man. 'I'm in Paris,' she said, 'reunited with my dashingly handsome husband, and the sun is shining. I have every reason to smile!'

He stopped abruptly and pulled her into his arms. 'Since, as you rightly point out, we are in Paris, the sun is shining, and I have been reunited with my beautiful wife, there is only one thing to be done.'

Her pulses leapt. She couldn't breathe. 'What is that?'

He dipped his head, blotting out the sun. And then in full view of the passers-by, he kissed her gently on the lips.'

It was the softest of kisses. Just the merest whisper of his lips on hers, but it made her head spin, forced her to cling to him, lest her knees give way, for she felt as if her bones had melted. And then the sound of an admiring whistle pierced the air, and it was over. Jean-Luc let her go, looking somewhat sheepish. 'Believe it or not, I have never done that in public before.'

'Believe it or not, neither have I. Shall we carry on walking, before we attract a full-blown round of applause?'

'We can go through the palace entrance here into the central courtyard, if you like. From there you can get a sense of the vast scale of the palace and the Louvre.'

'As you wish,' Sophia said compliantly. Unquestioning deferral was one of the earliest lessons Hopkins had inculcated in her. But she was no longer Hopkins's creature, and Jean-Luc did not deserve to be mentioned in the same breath, even if it was only in her thoughts. 'Actually,' she amended, 'I'd much prefer to see more of your beautiful city.'

'Your wish is my command.'

Jean-Luc smiled. By expressing her own wishes she had pleased him. Which was, Sophia thought as she allowed him to help her into the carriage, a truly novel experience.

* * *

The quay they drove along was very busy, forcing Jean-Luc to concentrate on his driving as they made slow progress, the Seine in contrast running at speed on their left, a muddy brown colour with grey choppy waves, and like the Thames, crowded with boats, barges and sculls. Despite this fascinating vista, Sophia was drawn to the view directly beside her of her erstwhile husband, his perfect profile, his disturbingly attractive person.

Very attractive, and very disturbing. She could easily have avoided kissing him, but she had not wished to. She, who had never in her life wished for such a thing had astonishingly, wanted Jean-Luc to kiss her. It was the way he looked at her. It was not lascivious. It was not covetous. It was not even that horrible, assessing kind of look of one weighing the odds as to her likely receptiveness, which she had always found revolting. It was a different kind of look altogether. As if he saw her—not the exterior which was her fortune and her misfortune, but the person inside. No man had ever looked at her in that way before. No man had ever made her feel this way before either. Tangled up inside, confused. Edgy, though not nervous but—anxious? No, not that either. Jumpy? She couldn't describe it. It was like looking forward to something while at the same time worrying it might not happen.

'The Place Louis Quinze,' Jean-Luc said, rousing her from her reverie and indicating a huge open space, dominated at the far end by two palaces. 'Or if you like, the Place de la Concorde, though you probably know it better as the Place de la Révolution.'

Sophia gazed at the innocuous civic space in horror. 'This is where the King was guillotined, and Queen Marie Antoinette?'

'And in the end Robespierre too, the man responsible for so much of the bloodshed—or at least the man who is most often blamed. Legend has it that for years afterwards, animals refused to cross the exact spot where the guillotine once stood.'

Sophia shuddered. 'I'm not surprised. Do you think this is where the Duc and Duchesse de Montendre met their end?'

His eyes were fixed on the *place*. She thought

he had not heard her, but the tightening around his mouth betrayed him. 'It is probable.'

A tiny shake of the head followed, a dismissal of whatever grim thoughts had momentarily possessed him. 'We are heading into the Champs-élysées now. Some of the biggest of the noble palaces are near here, over on the Rue du Faubourg Saint-Honoré. They put my humble little *hôtel* to shame, but you can't see anything, they are all hidden behind imposing walls. One of them, I believe, belonged to the Montendre family. I have yet to ascertain which, since so many have changed hands in the last few years.'

'Oh, so you have already started your investigations? '

'A tentative start, not much more. Tell me,' Jean-Luc said, nodding at the road ahead, 'what do you think of that?'

'I have no idea,' Sophia said, eyeing the huge construction. 'What is it?'

'The new Arc de Triomphe. It was to be Napoleon's biggest tribute to himself. As you can see, he didn't get to finish it.'

'Are there any plans to complete it?'

Jean-Luc laughed sardonically. 'I doubt it's a

priority for the King, and as for the people—Paris has far too many other urgent needs.' He drove in silence as they travelled the short distance towards the abandoned mass of stone covered in scaffolding, and once again pulled over. 'The Russian forces camped here during the occupation. Those were very dark days for Paris—to have foreigners claim our city—desperate times. It is a relief to finally put them behind us.'

'You really do love this city, don't you?'

'Yes. Though I have houses in London, Lisbon and Madrid, though I was raised in the southwest, it is Paris which is my home. I felt it here,' he said, touching his heart, 'from the first time I set foot here.' He consulted his watch, barking in annoyance. 'I'm sorry, but I must take you back now. I have urgent business to attend to.'

'Of course. We are supposed to be married, I would not expect my husband to sacrifice his business for me.'

'Then you will find that your expectations are aimed far too low. If I did not abandon my business—at least temporarily—for such a lovely wife, then I would be a fool. This meeting I have arranged, is to hand over some responsibilities to my secretary. Something which he believes long overdue, and will be delighted to accept.'

'But you must not—for my sake, you must not...'

'But I must. For my sake as much as yours, *ma belle*. Mademoiselle de Cressy must be utterly convinced of the veracity of our union. I promise you, Sophia, it will be no hardship at all to be seen to devote myself to you.'

The look he gave her made her skin heat. It made her pulses jump. He was a very good actor, she reminded herself. Was he acting? 'And I, to you,' Sophia said, allowing herself the briefest of caress, her gloved hand on his cheek, her fingers fluttering along his jaw. He inhaled sharply. Was he going to kiss her again? She didn't care if he was acting or not. She wanted his mouth on hers. A kiss. Such a simple thing to desire, wasn't it?

He caught her hand. He pulled her closer. 'Sophia?'

Her hesitation was fatal. He sat up. Why had he asked her! If he had simply kissed her! She was well and truly hoist by her own petard and now it was too late to change her mind. When her body had stopped this strange clamouring, she would be glad she had not. 'There is a gap in the traffic,' she said, pointing sightlessly and stupidly, for Jean-Luc had proved himself an excellent driver.

But though he drew her a look—one of *those* looks—he said nothing, merely picked up the reins and carefully edged back out on to the thoroughfare.

Chapter Five

Jean-Luc's business meeting kept him away from the *hôtel* until long after dinner, and in the morning he left apologies for his absence once more. Deciding that she had better make a start on assuming her role as chatelaine, Sophia arranged to meet with the housekeeper for the long overdue tour of her new abode, then took a simple breakfast in her bedchamber of coffee and buttered baguette while she compiled her own list of domestic tasks. Jean-Luc was not the only one with a methodical mind.

Just as she was perusing her limited wardrobe, Madeleine burst into the room followed by a small army of maids bearing a very large number of boxes. 'Your trousseau has arrived, Madame Bauduin,' she announced.

Sophia looked on aghast as the boxes began to pile up in the bedchamber. Madeleine, with an uncanny knack for divining the contents of each box, directed gowns, hats, shoes, undergarments and overgarments into separate piles. 'Now, *madame*, we will select a gown for you to wear this morning, and then I will have all this put away—unless you wish to inspect...'

'No! There is no need.' She had no ambition at all to see this mountain of unnecessary expenditure spread out for her delectation and delight. She couldn't imagine what Jean-Luc would think when faced with the bills. 'Not at the moment,' she said more temperately, realising that she had spoken sharply. 'I have promised to spend the morning with Madame Lambert. Madeleine...'

'*Oui, madame?*'

'How many gowns, exactly, did you order in the end?'

Her dresser frowned as she did a quick mental tally. 'Morning gowns, seven, and the same of afternoon dresses. Promenade dresses, four and four walking dresses. Evening gowns, six, I think.'

'Twenty-eight dresses?' Sophia said faintly.

'*Oui, madame*. We can always order more if you are concerned that is insufficient for your needs?'

Sophia poured herself the dregs from the coffee pot and swallowed them. 'I suspect it will be sufficient for the rest of my mortal days!'

Three hours later, Sophia entered the un-renovated wing of the *hôtel* alone. Though Madame Lambert had been very unforthcoming with her at first, by the end of the extensive tour of the house she was fairly certain that she had passed whatever examination the housekeeper had set her. The years managing house for her father had stood her in good stead—the early ones, at least, when there was still sufficient of Mama's money left to allow her to keep the house as it had been when Mama was still alive. Even then, their London town house had been nothing compared to this. Modest, is how Jean-Luc had referred to it yesterday, and she supposed it was compared to those on the Right Bank, or even compared to some of the grander houses she had visited with her father, when he was obliged to bring her along as his dining companion. Though none of those London houses had the spectacular light, the effortless sense of space of this house. None had those tall windows, the doors which opened on to the courtyard which, in summer, brought the outdoors inside.

Sunshine. Blue sky. Paris was not so very far away from London, yet even here, the air was different, and in the south...

A tear tracked down her cheek unchecked. Felicity had loved that fierce southern sunshine. 'I can feel it doing me good, heating my bones,' she used to say. She had a way of tilting her face up, as if she was drinking in the sun's rays, willing them to heal her. Her skin had become quite tanned. 'No respectable man will offer for me now,' she had said, laughing. 'I look like a peasant girl.'

She was always teasing. Always talking as if there was a future, as if there would be a time when marriage might feature, when tanned skin would then be an issue. She had the ability to live only in the present. Only occasionally could Sophia see that it was not a talent, but a hard-learned lesson. Only occasionally did she catch a glimpse of the other Felicity, the little sister who was terrified, and who tried so hard never to show it. So much life. And then, abruptly, none.

Tears cascaded down Sophia's cheeks. It was so unfair. So horribly unfair. She missed her dreadfully. It had been almost ten months now, but the pain felt so raw. She so rarely permitted herself to grieve. Since returning to England, all her efforts had been to survive without further compromising herself. Now here she was, on a beautiful day in a beautiful house in a beautiful city, and suddenly it overwhelmed her. With a sob, Sophia dropped her head on to her hands and gave way to a long overdue bout of tears.

It left her drained but oddly rejuvenated. She knew from experience that tears left no trace on her skin or eyes, a fortunate quirk of nature that had stood her in good stead many times in the past. She tucked her soggy handkerchief into the pocket of her gown. Enough tears! She had always prided herself on being firmly in control of her emotions. Those confrontations with her father had been very specific, always caused by the same contentious issue, and it had never been difficult to be anything other than patient with Felicity, who was adept at pretending all was well even when she was desperately unwell.

Jean-Luc would say that was a very English thing to do, but when it came to Felicity, Sophia's only motive had ever been a desire not to upset her sister by not being equally stoic. Pretence had become second nature to her, something else which had stood her in very good stead during the travails of her initial downfall and then the long endurance test which was her—did one call it a career?

She had never considered using this term before, and it amused her, in a dark way. Her father's career—his illustrious career, as he'd always referred to it—had brought his family to the brink of bankruptcy and left his daughters in abject poverty. Yet her choice of *career*—yes, she could, if she was so inclined, have labelled it illustrious with veracity. She had been successful. She had achieved what she needed to. It had been she who had instigated it on her own terms and ended it in the same way. Had she chosen to resume it on her return to London—ah, but she had not countenanced that. She would not live in shame ever again. Desperation had forced her down paths she would never have previously considered. The Procurer had provided a route to salvation.

She wandered over to the cracked mirror above the fireplace. The morning gown Madeleine had selected for her was an unusual colour of forest-green sprigged with white flowers, the hem weighted with white cotton lace. It was simply but beautifully cut, with a round neck and tightly fitting sleeves which tapered down to the wrist. It was not a colour which Sophia would have chosen, and as such, it quite transformed her. She was no longer any of her old selves, but someone quite new. Madame Bauduin was a confident woman, she decided, eyeing her reflection. Confident in her appearance. Confident in her ability to take up her new role. Confident in her husband's affections.

Her husband. Jean-Luc. It had become second nature for her to be on her guard with men, it should be a simple matter, especially since she had known him less than a week, but for some reason she was struggling. For a start, she felt as if she had known him for a great deal longer.

The effect, she supposed, of how much he had been forced to tell her, but also the effect of how much he seemed to understand her, despite her resistance to telling him anything. And if she were being honest, she wasn't so resistant. In fact, quite the opposite. She had found herself on several occasions wanting to confide in him. And twice now, she had wanted to kiss him.

Sophia shivered. Not in fear, but in anticipation. Twenty-six years old, and she had never been kissed. Not properly. There had been kisses, but they had been perfunctory to say the least, a token prelude to another act, with no interest in her response. Just as well, since she had none, other than the urge to shield her mouth with her hand. Jean-Luc's almost kiss had not been token. It had been given—or not given!—in anticipation of nothing more than a kiss.

A kiss which made no demands. What would a kiss like that be like? She shivered again. No, not a shiver but a *frisson*. A word she'd never understood before. *Frisson*. Sophia closed her eyes and wrapped her arms around herself. She could almost feel the brush of his leg against hers. The scent of him, a clean scent, but with an undertone of—of Jean-Luc. His eyes would be dark with desire that she would pretend was not an act. His lids would be heavy, his lashes thick black, no man should have lashes so beautiful. His breath would be soft on her cheek. And his mouth...

'Ah, here you are!'

Sophia jumped. Her eyes flew open. Heat flooded her cheeks. He could not literally read her thoughts, she reminded herself. 'Jean-Luc. I did not expect...'

'My apologies. It took more time than I anticipated, but I am pleased to say that my business affairs are now temporarily in the capable hands of my secretary. I am now, as they say, all yours.'

He strode towards her, his hands outstretched. It was perfectly natural to allow him to clasp hers. As for his smile, it would be a very beguiling smile, were she the type to be beguiled, which she was not. Still, there was no harm in smiling back, was there, nor in proffering, as any newlywed wife in love with her husband would, a welcoming kiss.

'Sophia?'

This time she did not hesitate. 'Husband,' she

said, disingenuously, closing the gap between them. 'It is lovely to see you.' And then she stood on her tiptoes, and she kissed him.

The touch of her lips on his made all thoughts of resistance flee. Husband, she had called him, Jean-Luc thought hazily, so this was part of their charade, though there was no one around and— and he didn't care. His senses were swimming at the nearness of her, at the light, fresh scent of her. And her mouth. Only then did he become aware that she was not actually kissing him, but simply pressing her lips to his. He could feel her breath, shallow and fast. Keeping one of her hands in his, he pulled her to him, wrapping his other arm around her waist, angling his head to kiss her properly. Her lips parted just a fraction. He kissed her, little darting kisses, all the way along her full top lip. She sighed, relaxing in his arms. He tried again, to kiss her properly. Her lips clung to his, but…

She was nervous, that was it. He slid his hand up her back, caressing the delicate skin on the nape of her neck, and fluttered more delicate kisses on her lips, until she followed his lead, giving fluttering, butterfly kisses in return. He caught one of them, his mouth moulded to hers, and moved gently. She followed his lead this time, opening to him, and he deepened the kiss just a little, ignoring the sudden clamour of his senses, the stirring of his erection, coaxing her into a response, concentrating on coaxing her a little bit more, and a little bit more, until she was kissing him, her free hand clutching at his shoulder for balance.

Her kisses were so delightful that Jean-Luc stopping thinking, losing himself in her embrace for a long, breathless moment, until the tiny gap between them became an agony to maintain, and the desire to deepen the kiss from desire to passion became almost irresistible. Almost.

He sighed deeply, reluctantly, and let her go. Her lids were heavy over her eyes, her skin flushed, her lips—*mon Dieu*, he had better not look at her lips or he would fall into kissing her again. 'Sophia?' It took a moment for her to focus. 'I thought that you wanted—did I misunderstand?'

She shook her head. Her smile was faltering. 'No, I wanted—you didn't misunderstand.'

Husband, she had called him. Had she been acting the innocent? He could not believe it. And yet there had been a peculiar naivety to her kisses. But The Procurer would surely never have sent him a virgin to play his wife. Unless—was this the reason for the terms she had imposed? Impossible. But if it was true, he had no designs on taking her innocence.

'Was it an act, Sophia? I need to know, because I am confused. The kisses,' he elaborated, for now she looked just as confused as he. 'Were you playing the innocent, the wife who had not yet been kissed or...?'

'Why do you ask?'

She looked so vulnerable, he was tempted simply to tell her it didn't matter. But it did. He had to understand, no matter how painful the conversation. 'Because if it was not an act,' Jean-Luc said gently, 'then I won't do it again. It would not be right.'

'Why not?'

'Because I am not the kind of man to take advantage of a woman's innocence. I thought that this—this fear you have of my touch, I assumed it was because some other man—but if it is because there has been no other man at all, then I will not take advantage of this situation, to be the first.'

She was quite ghostly pale now, her beautiful mouth trembling. He longed to pull her into his arms and to comfort her, though for what, he had no idea. 'I'm not an innocent. It is just that I...'

He waited, holding his breath, expecting her to change the subject, but to his surprise, she lifted her head to meet his gaze, reached out to touch his hand. 'You are a truly honourable man, Jean-Luc. I am not—I don't know if I have been unfortunate, but I have not met anyone like you before. I am not an innocent. You are not taking advantage of me.'

He took her hand in his. She did not resist, clutching at him as if she were drowning, and again, he had to fight his urge to pull her into his arms, to keep her safe, somehow, to protect her. He knew it was simply a reaction to her appearance. He'd noticed it the first day, hadn't he, that combination in her, of fragility and steeliness. It was simply that the vulnerable side of her was at the forefront at the moment. She didn't need him to protect her.

'Yet your kisses,' Jean-Luc persisted, 'were not the kisses of a woman experienced in the art of lovemaking.'

'I'm sorry to have disappointed you.'

He was surprised into a gruff laugh. 'I did not mean to imply they were not delightful. Merely unpractised.'

'Kissing is not—was not—I have limited experience.' Her colour had returned. 'Unlike you, I think?'

'How am I to answer that? I am not a gentleman but I am...'

'An honourable man.' Sophia astonished him by lifting his hand to her lips, pressing a brief but fervent kiss to his palm. 'Truly honourable.'

Their gazes were locked. The air around them seemed to sparkle with tension. He was breathing, he must be breathing, but it felt as if he was not.

Sophia raised his hand to her mouth again. This time her kiss lingered. 'I may be inexperienced, but that is not to say I would not be amenable to repeating the experience. Out of curiosity, you understand.'

He was hard. She had done nothing more than

kiss his hand, and he was hard. 'Sophia, there is nothing I want more than to...'

'Then please,' she said, with a smile that sent fresh blood surging to his groin, 'do.'

He did, and this time Sophia gave herself over to the kiss, because this time it felt like another step in their conversation, and in that conversation she had felt herself sparkle. Like the blood fizzing in her veins as Jean-Luc kissed her, those fluttering, teasing kisses were like an invitation. She accepted, pressing little kisses back, and then following his lead to open her mouth, shaping her lips to his and tasting him. She wrapped her arms around his neck, tilting her head to allow him to kiss her more deeply. And then his tongue touched hers, and there it was again, a *frisson*, the most delightful sensation. His tongue touched hers again and she liked it. She liked it very much. And then the kiss deepened further, and there was heat, and tingling and his hand feathering up and down her spine, and his hair was silky soft where her fingers tangled in it, and their kisses made her weak, so that she leaned against him, and brushed against the unmistakable evidence of his desire, and when that happened, her body instinctively froze and went limp. Jean-Luc released her instantly. 'Sophia?'

She could not meet his gaze. What could she say? Her throat was dry. She cleared it. She shook her head. 'Please, don't be angry with me.'

'I am not angry, I am confused.'

She nodded. Tears were horribly close. She would *not* cry. 'Understandably.'

He sighed. 'At least you admit I have cause, even if you won't explain it.'

'I can't.'

He took a step forward, his hand raised as if he would touch her cheek, but clearly thought the better of it. 'I have had lovers. To make love, it is something that two people share, two people enjoy. If you wished me to stop kissing you, you only had to say. And if it was more than that, if you thought for a moment that because you asked me to kiss you, I would have demanded more…'

'I didn't.' Mortified, she forced herself to meet his gaze. 'I promise you, that's not what I thought.'

He was not angry. It was worse than that. There

was pity in his gaze. 'You say that, but it's not how you acted.' He made a helpless gesture. 'You say you trust me. You say that you truly believe that I am an honourable man. But your actions reflect none of those assertions.'

'You are going to send me away,' Sophia said flatly. 'I've failed at the first hurdle, that's what you're trying to tell me.'

'For someone so very intelligent, you can be very foolish. Kissing is not part of your remit and we would probably both do well to remember that. I have no fault to find with you playing the role of my wife, and I am certain that when you meet Mademoiselle de Cressy tomorrow...'

'Tomorrow!'

'Tomorrow, we will easily persuade her that we are married.'

'We will, I will make certain of it.'

'Good.' He waited, but she had nothing she could think to add to this, and so to her utter relief, he shrugged, turning away. 'Well then, Madame Bauduin, perhaps you will share your wifely opinions on what should be done with this dilapidated wing of our home.'

* * *

They made their way through the connected rooms of the empty wing. Sophia, who had obviously inspected them already, had a host of ideas, which she recited from a notebook. They were excellent ideas, Jean-Luc thought approvingly. As he had suspected, she had impeccable taste, and what's more it chimed with his own, in her preference for maximising light, for muted colours, and for a lack of clutter. He listened. He encouraged her. He volunteered ideas of his own, which complemented hers. He occasionally disagreed with her. He gave the impression that his full attention was on the household renovation they were discussing, but mostly, he was studying her and trying to make sense of what had occurred between them.

The simplest solution would be to forget it. She was here to play his wife, he had no doubt that she would make an excellent job of it, but she was not actually his wife. He had the tangle of his own past to unravel without concerning himself with hers. But he was already far more intrigued than he should be. Was it precisely because she was so grudging with her history?

What did he know of her? She was clearly well born. Her mother died young, her father died relatively recently. Most likely he had left her in straitened circumstances, else she would not be here. But why was she not married? She was twenty-six, well past what society would deem to be an eligible age. Had she devoted her life to her father? Was that likely, given that she admitted to having a difficult relationship with him? Surely marriage would have been preferable, a convenient escape route. And if not, when he died—even if she had no dowry, a woman like Sophia could not have lacked offers.

Perhaps she had been married. Why hadn't that occurred to him before! There had been a strange comment when they were concocting their own story over dinner on the second night—what was it she had said? Something about lies offered in exchange for promises. But hadn't she implied that such a marriage was better avoided? Or had he misunderstood her? Yet she had admitted she was not an innocent. So she had been married then, and she regretted it—yes, that made sense. Her marriage had been unhappy. That would explain a great deal. Except the kissing. Or perhaps it did. A loveless marriage, such as the English gentry were reputed to routinely make, based on bloodline and on land and on influence. The consummation of such a marriage would be—Jean-Luc baulked at trying to imagine such a union. Not lovemaking, but breeding. *Sacré bleu*, that would indeed explain a good deal.

Then why not admit to it? She had nothing to be ashamed of. It could be, he supposed, that she wanted to put it behind her, to forget all about it, or even pretend it had never happened. Small wonder that her aim was independence. Smiling, nodding in agreement with her suggestion that this salon would make an excellent library or snug, Jean-Luc felt quietly satisfied that he was beginning to understand her. Whether these insights explained her kisses—now that was a very different matter.

Why had she kissed him? Husband, she had called him. Was she practising? But there would no call to kiss in such a way in public. Why had she broken her own rules? Was it a simple matter of attraction? She could be under no illusions about his desire for her, but hers for him? Any other woman, he would be happy to accept such a simple explanation. But Sophia…

'What have I said to amuse you?' she asked.

Jean-Luc shook his head. 'It is nothing you have said. I was just thinking that you are like no other woman I have ever met.'

'That is why you married me, remember.'

Which, in Sophia's language meant, let us not discuss the matter. Jean-Luc smiled in token acknowledgement. If his little paradox was more relaxed playing Madame Bauduin, then so be it. 'You are perfectly correct, *ma belle*, that is exactly why I married you.' He took her arm, leading her into the last of the rooms.

'Jean-Luc, why aren't you married—I mean why aren't you really married?'

'I told you, I have been too absorbed in my business. And I have never met the right woman.'

'Yes, but you know it's quite unusual for a single man to purchase a house like this, unless he is thinking of settling down.'

'That is a very good point. We will tell people that it is evidence that I was already contemplating marriage, so that when I met you it was a case of the fates colliding.'

Her smile was perfunctory. 'That is not the real reason though.'

'I'm afraid the real reason is rather prosaic. My business is not about selling a few bottles of wine to men to drink with their dinner, Sophia. I sell to suppliers and to wealthy connoisseurs—men who wish to stock their entire wine cellars. And my trade is international. It is expected that I entertain these men from time to time, and I could not do that while in lodgings.'

'So it is a business asset, then?'

'You could say so. That is one of the reasons I've left this wing untouched. Under the previous owners, it was the nursery.'

'Of course, I should have realised. I'm assuming that you don't foresee the need for it in the near future?'

'You assume correctly. I currently have a wife who is not my wife, and a woman who claims that she should be my wife. That is more than enough for any man to wrestle with. Taking a real wife, and populating a nursery is not something I care to contemplate at all, for the near, middle or even distant future.'

'So, no nursery then.'

'No nursery. Your suggestions, with the changes we've discussed, are perfect.'

She beamed. 'I am glad to have been of help.'

'You have.'

Her smile faded. 'I should tell you that my trousseau arrived today.'

'Good. Is that one of your new dresses?'

Her face fell. 'It is one of twenty-eight.'

'Well, it is an easy enough matter to arrange another appointment, there is no need to be upset.'

'I'm not upset that I've ordered too few, I'm upset that I've ordered far too many,' Sophia exclaimed. 'Twenty-eight gowns and heaven knows how many pairs of shoes and boots and hats and coats and—and other items that need not concern you.'

Those *other items* interested him the most, but he doubted Sophia would wish him to tell her so. Nightgowns. Stockings. Chemises. Petticoats. Unfortunately, he'd never get to see her wearing any of those most alluring garments. 'I told you not to worry about the expense,' he said. 'It is important that you are adequately clothed.'

'What I consider adequate, and what Madeleine—but it is not her fault,' Sophia amended quickly. 'The fault is mine. I am so very sorry. I don't know if some of it can be returned, but…'

'You will do no such thing. How do you think that would look, for my bride to be sending back her trousseau?'

She grimaced. 'I hadn't thought. But you can have no idea how much such clothing costs— oh, or perhaps you do.'

'No, I don't,' he snapped. 'I have never purchased any item of clothing for a woman in my life. I have had lovers, Sophia, not mistresses.' She flinched. 'I do not mean to offend you by being so blunt, but it is an important distinction to me.'

'And to me.' She bit her lip. 'Being Madame Bauduin is taking some getting used to.'

'Perhaps I was too modest when I informed you of my status. Let me assure you that I am a very, very, very rich man, and you, *ma femme*, must dress like the wife of one. Twenty-eight gowns does not seem to me such an outrageous number.'

'It does to me, but to Madame Bauduin—no, perhaps not.'

He smiled. 'Then that is an end to the matter. I trust there is something suitable in that vast collection to impress Mademoiselle de Cressy.'

'Oh, dear heavens, I had forgotten. Where is the meeting to be held? And at what time? Will it be just the three of us?'

'At Maxime's office, in the morning, so there will be four of us.'

'And what will you—what will we...?'

'We will tell our story. We will show to Mademoiselle de Cressy that we are madly in love. And we will tell her that though she is the first to have the honour of making your acquaintance, we have accepted any number of invitations. Soon all of Paris will be talking of the beautiful Madame Bauduin.'

'Will they? What invitations?'

Jean-Luc shrugged. 'They will arrive in numbers, once the marriage announcement, which Maxime has placed in today's newspapers, is circulated.'

'So you can't get rid of me now, even if you wanted to.'

'If that was a joke, it was a very poor one.'

'It was, a very poor one, I mean. I've lost my sense of humour of late.'

'And your self-esteem,' he riposted, 'has that been a recent loss too?'

He had not meant to speak so harshly, would have retracted the question instantly, but Sophia forestalled him. 'No,' she said, 'that is something I doubt I had to lose in the first place. My father,' she added, further astonishing him, 'was a man whose high opinion of himself could only be maintained by a correspondingly low opinion of everyone else.'

'He sounds like a man most *charmant*,' Jean-Luc said sardonically.

'He could be, actually, when it mattered. His public persona was very *charmant*.' Sophia's smile was mocking. 'At home, behind closed doors, we experienced the other side of his personality. Although you could say Mama had the last laugh. The greater part of her trust fund returned to her family when she died. My father blamed me for that. She had taken me for a walk in the park, you see. I slipped and fell into an ornamental pond. She fished me out but subsequently took a chill and never recovered. I don't know why I'm telling you all this, you can't possibly be interested.'

'And it is against the rules, do not forget that.'

'I did though.' She smiled tentatively. 'I have broken them twice today.'

'Once, to allow me to get to know you better and once, most delightfully, to allow me to kiss you. Do you regret your lapses?'

'No, because I know that you won't press me to confide in you unless I want you to, and I know that you won't kiss me again unless I ask you to. You really are an honourable man.'

'I fear your prior experience of men has led you to adopt very low standards. From what you have said of your father...'

She laughed at that, but shook her head. 'That is true, but I don't compare you to him or to...' She gave herself a little shake. 'It occurred to me that it might be a good idea for us to host a dinner or soirée. It is the custom, you know, for newly married people to do so, and since you said that it was vital that people believed in our marriage—what do you think? I'd be happy to take care of it. I have experience of both arranging and hosting such social gatherings. All you have to do is give me a list of the people you wish to attend. Obviously we can accommodate a good many more if it is a soirée.'

'Then it shall be a soirée. That way we can spend less time with more people.'

'Very well then. Canapes and a supper. I shall ask Monsieur le Blanc to compile a menu. How exciting!'

'My wife, the gourmand. I forgot. I think you were born in the wrong country. I'll tell you what, we will visit the market together, and you can instruct me on the best produce.'

Her eyes lit up. 'You don't need to, you know. I can go shopping with Madame Lambert.'

'I am perfectly happy that you do, but I would prefer you to enjoy your first taste of our renowned food markets in my company. You will find it both fascinating and enjoyable.'

'Won't you find it a chore?'

'How can making you happy ever be considered a chore?'

Chapter Six

For the momentous encounter with Mademoiselle de Cressy, Sophia chose a full-length pelisse of navy-blue satin, the bodice cut and fitted in the military style, softened by full sleeves, which were gathered at the wrist with a band of satin ribbon and trimmed with white lace. White braiding and large white buttons maintained the military effect, while the matching poke bonnet had a jaunty white feather. Tan leather boots and gloves completed the outfit.

She and Jean-Luc were driving to Maxime Sainte-Juste's office in a town carriage pulled by two horses and manned by two grooms, but Sophia was far too distracted to notice Paris passing outside the window. She had hardly slept, had been unable to eat her breakfast, and by now was quite sick with nerves. This was not a game they were playing, not a play they were enacting. In very different ways, this meeting could be the key to both Jean-Luc's future and her own. And also, she supposed, that of Mademoiselle de Cressy.

Beside her, his leg brushing her skirts, Jean-Luc was also carefully dressed. A dark blue double-breasted tailcoat showed off his broad shoulders to perfection. The high, starched collar of his white shirt enhanced his tanned skin. Fawn-coloured knitted pantaloons and glossy, tasselled Hessian boots encased his long, muscular legs. Like hers, his gloves were tan. He held on his lap a simple, black beaver hat with a narrow curved brim.

'There is no need to be nervous,' he said. When we rehearsed our little romantic fable last night, you were word-perfect.'

'Yes, sitting at home, with no witnesses. Your friend, Maxime, what have you told him of me?'

'Nothing at all. Maxime is on our side, Sophia.'

On Jean-Luc's side, more specifically, she thought but did not say. The lawyer, she knew, had been party to Jean-Luc's signing The Procurer's contract. He would likely assume she was an actress, and he would probably assume that 'actress' meant courtesan, which was, Sophia thought slightly hysterically, a horribly reasonable assumption.

'*Ma belle*, you must stop worrying. You are my wife, remember.' Jean-Luc kissed her gloved hand. 'My beloved wife. Remember that too.' He kissed the tip of her nose. 'And most of all remember that you are my much-desired wife,' he said, his hand fluttering on her cheek, on her jaw. His mouth hovered over hers. 'Even though we have already made love this morning…'

'Jean-Luc!'

'Sophia.' His smile had a wicked edge to it that dissolved the butterflies in her tummy and made her blood tingle. 'I should warn you, Wife, that your husband is about to kiss you.'

He was not kissing her. He was kissing his wife. And as his wife it was her duty to surrender her lips to his. And to pretend to enjoy his touch. And if she did not have to pretend, it was simply because she was enjoying the novelty of it, and because it was just a kiss, nothing more, and…

His lips touched hers. Not just a kiss but kisses, gentle soft kisses, making her mouth soften, mould itself to his. Another kiss, a proper kiss now, his tongue barely touching hers. Her hands reached for him, pulling him towards her of their own accord, and their lips clung together and she felt the oddest sensation, of a connection, a yearning for something she didn't recognise, and when the carriage came to a halt, for a long moment their eyes met and he looked as surprised as she felt.

'Now you look exactly as a newlywed bride should,' Jean-Luc said, retrieving his hat from the carriage floor. 'Are you ready?'

A newlywed bride. She was his wife. He had not been kissing her, but his wife. He could not kiss her, because her own terms forbade it. Sophia straightened her bonnet. She was Madame Bauduin. Confident in her appearance. Confident in her position as the wife of one of France's richest men. Confident of her husband's deep affection. *'Absolument, mon cher.'*

* * *

'It was a *coup de foudre*, for both of us,' Jean-Luc said, casting Sophia a yearning look. 'One glance was enough.'

'It was in Bond Street, wasn't it, *mon cher*?' Sophia returned his look. 'I was looking to match some ribbons for a new hat.'

'I had business with Berry Brothers, the wine merchants in St James's Street, and I was walking back to my town house.'

'He ran right into me. I dropped my packages. You picked them up did you not, *mon amour*?'

Jean-Luc raised her hand to his mouth. 'Our eyes met, just like this. And we knew.'

Sophia smiled beatifically into her husband's eyes. 'We knew.'

'I took her to tea,' Jean-Luc said, returning his gaze to the other two interested parties. 'And then the next day for a drive in Hyde Park, and we met every day after that, until a week before I was due to return to Paris I realised that I could not live without her.'

'And so he proposed, on the spot.' Sophia clasped her hands together ecstatically at her breast. 'And of course I did not hesitate to accept. We were married just two days later by special licence. It was the happiest day of my life.'

'Until we were reunited four days ago, that is,' Jean-Luc chided her gently. 'Surely that became our happiest day?'

Sophia sighed. 'I think that every day we have together will be happier than the one before.'

There was a smile lurking in Jean-Luc's eyes. She dropped her gaze demurely, lest she betrayed herself by bursting into laughter.

'And there you have it,' Jean-Luc continued. 'The story of our whirlwind romance.'

'It is certainly a highly romantic story.' Maxime Sainte-Juste spoke with just sufficient irony to make Jean-Luc cast him a reproving glance.

The lawyer was not at all the stern, scholarly man Sophia had imagined, but rather boyishly good-looking, with dark brown wavy hair, blue eyes, and a mouth that seemed to smile, even when, as now, he was not doing so. As Sophia had suspected, the man had clearly made his mind up about her before she walked into the office. She treated the lawyer to one of her sweetest smiles. 'All the more remarkable for being a true story, *monsieur*.'

'But of course, Madame Bauduin, I did not...'

'You were married in March, you say, Madame Bauduin? Yet you did not arrive in Paris until four days ago,' Juliette de Cressy interjected.

As Jean-Luc smoothly launched into the story of Sophia's mythical companion and the need to settle her in the English countryside, Juliette de Cressy became increasingly agitated, and Sophia struggled not to feel sorry for her. Though only twenty-two years old, the French woman had about her a quiet air of sophistication, a poise and an elegance, combined with a cut-glass accent that lent a great deal of credence to her claim to be the daughter of nobility. She was also very beautiful, with hair which had the same blue-black lustre as Jean-Luc's, and skin like porcelain. She was tiny, of delicate build, with huge eyes, a retroussé nose, and a full mouth. The perfectly bred wife for a duke, rather ironically, Sophia thought.

'My husband was so kind,' she said, recognising her cue, 'as to purchase a little cottage for her, in the village where she grew up and though it was my heart's desire to be with him in Paris, it was a small sacrifice to make, to remain with her for a few weeks to ensure that she had every comfort.'

'And for me,' Jean-Luc chimed in, 'a small sacrifice to make, to ensure that my wife came to me knowing she had done her duty at home. Though I counted off every day on my calendar.'

'And I on mine.'

'And yet, despite your excitement and joy, you shared your happy news with no one,' Juliette de Cressy said, frowning.

'Maxime knew, for he drew up the settlements, didn't you, Maxime?'

'As you say.' The lawyer fidgeted with a brass paperweight, obviously deeply uncomfortable even with this half-lie.

'And the formal announcement was in the press yesterday. You will no doubt have seen it, *mademoiselle*? Yes, I thought so, though I brought a copy for you, just in case it had escaped your notice.'

'It did not.' Mademoiselle de Cressy was very pale. 'You are aware, Madame Bauduin, of my prior claim?'

'I know of the marriage contract to which you claim my husband is a party.'

'Ah. And like your husband, you think that I am a fraud, no? But of course you do. You are his wife, and it is very obvious that you are besotted with him.'

Which statement should please Sophia very much. Clearly Juliette de Cressy believed their story. Unfortunately, it was equally clear that she believed her own too. 'No one is accusing you of fraud, *mademoiselle*,' she said gently.

'Your husband…'

'My husband,' Sophia said, putting her hand on Jean-Luc's to forestall him, 'most understandably, is extremely unsettled by your various claims. You will admit, will you not, that they are extraordinary?'

Juliette de Cressy shrugged. 'To me, no. It is a story Maman and Papa told to me, like many they told, of the days before the Revolution. Of course, I never thought that I would be forced to honour the marriage contract, but then I never thought that I would lose Maman and Papa while I am still so young.' She dabbed at her eyes with a delicate lace handkerchief. 'We were very happy in Switzerland. I was their only child, and they loved me very much, Madame Bauduin. Their loss, I feel it still, though it has been almost nine months now, since Papa—excuse me, I find it very difficult to talk about.'

'There is no need to apologise, *mademoiselle*. When one loses someone close, time has no meaning.'

'That is so true. However...' The Frenchwoman tilted her chin determinedly at Jean-Luc. 'We are not here to discuss my loss, but the consequences of it. Though I have no particular desire to be married to a complete stranger, none the less this particular stranger was selected as suitable for me by Papa, and so I must trust that he has, as in all else, my best interests at heart.'

'So close to his heart,' Jean-Luc said, 'that he died without making adequate provision for you.'

'Papa did make provision for me,' Mademoiselle de Cressy exclaimed. 'He provided me with you!'

'You cannot have me, *mademoiselle*, because I am already married.'

'But you cannot be, when you were already

contracted to wed me!' Mademoiselle de Cressy wailed. 'I am very sorry, Madame Bauduin, but I do not see how your marriage can be legal. My marriage contract was made in good faith, and must take precedence. You must have your marriage annulled. Or you must obtain a divorce. Or you must—you must do something—because this man is obliged to marry me.'

'*Mademoiselle*, you must try to calm yourself. Hysteria will get us nowhere.'

'Calm myself! How can I calm myself? What do you think I will do if I cannot be married? I have nothing, *madame*, absolutely nothing, save the arrangement my father made for me with his best friend. And, yes,' she said, turning on Jean-Luc, 'it is true that he made no attempt to enforce the contract when he was alive, I admit that, but that is because he was loath to let me go. I was sixteen when Maman died. For the last six years, it has been just the two of us, myself and Papa. There was time, we both thought there was plenty of time, for me to find a husband of suitable standing of my own choosing, or for him to contact the one he had already agreed for me.'

'So I was your insurance policy? How romantic,' Jean-Luc said sardonically.

'I do not mean to sound calculating, but as it turns out I need to cash in my insurance policy after all. I am left alone and quite bereft, with no dowry and therefore no prospect of making a match with any respectable gentleman. All I ask for is what is rightfully mine, the marriage Papa arranged for me. Do you understand?'

'Mademoiselle de Cressy...'

'No, Jean-Luc, let me answer her.' Sophia got up to take the seat beside Mademoiselle de Cressy. 'I do understand, I assure you. I know that there are very few options open to gently bred women who find themselves on their own. I can see that you do feel quite desperate.'

'*Oui.* I do. It is not that I wish to deprive you of your husband, Madame Bauduin, I can see that you love him, and that he loves you, but he has no right to do so.'

'*Mademoiselle...* Juliette—may I call you Juliette?' Waiting for her nod, Sophia angled her body to give the illusion that they were alone. 'Your papa was very proud of your family name, your heritage, I think? Yes, I thought so. He would wish you to marry a man with a heritage he could be proud to be associated with, wouldn't he?'

'That is why he contracted me to marry the son of the Duc de Montendre.'

'But my husband is not that man.'

'He is.' Juliette crossed her arms and pursed her lips. 'I assure you, he is.'

And Sophia was forced to accept that Juliette truly did believe so. Aware that Jean-Luc and his lawyer were watching intently, she tried a different tack. 'Surely you would prefer to choose your own husband.'

'As I have already pointed out, despite being the daughter of a comte and of noble birth, I have no dowry whatsoever. That fact renders me unmarriageable in polite society, so choice doesn't enter into it.'

Maxime coughed. 'As to that, Monsieur Bauduin has already offered you a financial settlement which you rejected out of hand. My client has authorised me to table an improved offer comprising a lump sum dowry and an annual income. Which, if I may say so, is a remarkably generous gesture given he is under no obligation to offer you anything. I urge you to accept, so that all parties may move on from this most unfortunate situation.'

'No!' Juliette jumped to her feet, her eyes blazing with anger. 'What kind of woman would I be, to accept money to conveniently disappear? I am not some—some trollop to be paid off. If I accepted Monsieur Bauduin's offer, essentially a bribe to keep me silent, then I would be left quite without a character.'

'I'm sorry, I don't understand,' the lawyer said, 'why then are you so set on marrying my client?'

'I am not at all interested in marrying Monsieur Bauduin. I want to marry the Duc de Montendre.' Juliette twisted her lace handkerchief into a tight ball, breathing heavily, clearly trying desperately to regain control of herself. When she spoke again, she was still shaking, but her voice was calm. 'I cannot accept money, because it would confirm what you think, that I am a charlatan. I am not. My claim on the Duc de Montendre is a valid one, and your client is the Duc de Montendre.'

'Mademoiselle de Cressy, if you would permit me, I would like to consult with Monsieur Bauduin,' Maxime said hesitantly.

'No, there is no need,' Jean-Luc said firmly. 'Here are my terms, Mademoiselle de Cressy. I assume that you are determined to press your claim?'

'I have no option.'

'Very well then, you will remain here in Paris for the time being. Maxime will ensure that you have sufficient funds to keep you in respectable lodgings along with your maidservant. The arrangements will be made in such a way that the proprieties will be observed. I leave that with Maxime to discuss with yourself. I will have no dealings with you other than through Maxime, and I will require your promise that you will speak to no one other than Maxime on this matter.'

'But why should I agree…?'

'I am coming to that, *mademoiselle*. I sympathise with your predicament. I understand that you are overwrought. I understand that your circumstances are straitened. But you must see that the solution is not for me to abandon the woman

I love...' Jean-Luc paused to press a kiss to Sophia's hand '...for a complete stranger.'

'In our circle, such marriages are not uncommon. Maman said that she met Papa only twice before they were married, and they were very happy.'

'But your father was not in love with another woman,' Sophia pointed out.

'Of course not!' Juliette said indignantly. 'But...'

'I have not yet finished.' Jean-Luc spoke with quiet authority. Juliette, who was, Sophia was beginning to suspect, rather too used to getting her own way, stiffened, pouted, but was silenced.

'My wife and I have only just been reunited. We have better things to do than set about trying to disprove your claim, but none the less, that is what we will now do. I do not know how long that will take us, but I can promise you, Mademoiselle de Cressy, that we will succeed, and I will give you my word of honour that when we are done, we will lay all the evidence before you. You will now give me your word of honour that when we do, you will accept the proof and withdraw your claim.'

'The only evidence you will find will prove that I am telling the truth. And then—'

One look at Jean-Luc's face, and Juliette broke off.

'I think that Mademoiselle de Cressy understands,' Maxime Sainte-Juste said, breaking the short silence. 'Do you not, *mademoiselle*?'

Juliette nodded.

'And you are happy to give Monsieur Bauduin your word,' the lawyer said, encouraging her with a gentle smile, 'that whatever evidence he uncovers, you will accept the findings?'

Juliette heaved a sigh. 'I have no option.'

'That was ungracious, *mademoiselle*.'

Juliette turned to the lawyer in surprise, her big eyes wide. 'I'm sorry. I did not mean...' She heaved another sigh. 'You are quite right, it was most ungracious.' She turned to Jean-Luc. 'My apologies. You have my word of honour that I will accept your findings and my word that in the meantime, I will say nothing of this to anyone. Since I have no acquaintance in Paris anyway...'

'My sister,' Maxime Sainte-Juste said, 'will I am sure be most happy to make your acquaintance, and to show you the city. She is about your age, *mademoiselle*, and a most respectable young woman. As to your lodgings, I am sure that my mother will be able to recommend—' Sensing his employer's astonishment, he broke off. 'But we can discuss the matter later. I can see that Monsieur Bauduin is anxious to be away.'

'Monsieur Bauduin, it appears, can happily leave matters in your hands, Maxime,' Jean-Luc said, giving his friend a quizzical look. 'But you are quite right, I have a great many things to attend to, not least presenting my wife to Parisian society.' He bowed briefly over Juliette's outstretched hand. 'Your servant, *mademoiselle*.'

'Goodbye, *mademoiselle*.' Sophia dropped a curtsy.

'I am truly sorry,' Juliette said, returning the curtsy. 'If I had any other option, believe me, I would pursue it. I have no desire to ruin your life.'

'Which proves,' Sophia said to Jean-Luc as they settled into the waiting carriage, 'if nothing else, that she truly does believe her story, and more worryingly, is convinced that any evidence you produce will support it, rather than discredit it.'

'All it proves is that she is deluded.' Jean-Luc took her hand. 'Though I do believe that she is now in no doubt of our marriage and our feelings for each other.'

'Yes, but it hasn't made any difference.'

'I didn't expect it to, not really.'

'Jean-Luc, you don't think her claim might have substance?'

'I don't think for a moment that I am a duke.'

'But?'

He shrugged, but it was unconvincing. 'Why do I know so little of my true heritage? Why did it never occur to me to ask questions of my parents when they were still alive?'

'Because you had no reason to.'

'Until Mademoiselle de Cressy came along,' he said wryly. 'And now, not only am I plagued with having to prove I am not a duke, she has inadvertently plagued me with doubts about who I really am. I always thought my parents were simply very private people, content in their own company, you know? But looking back, I wonder if there was more to it? Were they hiding something?' He sighed impatiently. 'It is driving me mad, the questions I should have asked them and now cannot.'

'But not so mad that you are imagining yourself the Duc de Montendre?'

He laughed. 'No. Mademoiselle de Cressy is—how do you say it, barking at the wrong tree?'

'Maybe so, but she is utterly convinced it is the right one.'

'She is also now convinced that we are married, and that we are madly in love.'

'That is very true.' Sophia leaned back on the squabs with a sigh. The parallels between Juliette and herself could not be ignored. Though Juliette's papa had loved his daughter, ultimately it had made no difference. She was left quite alone and without practical resources. For both of them, marriage was the obvious solution. Ironically, marriage was not a solution for either of them. Despite the shame and degradation Sophia had suffered, she had not once regretted her decision to forgo matrimony in favour of the less formal contract she had entered into. That, at least, she had been free to terminate when it had served its purpose. She shuddered to think of the alternative, which would have bound her for the rest of her life.

'I can see the wheels turning in your mind. What are you thinking?'

She opened her eyes to discover Jean-Luc resting his head beside hers. 'Poor Juliette,' Sophia said. 'You won't understand, but when she said she had no option but to press her claim, she spoke something close to the truth. Women in her position are reared only to be wives. Without a proper education, without any marketable skill, they have so few resources, only their body, their blood, their pedigree to barter with. You must not blame her for being so persistent, Jean-Luc.'

'I don't. When I said that I sympathise, I meant it. It does not square particularly well with my conscience to deceive her as we are doing, but she has given me no option. I will not solve her predicament by surrendering my own freedom.'

'No, that's not what I meant. Such a marriage, resented from the very beginning, would be doomed to failure. But the alternative for Juliette, to sell herself to a different kind of bidder...'

'It won't come to that! Whether or not she is

the daughter of the Comte, as she claims, she is clearly gently bred. Women like that do not become courtesans, if that is what you meant. She is young, she is beautiful, she will find another man to marry her—with or without the dowry which I still intend to pay her. Though whether she will accept...'

'That is very generous of you.'

Jean-Luc shrugged. 'It's not. I can afford it.'

But he did not have to, Sophia thought. An honourable man. She smiled at him. 'She is very beautiful, quite exquisite in fact, and as you said, obviously gently bred. Were you the Duc de Montendre, she would be the perfect wife for you.'

'Well, I'm not. I'm Jean-Luc Bauduin, and the perfect wife for me is sitting right beside me. Thank you, *ma belle*, but I have had enough of Mademoiselle de Cressy for the moment. May I say that Madame Bauduin played her part to perfection.'

'Thank you. As did Monsieur Bauduin, which made my part considerably easier. There were times when I really believed you.'

He laughed. 'I almost convinced myself.

'We were good, weren't we?'

'Better than that. We were excellent.'

Their foreheads were almost touching as they rested on the squabs, his mouth only inches from hers. She felt that odd fluttering tension in her belly that she couldn't find a name for. She wanted him to kiss her. She knew, from that slumberous look in his dark brown eyes, that he wanted to kiss her, though he would not make the first move. Was there anything wrong with a kiss? There was a great deal right with it, she had learned yesterday. And no harm, not really. Compared to all the other physical intimacies she had been forced to endure, quite innocent. Innocently pleasurable, in fact, she reasoned.

'We were so good,' Sophia said, 'that were I really your wife, and were you really my husband, I think you might kiss me right now, don't you?'

'I think I might.'

She smiled. 'Then I think you should. In the name of authenticity.'

'In the name of veracity, I should tell you that I don't give a damn about authenticity. I simply want to kiss you, Sophia.'

'I'm not sure that I much care why you do, Jean-Luc. I just wish that you would.'

'Then it will be my pleasure,' he said. And did. Kisses like before. Sweet kisses. Kisses that were safe, because they were only kisses, and because he had promised they would never be anything more. Safe kisses which felt dangerous in a dizzying way, as if she was on a precipice looking down. She knew she would not fall, but there was delight in imagining the thrill of tumbling into the abyss. That's what those kisses did. Kisses that took no liberties, and so she was free to return them. And when she did, and the kisses took on a more dangerous note, Jean-Luc stopped kissing her, releasing her before she even knew she needed to be released. Then she rested her head contentedly against his shoulder, feeling safe, for the first time in her life.

Chapter Seven

The next week was spent paying social calls in response to the flurry of invitations which, as Jean-Luc had predicted, poured in following the announcement of their marriage. His friends, business colleagues and acquaintances had all read the announcement of their nuptials in the newspaper. They were, to a man and woman, astounded to discover he was married. They could all, having now had the pleasure of meeting his English wife, understand perfectly his desire to renounce his bachelordom. After another exhausting round of visits earlier that day, Jean-Luc had declared that they had earned a treat, in the form of a night on the town.

Their destination was on the other side of the river in Le Marais, an area which had, before the Revolution, been popular with the nobility but which was now, he informed Sophia, notoriously unsafe and awash with unsavoury characters. 'Welcome to the Boulevard du Crime,' he announced as their carriage came to a halt. 'Named for the number of farces and melodramas performed here nightly, and not for the criminal activities which take place in the surrounding area.'

The wide boulevard was crammed with jostling carriages, lined with theatres from which lights and braziers blazed, the pavements awash with milling people from all walks of life. 'Goodness,' Sophia said, clutching his arm, 'it is busier than Drury Lane.'

There were hawkers selling nosegays, oysters, wine, cherries and a pale, potent spirit from the south which Jean-Luc informed her was called pastis. Outside each of the theatres, actors touted their shows, their cries and competitive banter adding to the general hubbub. Some people were strolling idly, enjoying the raucous atmosphere, while others were studiously examining the bills of fayre each theatre had to offer. There were groups of men in formal evening dress standing alongside groups of men still in their working clothes. There were courting couples in their Sunday best, oblivious to the hive of activity, with eyes only for each other. Women, in the tawdry plumage that formed the uniform of the street walkers called out their wares in competition with the other hawkers.

'Sophia, *ma belle*.' There was a warning note in Jean-Luc's voice. 'Two gentlemen of my acquaintance approaching. Jacques, Marc, may I have the pleasure of introducing you to my wife. Monsieur Jacques Burnell, and Monsieur Marc le Brun are rivals in the wine trade.'

'You flatter us, Jean-Luc,' the younger man said, bowing low over Sophia's hand. 'No one rivals your husband in the wine business, Madame Bauduin.'

'And now, it seems, none of us can rival him in the marital trade either,' the other vintner said, making his bow. 'Your husband has, as ever, picked the cream of the crop. It is a pleasure to make your acquaintance, Madame Bauduin.'

'We read the announcement of your marriage in the newspaper, didn't we, Jacques? None of us could believe it, but now the reason is very clear. No wonder he kept quiet about you.'

'You flatter me, *monsieur*.'

'Not possible, *madame*. Do I detect a trace of an English accent?'

'You do.'

'We met when I was in London on business,' Jean-Luc said. 'In February, as you may recall, for I missed your wife's birthday party, Marc.'

'Ah yes, how could I forget. My sister was most upset, Madame Bauduin. She has a little soft spot for Jean-Luc. She will be your sworn enemy now.'

'I should tell you, *ma belle*, that Marc's sister is only six years old.'

'And showing very early signs of excellent taste,' Sophia said, casting her husband a melting look to which he responded by kissing her hand.

'For pity's sake, Jean-Luc, you will melt her glove. I hope you have had the sense to purchase a box with a curtain at the theatre, else you will be providing the show.' Marc made Sophia another bow. '*Madame*, we must leave you or we will be late for our own show. I hope that you will allow my wife to do you the honour of calling on you? She will be delighted to be able to practise her English.'

'I look forward to it, Monsieur le Brun.'

'Alas, I do not have a wife to call upon you,' Monsieur Burnell said. 'But I dine tomorrow with the Corneilles, you will be there, I hope? Excellent. I look forward to it. Until then.' He made his farewell bow, and the two sallied off in the direction of the Théâtre de la Gaîté.

'You played the loving wife perfectly, as always,' Jean-Luc said, taking her arm once more. 'Now, hopefully we can relax and enjoy the show.' He directed her towards the foyer of the smallest of the theatres on the boulevard. 'I am hoping it will be a new experience for you.'

'Théâtre des Funambules,' Sophia read, frowning. 'What does that mean?'

'Theatre of Tightrope Walkers. You don't know what that is?' When she shook her head, he grinned. 'Then you are in for a real treat.'

The tiny theatre was packed to the rafters. In the stalls, men were crammed in, standing shoulder to shoulder. Fortunately, Jean-Luc had secured one of the few boxes. As he helped her out of her evening cloak, Sophia was relieved to discover that she was not, as she had feared, overdressed. Though many in the audience were plainly garbed, a significant number were in evening clothes. Her own gown was of cerise-pink satin with an overdress of net, the hem and puff sleeves embellished with an embroidered design of black poppies. Her long gloves had been dyed to match the gown, an extravagance which Sophia would never have permitted herself but which, since Madeleine had taken it upon herself to order them for her, she guiltily treasured. They fitted so very perfectly, the soft leather encasing her arms like a second skin, that it was a pleasure to wear them. She couldn't resist running her fingers up and down the length of her arm. Looking up, she caught Jean-Luc staring at her. 'They are very nice gloves,' Sophia said, embarrassed.

'You certainly wear them beautifully, though I think you could make a hessian sack look fashionable.'

He took her hand, opening the two tiny pearl buttons which fastened the glove at her wrist, pressing a kiss to her pulse. For heaven's sake, she thought, it was absurd, to catch her breath over such a fleeting touch. Then he kissed her again, a mere caress of a kiss, but his lips lingered just enough for him to sense the delightful *frisson* which rippled through her.

'People are staring,' Sophia cautioned. 'Oh. That is why you are doing it.'

But he shook his head, smiling at her in a way that, oddly, made her stomach knot. 'It is a happy coincidence that what I wish to do is what I ought to be doing Namely making love to my wife.'

'Jean-Luc! One cannot make love in a public theatre.'

'Sophia.' The way he spoke her name was a caress. 'Don't you know there are any number of ways to make love?'

Any number, and she thought she had endured them all, but this was a completely new experience. Not a performance, but a duet. The way their eyes met. The latent heat in his gaze which heated her blood. The tingling of her skin where his lips touched her wrist, surely the most innocuous of places, yet her pulse leapt in response, her body inched closer to his until their knees were touching. His smile, such a wicked smile, seemed to connect directly to her insides. It made her light-headed, that smile, made her want something she could not name, or did not care to.

'Sophia.'

He breathed her name again, his lips against her ear, the whisper of his breath on the nape of her neck another caress, so sweetly arousing. Arousing? He pressed another of those fluttering kisses to the skin behind her ear. And more, down her neck. And her hand lifted of its own accord to touch his cheek, and her mouth was already anticipating his kiss when there was a roar from the audience, and their private performance ended as the public performance got underway on the stage below.

'*Mesdames et messieurs,*' the Master of Ceremonies intoned from the stage, 'tonight, at the Théâtre des Funambules we have for your delectation a very special performance, a farewell to the European stage from one of its most talented duos. Tonight, for one night only, it is my great privilege to present the most extraordinary, the most graceful and indeed the most flexible acrobatic performers in the civilised world. Prepare to be both astounded and amazed. I give you brother and sister, Alexandr and Katerina, the fabulous Flying Vengarovs.'

The shouting and cheering subsided. Clothing rustled as the audience settled back in their chairs in anticipation. Painted fans wafted faces hot from the heavy, still air of the tiny candlelit auditorium. Tension, as taut as the rope stretched between two poles on the stage, was palpable. Sophia edged forward on her seat, leaning on the balcony of the box. Beside her, Jean-Luc also edged forward. She reached for his hand. His fingers twined with hers.

The Flying Vengarovs were a striking pair, he so tall, and she so tiny in comparison. Both wore long cloaks, hers dark blue and his jet black, studded with paste diamonds that sparkled and shimmered in the stage lights. There were paste diamonds in Katerina Vengarov's burnished auburn hair too. The couple seemed to float across the floor together like a constellation of stars tracking across the night sky. For a long, tense moment, they simply stood together in front of their tightrope, facing the expectant crowd. Then they made their bows and dropped their cloaks.

There was a collective intake of breath. The male half of the duo was half-naked, wearing only a pair of tightly fitted knitted pantaloons. His muscled torso gleamed, his sculpted physique drawing a chorus of whistles as he flexed his arms, the gesture rippling through his chest and stomach muscles. Beside him, tiny in comparison, the female acrobat looked quite naked. Closer inspection allowed Sophia to discern that she was wearing a flesh-coloured tunic studded with more paste diamonds clinging to her perfectly proportioned body. The pair were positively indecent, but Sophia found herself excited. They had an exotic allure that set them quite apart from their audience, as if they came from quite another world. She gazed rapt, as the girl put her bare foot on her brother's linked hands and he propelled her upwards on to the tightrope. He followed her, too quickly for Sophia to work out how he'd managed to leap so high, and the show began.

* * *

'I've never seen anything like it,' Sophia said for the third time, 'They seemed to fly through the air, as if they really did have wings. So graceful. So fluid. It was quite breathtaking.'

As was she, Jean-Luc thought, seating himself on the sofa beside her. They were back at the *hôtel*, sharing a nightcap in front of the fire in the small salon off the main dining room. Sophia had removed her precious gloves and had curled her feet up under her skirts. He had hardly been able to watch the Flying Vengarov duo for watching her, eyes wide with wonder, lips parted, her hand tightening in his, her breath held every time the brother released his sister to hurtle through the air. And every time he caught her safely, Sophia turned to him to share her relief and her joy, and he had been hard put not to kiss her on those pouted, parted, delightful lips, for his own sheer joy at being there with her.

'It was magical,' she was saying now, clasping her hands together at her breast. 'To see the perfection of the human body, such control, such shapes as they made together. I could have watched them for ever, they were so—so, beautiful, they made me feel so—' She broke off with an embarrassed laugh. 'What I'm trying to say is thank you.'

'There is no need to thank me, *ma belle*, your pleasure is my pleasure.' She smiled at him uncertainly. 'I mean you,' Jean-Luc hastened to reassure her. 'I wanted to please you, not my wife.' Though the boundaries between the two, the real Sophia and the part she was playing, were becoming increasingly blurred in his mind.

'It was a lovely thing to do and I'm very grateful but there was no need to.'

'Perhaps not, but I wanted to.'

'Oh.' She reached out to touch him, her hand resting fleetingly, disturbingly, on his knee. 'It was a—a pleasure, to watch them perform. It should have been shocking, they were all but naked, but it was...'

'Exciting?'

She blushed delightfully, nodding. 'Each time she flew through the air, there was a moment when I thought he wasn't going to catch her, a moment when she might fall, though she must know she would not. I was holding my breath every time.'

'I know.'

'You were watching me? But you must have missed...'

'I saw the entire performance reflected in your face. I assure you, I missed nothing. You were every bit as exciting to watch as the Flying Vengarovs.'

'It was like kissing,' she said softly, under her breath. 'That feeling. I've been trying to find words for it ever since we first—and that's what it was like.'

She smiled at him, and blood surged to his groin. A smile, that's all it was. He shifted on the sofa, preparing to get to his feet. 'It's late.'

Her face fell. 'Of course. We've probably had quite enough excitement for one day.'

'Sophia, it is more excitement that I am trying to avoid! I have no wish to break our agreement. If only you had not mentioned kissing...'

'But I did.' She shifted on the sofa, leaning towards him. 'Would it be wrong of us to kiss goodnight? As your wife...'

'No.' He eased himself away from her distracting presence. 'I want to kiss you, Sophia, and I won't pretend it is part of our act.'

He made to get to his feet, but she stayed him with a hand on his arm. 'Don't go just yet.'

'Sophia, what I'm trying to say is that you are a temptation I am finding increasingly difficult to resist.'

'You don't have to resist.' Sophia knew she was blushing, but she forced herself to hold Jean-Luc's gaze, her heart thumping at her boldness, the tension she would rather not name knotting in her belly. It was her own fault that he hesitated. He was playing by her rules. 'A kiss is not temptation,' she said, 'it is simply a kiss.'

Jean-Luc's smile had a sinful twist to it. 'Simply a kiss.' He pulled her into his arms. '*Ma belle*, I hate to contradict you, but I am fairly certain that there is no such thing.'

His mouth covered hers and her lids drifted closed as their lips met and the sweet, aching feeling that she could easily become addicted to flooded her veins. They kissed. Feathery kisses mirrored by the feathery touch of his hands on her bare arms, sending little *frissons* of delight shivering through her. Then deeper kisses, lips clinging, and her hands crept up around his neck, her fingers curling into the silky softness of his hair. Heat spread through her body as their kisses merged one into another, and she sank back on to the sofa, pulling him with her. Deeper kisses, and his tongue touched hers, sending a shock through her that made her nipples tingle and tighten. She followed his lead, sliding her tongue into his mouth, registering the answering sharp intake of his breath, the way his hands tightened on her arms, leaving her in no doubt of the pleasure she gave.

They were only kisses. Simply kisses. Nothing more. And so a complete delight. She let her hand drift down his body, smoothing over the line of his back, enjoying the presence of him, muscular, taut, reassured by the layers of clothing between them and at the same time revelling in it, the heat of his body, the roughness of his cheek, the day's growth of stubble rasping against her palm, the scent of his soap and his linen and the underlying, elusive Jean-Luc scent she could not even begin to describe.

He dragged his mouth from hers, but before she could protest, there were more kisses. On her lids. On her cheeks. The line of her jaw. The lobe of her ear. Kisses where no one had kissed her before, where she hadn't known kisses could be bestowed. Simply kisses, but they were making her restless now, sending her hands fluttering up and down his back, across the expanse of his shoulders, in search of something more. His hand skimmed down her body, brushing the side of her breast, and his mouth trailed kisses down her throat, to the swell of her breasts above the décolleté of her gown. She stiffened. He hesitated. She made no move, waiting. And then he kissed her again, his mouth gentle on her breasts, and his hand, cupping one of them through her gown, so gently, so carefully, that she knew she had only to move, to utter the tiniest word of protest, and he would stop.

She knew he would stop if she asked, and so she did not protest. She knew he would stop, and so she didn't want him to. Instead she surrendered to the sensation of his gentle caress, of his thumb, circling her nipple through her clothing, the delicious, delightful feeling of her nipple tightening, the tension connecting with the knot in her belly, sending new ripples of sensation through her. She bit her lip hard as an involun-

tary moan caught in her throat, and the echo of
it, a noise which she had manufactured so often
to order, threatened to rupture the mood. She
opened her eyes, met Jean-Luc's gaze, his lids
heavy, his desire reflected in slashes of colour
on his cheeks. Jean-Luc, this was Jean-Luc not
that despised other.

'Do you want me to stop, Sophia?'

He could not have said anything more reassuring. She shook her head. She caught his face
between her hands, kissing him, her tongue
sweeping over his lower lip, her kiss urgent, de-
manding. It was returned fervently, urgently, and
her eyes drifted closed once more, and she was
lost in a dark, vibrant, sensual world of endless
kisses. His hand on her breast jolted new sensations from her, making her arch against him, as
if her body was searching for something, seek-
ing some place high up, where she must cling
and kiss and where her hands must find skin beneath his coat and his shirt, where she must feel
the ripple of his muscle with no barrier between
them. She was lost in his kisses now, her mouth
clamouring for more, her body clamouring too
in a different way, coiled tight as a ship's rope.

And then, before she knew what was happening, she unravelled, the tension inside her rent her apart, as if a knife had slashed through the ropes lashing her together, casting her adrift on a strange foreign sea.

Sophia cried out, a wild sound, which she caught instantly, covering her mouth, pushing herself free of Jean-Luc, and catching the wave of pleasure rippling through her before it had time to crash again. Mortified, she concentrated on suppressing everything that her body was intent upon doing to her, frantically gathering all the pieces together, wrapping her arms around herself, keeping her gaze fixed firmly on the ground, all the time aware of Jean-Luc beside her, keeping his distance, making no attempt to touch her, but watching silently.

She felt exposed. She felt both wildly elated, and at the same time on the verge of tears. She had always been able to hide her revulsion from Hopkins, why was it so difficult to hide these very different, utterly opposing feelings from Jean-Luc? She stumbled to her feet. 'It's late. I'm going to bed.'

'Sophia.' He got to his feet, though he made

no attempt to touch her. 'There is nothing to be ashamed of.'

'I'm not,' she said, though even to her own ears, the lie was clear enough. She crossed her arms. 'You have made your point, Jean-Luc, if that is what you're trying to say.'

'My point?' He looked genuinely perplexed, and then he swore. 'Simply kisses. You think that I set out to prove you wrong? I had quite forgotten—Sophia, you cannot possibly be imagining that what you are feeling was one-sided? I assure you, I am every bit as aroused by our kisses as you are.'

Her cheeks burned 'I am not—you are not—you did not...' She stuttered to a halt. He had not made any attempt to demonstrate his arousal to her. He had, in fact, made every effort to keep sufficient distance between her and that part of him.

'You offered me kisses. I promised I would not take anything more than you offered.'

An honourable man who had not taken, but who had given. 'I'm sorry,' Sophia said helplessly. 'I didn't know. I have never....'

'That much is obvious,' he said gently. 'Your husband has a great deal to answer for.'

'My husband?'

'Arranged match or no, he should at least have tried to make it a pleasurable experience,' Jean-Luc said tightly. 'You may have been without experience, but that would almost certainly not have applied to him.'

He thought she was married. Or had been married. When she'd told him that she was not innocent, that was what he had surmised. She didn't know whether to be appalled or relieved. It didn't matter, Sophia told herself. What he thought shouldn't matter. But it did, and the sordid truth would appal him. It was kinder by far not to contradict him.

'It really is late,' Sophia said, pretending to yawn. 'And we have an early start tomorrow.' She forced a bright smile now. 'It has taken a considerable effort for you to obtain permission for us to cross the hallowed portals of the Montendre town house. I want to be fresh in order to help you make the most of it.'

'And you want me to discontinue this too painful conversation. As you wish, *ma belle*. I will bid you goodnight.'

He looked hurt, but there was nothing she could do about that. *'Bonne nuit,'* Sophia said, and turning on her heel, fighting the urge to flee, she left the room without a backward glance or another word.

Once alone, Jean-Luc retired to his study. Pouring himself a cognac, he leaned his head against the cool glass of the window. Light flickered through the curtains which had been drawn across Sophia's window. He knew her well enough by now. Any attempt to force a confidence would result only in her retreating further. That brittle smile of hers betrayed her every time. Was it his fault that their kisses had got out of hand? He sighed, taking a deep draught of his very excellent brandy. He hadn't intended them to, though he was forced to admit that he had, shamefully, wanted to prove a point. Which wasn't like him. He took another, smaller sip of his cognac and dropped wearily on to the window seat, turning his back on that flickering reminder that his wife was in the process of undressing.

His wife. Sophia had been here, playing that part for less than two weeks, but he felt as if she had been here much longer. He could not have said what it was she had done to change the already efficient running of the household, but there had been subtle changes. Dinners were less formal and more delicious. Breakfasts too, were more intimate affairs, taken not in the dining room but in a small parlour he didn't remember ever using before, but which caught the morning sun. At breakfast they planned their day, the time to be spent both together and apart—for his business, and the painfully slow process of trying to negotiate entrance to the town house belonging to the Montendre family, occupied him for a proportion of every day. Tomorrow, if matters went as planned, they would finally breach those hallowed portals together. He and his wife.

He had moved well beyond a passing interest in Sophia. He had desired her from the first, but he had very quickly come to enjoy her company. No, that was putting it too mildly. He relished her company. He looked forward to it. He wanted to please her. And those kisses—yes, he had been trying to prove a point. He wanted her to admit that they were not simply kisses. He wanted her to admit what he felt. That they meant something more.

Even though there could be nothing more. Sophia was here to help him escape marriage yet ironically, Sophia was making him wonder whether marriage would be such a bad thing after all. Ridiculous! Jean-Luc drained his cognac. Absolutely ridiculous. He was frustrated, that was all. Though he did not like to think of himself as in any way a typical man, in this instance he was, wanting what he was told he could not have. Masculine pride was what motivated him, nothing more. He was certainly not falling in love with her. That was inconceivable, especially in such a short period of time. Now *that* was a preposterous notion!

Sighing, he allowed himself to look out of the window again. Sophia's bedchamber was in darkness. She was in bed. Asleep, or reflecting on what must surely be her first experience of pleasure? Could it be called pleasure, when she seemed to enjoy it so little? Maybe gratification was more appropriate. But that sounded too cold for what had been a shared sensual experience. Her response had clearly unsettled her. If only he'd known, he would have been more careful, but he had been so lost in the delight of arousing her, in watching her surrender to sensation, in wishing only to please her more and still more, that it hadn't occurred to him that the climax would be new territory for her.

Unwelcome territory? The clock on the mantel chimed the hour. One in the morning. The very morning in which he was to visit the Montendre town house, and perhaps finally obtain the evidence he needed to prove to Juliette de Cressy that he was not the man she wanted him to be. Though who he was—now that was a very different question. Not, however, one to ponder tonight. He should be asleep, so that he would be sharp, fully alert in the morning. He was wasting far too much time thinking about his wife, who was not his wife, and whom he would no longer require to be his wife, perhaps as soon as tomorrow. Which thought should make him happy. And not make him feel—no, he was not going to explore what it made him feel. He was going to bed. And to sleep. And he was not, most definitely not going to lie awake and think about the distracting, beautiful, intriguing woman lying alone in bed in the adjoining room.

Chapter Eight

To her surprise, Sophia had slept deeply, awaking as the morning light crept through a gap in the curtains, in a very different mood from the one in which she had fled from Jean-Luc the previous night. Pulling on a wrap, she padded over to the window and pulled the heavy curtains apart. The sky was changing from grey to pale blue, the few scattered clouds white and fluffy. She opened the window to lean out, relishing the welcoming kiss of the sun on her skin. It was going to be a lovely day.

She closed her eyes, surprised to discover that her memory of the previous evening's events was no longer tainted by embarrassment. Last night had been a revelation. Jean-Luc had been right, there was no such thing as simply a kiss.

Until that shocking moment of release, she had been quite lost in those kisses and Jean-Luc's touch and his taste. Her hands roving over his body, she had relished the effect she was having, because it was an echo of the effect he was having on her.

Was that why it had happened? Startled, her eyes flew open. Last night, she had not set out to induce pleasure, but she had done, almost effortlessly. Last night, there had been none of the physical intimacies she had experienced before. They had been fully clothed, for heaven's sake, and yet she had surrendered to the wave of passion, the surging crescendo, in a way she never had before. She was not an expensively purchased toy for Jean-Luc to play with. She was not a well-trained automaton, dutifully responding to his cues. He had given her no directions, and he had expected nothing from her. He would have ceased at the merest indication from her. He had not gone galloping off intent on his own journey to completion. It was she who had galloped off uncontrollably! It was perfectly natural, Jean-Luc had said. And in the bright, revealing light of this June morning, Sophia saw that he had spoken the truth.

Hopkins, she supposed, had earned the right to affect indifference, having bought her body to do with as he wished, requiring only that she appeared to enjoy what gave him pleasure. It should have been different with Frederick. He had professed to care, but in the end had proved he cared only for himself. His subsequent behaviour demonstrated that beyond doubt. She'd thought it was the province of the male, to take pleasure from the female. She'd assumed that every woman did as she had learnt to do, to simulate her enjoyment. And she'd been wrong.

Though the circumstances, Sophia thought bitterly, until now had hardly been conducive. With both Frederick and Hopkins, she had been burdened by the bargains she had struck. She had knowingly sold herself twice, albeit the nature of the arrangements had been very different. Jean-Luc was also paying for her services, but on an entirely contrasting basis. He had no rights to her body. That was the enormous and very significant difference.

Last night. Tension curled in her belly, an echo

of what had happened. Her first ever climax, and she had smothered it. She didn't want it to be her last. She was only twenty-six. When she left Paris, when she was no longer Jean-Luc's wife, then she would be free to take a lover if she wished. She tried to picture him, this mythical, considerate man, but she could only picture Jean-Luc. She didn't want another lover. She wanted him. Dare she dismantle the barriers she had been so determined to erect between them? What if she discovered it was a mistake? What if last night was unique? Could a yes become a no once more?

'Bonjour, Madame Bauduin.'

Madeleine's appearance with her morning coffee saved Sophia from answering this tricky question. But Madeleine's sidelong glances at the neat, undisturbed bedclothes as she poured the coffee and straightened the curtains made it clear that she was not the only one considering the subject. She knew that her dresser would not betray her to any of the other servants, just as she had assumed that Jean-Luc put similar trust in his valet, but it was clear that those two most personal of servants knew that their master and mistress were not sharing a marital bed. If she allowed Jean-Luc to make love to her it would enhance the charade of a happy marriage.

Sophia set her coffee cup down with a clatter. No! She would not sully her feelings for prosaic purposes. If she made love to Jean-Luc it would be for no reason other than genuine desire. And it was very much a question of *if*, for even if she wanted to, after last night there was no certainty that he would feel the same, she reminded herself, picking up her coffee again.

'I think the powder-blue half-pelisse, with the white promenade dress would be a good choice for today,' Madeleine said, holding up the garments for her inspection. 'Monsieur Bauduin has ordered the carriage for ten. He is taking you out to see more of our beautiful city?'

'No. I mean, yes.' Sophia set down her cup. 'And, yes, that combination will work perfectly.'

'You could wear the pale blue muslin with this pelisse, but I think…'

'No, the white is perfect. You have excellent taste, Madeleine. Thank you.'

'It is my job, *madame*, and you make it very easy for me. When Monsieur Bauduin engaged me, I had no idea that I would be working for such a very beautiful mistress. To be honest, I was very surprised to be engaged by the master of the house and not the mistress. It is very unusual, but yours is a most unusual love match, no?'

'Yes.' Sophia smiled thinly. She liked Madeleine, and did not like lying to her. 'I didn't realise you had heard the story of how we met.'

'*Monsieur*'s valet regaled us all with it. He had *monsieur*'s permission, rest assured. Some of the servants were a bit dubious—it seems *monsieur* had not even mentioned your name. But now all is clear. Such a *coup de foudre*, of course he wanted to keep you secret, in his heart, until you were reunited.' Madeleine sighed and clasped her hands to her bosom. 'I think it is *trés, trés* romantic.'

'Yes.' Sophia busied herself with a second, unwanted cup of coffee. Jean-Luc hadn't told her he'd disseminate their invented history to the servants. She understood why, but it made her uncomfortable.

'*Madame...*' Madeleine too was looking uncomfortable. 'I hope you will forgive me for being so bold, but I cannot help but notice *monsieur* does not...' She indicated the pristine bed. 'I am a married woman myself, *madame*. I know that even when one is in love as you are, the nature of—to some, it is a shock. If there is anything I can do to help, if you wish to talk...'

'No! There is nothing—I am perfectly—you must believe me, Madeleine, there is nothing to be concerned about.'

Her dresser looked unconvinced.

'Nothing at all,' Sophia said firmly. 'Now, if you would be so good as to fetch me some hot water, I do not wish to keep my husband waiting for his breakfast.'

The *hôtel particulier* which belonged to the Montendre dynasty had been closed up at the height of the Terror by the Duke, when he realised he had left it too late to escape Paris. Provision had been made for its maintenance if he were arrested, until such time as either he was released, or, if the worst should befall him, it was subsequently reclaimed by his son. This much Jean-Luc had managed to establish from the firm of lawyers engaged by the Duke to act as trustees, he informed Sophia over breakfast, 'Though the whereabouts of the son and heir are entirely a matter of indifference to them. They are paid on an annual retainer, as are the skeleton staff of the *hôtel*, and all seem content to continue with this arrangement indefinitely.'

'So if the long-lost son did turn up, it would be an inconvenience to them?' she asked.

'It would, but after all this time they don't believe it will happen.' Jean-Luc set aside his half-finished plate of eggs. 'They assume he must be deceased, and they are very likely correct in that assumption, though naturally, they don't wish to be proved so, for that would put an end to their stipends.'

'Which is why they have been obstructive, presumably?'

Jean-Luc grinned. 'Fortunately, I can be very persuasive.'

'And money talks,' Sophia added acerbically. 'As do servants. Madeleine told me this morning that you had shared our romantic history with your valet, who then told the entire household.'

'Best to put a stop to gossip before it begins. Not that I think our servants would gossip beyond the confines of the *hôtel*, but—as I said, it's best not to take the risk.'

'You think of everything.' No, not quite everything. Sophia thought, biting her lip as she recalled the rest of her conversation with Madeleine.

'What is it, *ma mie*? You have that look of yours, the one where you are thinking dark thoughts and wondering whether or not to share them with me. If it is about last night…'

'No, it's not.'

'I went too far,' he continued, heedless, 'I know I did. I knew that with you there would be no such thing as simply a kiss—not for me, anyway. I should have stopped long before…'

'No.' She leaned across the table to touch his hand. 'No, I won't let you take the blame, that's not fair. I knew, you see, that you would stop any time, and I chose not to ask you to. I wanted you to continue, even though I did not know…' Her face was hot, but she was determined to carry on. 'Even though I was not aware of the—the strength of my reaction. In fact, I had no idea, and it—it took me aback.'

Jean-Luc laughed gruffly. 'Your English way

of talking is some times—it took you aback? That is something of an understatement, no?'

'Just a little.' She was obliged to smile. 'I was angry this morning. Not with you,' she added hastily, 'but with—you see I really didn't know I could experience such release.' And she had thought she'd known it all. Why had no one told her? There had been opportunities, in the early days when she had been forced to ask so many mortifying questions, yet none of the so-called experts she had consulted had seen fit to enlighten her about that.

'And now you do,' Jean-Luc said. The silence between them stretched uncomfortably. 'I'm your husband, Sophia. You can tell me anything, ask me anything.'

'You are not really my husband. And even if you were, I can't, because even if you wanted to, which you probably won't…'

'But how will we know, if we don't discuss it, whatever it is?'

He was smiling, but he was not teasing her. There was tenderness in his expression. 'The fact of the matter is that I don't want last night to be the first and the last time,' she whispered. 'I

know that the terms I insisted on forbid us to…'
She paused to take a deep breath. 'What I'm trying to say is that I trust you enough to want to
amend my terms. If you are amenable, that is.'

Jean-Luc exhaled sharply. 'Amenable? You can
be in no doubt what I want. Ah, but of course
you can, being you,' he added, studying her carefully. 'I think that your experience in affairs of
the heart has been unsatisfactory, *ma belle*, am
I right?'

'To put it mildly, which is why I want…'

'As I do.' He pressed her hand. 'Very much,
but it would be a mistake to get too far ahead
of ourselves. It is a leap, not just of faith, from
what happened between us last night, to sharing a bed.'

'I know what size of step it is. I told you, I'm
not an innocent.'

'But you are. You may not be a virgin, but you
have no experience of making love. And now
you are thinking, what an arrogant man my husband is, thinking that he can tutor me, but that's
not what I'm saying.'

'What are you saying?'

'That to learn together, to make the journey

slowly, to discover what pleases you, and what pleases me, would be so much more enjoyable.' His expression became serious. 'And for you, knowing that at any point you could call a halt, I think that is important, yes?'

'Yes.' She forced down the lump which had risen in her throat. 'And I know that you would. You see, I can trust you.'

Jean-Luc pulled out his watch with a groan. 'You do pick your moments. The carriage will be at the door in five minutes.'

'I need only three to get ready.' Sophia jumped to her feet, catching him unawares and pressing a kiss to his lips. 'I do not forget the reason you brought me here. A journey of a different kind for you. This could be a significant step, a momentous day.'

The Montendre town house, Sophia noted, was on a grand scale, a palace rather than a *hôtel particulier*, and one of the most opulent on the very opulent Rue du Faubourg Saint-Honoré. They were expected. As Jean-Luc drew the horses to a halt, the huge gates were opened by a liveried servant. Another awaited at the front door, ready to take charge of the carriage. And another stood at the top of the shallow flight of stairs.

'Welcome to the Hôtel Montendre, Monsieur Bauduin, Madame Bauduin. I have been instructed to show you around. You understand, there has been no one staying here since the Duke and Duchess were taken?'

Jean-Luc reassured the man that they understood perfectly well. In the drive across the city, he had been business-like, going over the little they had learned of the Montendre family and the questions which he hoped they would find answers to. He seemed not in the least nervous, while Sophia struggled to hide her own increasing tension. So much depended upon this visit, not least, the termination of their marriage. Which was the last thing which should be occupying her mind at this moment in time, she chastised herself, as Jean-Luc asked the servant whether there was anyone on the premises who had personally served the Duke and Duchess.

'No, not a single one,' the man replied. 'Some went with them to their fate, alas, and the others left Paris in order to avoid doing so. As far as I am aware, the château in Bordeaux is a ruin.

Though the Duke made provision for a small staff here, he left limited funds for upkeep. The roof leaks like a sieve and the whole place is in dire need of repair. Now, would you like to begin your tour with the state rooms?'

'Actually, I wonder if it would be possible for us to inspect the place unaccompanied,' Jean-Luc said, slipping a coin into the servant's already outstretched hand.

'I see no reason why not, *monsieur*. If you have any questions, I'll do my best to answer them. The bells in the main rooms are still in working order. You only have to ring to summon me.' The servant bowed and withdrew.

'I had hoped there would be some survivors from the Duke's time,' Jean-Luc said, looking bitterly disappointed. 'Never mind, let us see what we can uncover.' He produced a scroll of paper tied with a dusty red ribbon. 'A plan of the *hôtel* I managed to acquire at considerable expense,' he said, unrolling it on the huge circular table which was the only piece of furniture in the reception hallway. 'As you so rightly said this morning, money talks. Come and take a look.'

* * *

It was a melancholy and dispiriting experience, Jean-Luc thought, as he and Sophia climbed the stairs to the third floor. On first impression, the vast, ornate, interconnected state salons were awe-inspiring, seemingly palatial with their gilded cornicing, hand-painted wall coverings and brocade curtains. Some of the floors were marble. Others had oak floorboards. All were elaborately inlaid, the Montendre crest appearing repeatedly, not only on the floors but on the pediments above doors and windows, in the plasterwork, and in the very few pieces of dusty furniture that remained, presumably because they were too heavy and too large to sell. The portraits which had been taken down had left their ghostly outlines on the walls. On closer inspection, dark brown stains could be seen in the cornicing where water had made ingress. There were cracks and cobwebs everywhere. Many of the windows had been boarded over.

'The caretaker didn't exaggerate when he said this place was in dire need of repair,' Jean-Luc said, pulling up a rotten piece of floorboard in the window embrasure of one of the bedchambers.

'It must have been very beautiful in its day,' Sophia said, brushing a cobweb from the bonnet of her hat, 'though I must confess, I wouldn't like to live here. I would need that map with me at all times, to stop me from getting lost.'

'I don't know. It has a certain something.' Jean-Luc pulled back the shutters, sending several startled spiders scuttling off. 'Look at those gardens.' They were at the rear of the house, looking out over what once must have been a magnificent garden. An ornate fountain, now filled with filled with leaves rather than water, stood at the centre of a network of geometric paths, the outline of the formal beds still barely visible. 'It's reminiscent of Versailles on a much smaller scale.'

'Decrepit magnificence,' Sophia said. 'Do you think ghosts haunt these halls and corridors?'

'I wish they did. Then we could talk to them, ask them a few pertinent questions. We haven't even come across a single portrait. I had hoped we'd at the very least get a likeness of the elusive Duke and his wife.' Jean-Luc pulled the shutters back across the room. 'Come on, we've still got the attics to investigate. Perhaps we'll find a helpful ghost lurking up there.'

'There are no such things as ghosts, you know,' Sophia said.

He had pulled out the map again, was casting an eye over the layout of the attics. It was the tone of her voice rather than the words which caught his attention, a terrible yearning that tugged at his heart.

'Death is final, no trace remains,' she said, turning away, making it clear she was speaking to herself. 'I wish that it were otherwise.'

And then she gave herself a little shake. And she flashed him her brittle smile. And he knew better than to ask her what she had been thinking, *who* she had been thinking of, though he longed to know. Her husband? Her father? She had not cared for either men, as far as he was aware. But absence, he supposed, gilded many memories.

Jean-Luc rolled up his map and took her arm, pulling Sophia tightly against his side as they left the room, which was all the comfort he dared offer. 'One conclusion we can draw,' he said as they made for the service stairs. 'is why there has been no pretender claiming the Montendre title. No one in their right mind would take this financial millstone on.'

The attics were, like the rest of the palace, built on a very grand scale, and similarly all but empty. Only one room, at the furthest end, contained a number of boxes and trunks. All of which, save one, contained woman's clothing.

'Shoes,' Sophia said, inspecting one trunk. 'Gloves. Petticoats. Goodness, look at this lace. Sleeves and jackets. These must be decades old. Stoles and scarves. Feathers. Oh, and look at this, Jean-Luc. How lovely.'

He turned from his inspection of the final trunk to find her standing beside him, holding a gown against herself. It was dark red velvet trimmed with gold thread. The sleeves were full, slashed to reveal a gold under-dress. There was nothing at all familiar about it, yet he had the oddest feeling. 'It's probably infested with moths.'

'No. I think there must be some sort of pomander in the boxes. Here, smell.'

Before he could turn away, she thrust the dress at him. His stomach lurched. And then he remembered. 'Bergamot,' he said, with relief. 'Maman had a little bottle of it, though she rarely wore it.'

'I'm not surprised. It's very expensive.'

Jean-Luc shrugged. 'We were comfortably off at one time, I thought I mentioned that.'

'You did. What happened to change your family circumstances?'

'I've no idea. Investments gone wrong, perhaps.'

Sophia bit her lip. She did that when she was pondering. 'Whatever the cause, I had to leave school go into the business—but you know all that,' Jean-Luc said impatiently, 'and it's hardly pertinent. I don't know why you've brought it up.'

He turned away, squatting down by the trunk to pick up a sheaf of papers that looked to be part of a set of household accounts. He made a show of examining them, confused by the nervous churning of his stomach. He heard the rustle of silk and damask as she folded up the gown, the soft sigh of the trunk being closed, and then felt her hand resting lightly on his shoulder. 'I think we have seen enough. We have found no evidence,' she said.

His relief was inexplicable. He smiled up at her. 'Nor any ghosts.'

The manservant was waiting for them in the reception hall with a decanter and glasses. 'One of the last bottles from the Duke's estate,' he said, pouring the wine. 'See what you think, Monsieur Bauduin, would it be worthy of your own prestigious cellars?'

Jean-Luc took a cautious sip, quickly setting the glass aside. 'I'm afraid it's corked, but thank you, I appreciate the gesture.'

'It was the gardener who recognised your name,' the servant said. 'I didn't make the connection with the celebrated Bauduin vintners. It is a pity the wine has deteriorated, but not surprising since there is no Duke in situ and our long-lost heir is highly unlikely to turn up now.'

'What will happen to the place?' Sophia asked, following Jean-Luc's lead and setting her own glass down untouched. 'If the heir never appears to claim it?'

'The annuity that pays our wages will run

out eventually. Then I suppose the place will be closed up completely and left to fall into ruin. It's a real shame, but it's not exactly an uncommon story, though most of the other neighbouring town houses have been reclaimed. With these titled families, there's usually a third cousin twenty times removed happy to come forward, but the Montendre family pretty much all went to the guillotine. Save the boy.'

'And nothing is known of his fate at all?' Jean-Luc asked.

'Nothing. According to old Marie Grunot, he was sent away for his own safety, no one knows where, a couple of years before Madame Guillotine claimed his parents. But to be honest, Marie wasn't the most reliable of witnesses. Her husband, the Duke's valet, went to the guillotine along with the Duke and she was never the same again.'

'None the less I would be interested in speaking to her, out of curiosity you understand,' Jean-Luc said guardedly.

'Not possible, I'm afraid. She passed away last winter. Now, if there's nothing further, time is getting on, and my dinner…'

'What was the husband's name?' Jean-Luc asked sharply.

'Henri Grunot.'

Sophia shot Jean-Luc a startled glance but he shook his head imperceptibly.

'And the boy, do you know what age he was when he was sent away?'

The man puffed out his cheeks. 'Two? Three? Four, maybe? No, couldn't have been four, because the Duke and Duchess were taken in March of 1794, I know that because we were all appointed three months later, when the lawyer had the proof that they were both dead. He'd be—what, thirty years old now, the lad, if he'd survived.'

'How do you know that?'

'Because he was born in June 1788. It's recorded in the family bible. We keep it downstairs. Our gardener is very fond of a good pray at the end of the working day.'

'So my memory was not playing tricks on me?' Sophia asked. 'Henri Grunot, the valet, was indeed one of the signatories to the marriage certificate. Which proves it is authentic.'

Jean-Luc poured himself a glass of cognac, handing Sophia her preferred madeira, before sitting down beside her on the sofa. 'We always suspected it was. Now we also know that one of the witnesses is dead, but we still have no idea of the identity of the other.'

It was late afternoon. The sun cast shadows through the tall windows of the salon. Sophia took a small sip of her wine. It was honey-sweet, and as she had come to expect from Jean-Luc, a first-rate vintage. 'June 1788 is the date recorded for the birth of the Duke's son, and you were born in May of the same year.'

'Coincidence, nothing more. It's not even the same month.'

'That doesn't necessarily prove anything,' Sophia said carefully, for he had been in a strange mood since they left the Montendre residence, on edge, impatient, dismissive. 'The date recorded in the bible is that of the birth of the boy. Quite often what we call our birthday is actually the day we were christened or baptised. So it could be...'

'What?' He jumped to his feet, swallowing the cognac in one draught. 'You saw the list of names, not one of them refers to a Jean-Luc Bauduin.'

'No, but…'

'I know what you're going to say. Cognac is in the same part of the country as Bordeaux, but what of it? There are any number of towns near Bordeaux, no doubt full of numerous men my age, who could just as easily pass for the abandoned son of a long-dead duke.'

'Though it was you Juliette claimed,' Sophia said tentatively. 'It is Jean-Luc Bauduin from Cognac who was named in the de Cressy family legend.'

'Legend, or a fable she has invented.'

'I don't believe she is a fraud, and I don't believe you think so either.'

'I don't know what to think any more.' Jean-Luc sighed, stretching his legs out in front of him. 'You were right, we are not just chasing one wild goose but a whole flock. I don't want to have to go to Bordeaux, but I can't think what else to do. You've been to Bordeaux before, I think you said?'

'I've passed through it.'

'It's a beautiful city. Not as beautiful as Paris, but lovely. You will like it.'

'I?'

'You don't think I'd go on my own, *ma belle*? We are only just reunited. I could not bear to tear myself away from you again so soon.'

'But we are due to host our soirée in three days' time.'

'And we shall. I'm not suggesting we leave immediately. You have put a great deal of effort into organising our soirée. I am, strangely, looking forward to it. I was thinking that tomorrow morning would be a good time to visit the market. You can see what there is, taste and try, as we say, and then send Madame Lambert off to do the shopping on the day with complete confidence.'

'If I wished our chef to tender his resignation. Sourcing ingredients is his province,' Sophia said, laughing, relieved to see his mood lifting. 'I can easily go to the market myself, Jean-Luc. You are not particularly interested in what food we serve.'

'But I am particularly interested in pleasing you, and I think that the way to your heart might well be through your stomach. I'm going to test that theory at the market, I warn you.'

'Oh, if you intend to feed me oysters and snails and *foie gras*, then my heart will melt like a perfectly ripe camembert,' she teased.

'Will it?' Jean-Luc touched her cheek. 'I have an insatiable appetite for camembert.'

There was something in his eyes that made her catch her breath, but she was spared the necessity of a response by a discreet tap on the door. A message had come from the *halle aux vins*, the footman informed Jean-Luc. A problem with a shipment required his urgent attention.

'I'm sorry, I'm going to have to leave you,' he said, after reading the note.

'May I come with you?' Sophia asked impulsively.

'It's likely to take some time to resolve.'

'I'm your wife,' she said, tucking her hand into his arm. 'My place is by your side.'

Chapter Nine

Sophia awoke as the dawn light filtered in through the windows. Bleary-eyed, she sat up, realising as she did so that she was wearing her petticoats and shift, not her nightgown, that she was lying on a leather sofa under her cloak and Jean-Luc's greatcoat, and she was not in her bedchamber but her husband's office in the *halle aux vins*.

Jean-Luc got up from the chair behind his desk to perch beside her. His chin was dark with stubble, his hair tousled, his shirt open at the neck to reveal a dusting of rough dark hairs on his chest. 'Good morning. Dare I ask if you slept well?'

'I am ashamed to say that I did, though I take it you did not?'

'Which is a polite way, I think, of telling me that I look a sight.'

'You look boyishly dishevelled,' she said, smiling shyly. 'It suits you.'

He smoothed his hand over her tumble of hair, pulling out a stray pin. 'Your crumpled, barely awake appearance is strangely appealing too.'

'With my hair on end, and my face creased? Thank you.'

He laughed softly, leaning towards her, sliding his arm around her waist. 'Sophia, you are adorable whatever the circumstances. Will you grant your husband a good morning kiss?'

She was not primped and prepared, yet there was no mistaking the heat in his eyes. And she could admit to herself, couldn't she, that she liked this unkempt version of her husband very much. She twined her arms around his neck. 'Good morning,' she said, and kissed him.

He tasted vaguely of the wine he had been sampling the night before, and of toothpowder too. He must keep a supply here, she thought hazily. He must be accustomed to spending the night on this sofa, where she had slept. He returned her kiss slowly, his fingers combing through her hair, freeing it from the remainder of her pins, and she slid her hand under the loose neck of his shirt, feeling the heat of his skin against her palm for the first time. Their kisses deepened, their tongues touched. She lay back on the couch, pulling him with her, for the first time wanting to close the space he maintained between them, sliding her hands down his back to pull him against her. Their kisses were languorous. Early morning kisses, slumberous, yet rousing every one of her senses.

She tugged his shirt free from his breeches, running her hand up his back, relishing the way his muscles tensed under her touch. More kisses, deeper kisses. He cupped her breast, circling her nipple through the thin cambric of her chemise. She shuddered with delight.

'More?' he asked, his lids heavy, his eyes dark with passion, and she nodded. 'More, please.'

He undid the ribbons to loosen the neckline of her chemise. He kissed her breasts, his mouth tasting every inch of her flesh, kissing as if there was no rush at all, which was both delicious and agonising. When his mouth covered her nipple, sucking, licking, she had to stifle a cry of delight. Her back arched, and she felt the ridge of his arousal, hard against her thigh, and it almost catapulted her out of her blissful bubble, but she screwed shut her eyes and refused to let the past spoil the present, shaking her head to forestall his question, pulling him back on to her, pressing her mouth fervently to his, and losing herself once more in their kisses.

Her nipples were tight, sweetly aching, with his ministrations. Her hands roamed more freely over his back, then, as he angled himself on to his side to lie beside her, on to the contours of his chest. She could feel his heart beating steadily, could feel the rough hair, then the flat, hardness of his nipples, and the sharp intake of his breath as she smoothed her hands over them. It was all so new, and all the more delightful for that.

The tension she now recognised was building steadily low inside her. She was hot. Restless. Wanting, but not wanting to think, afraid to act, anxious that Jean-Luc would misinterpret, that he would not know what she wanted, though how could he, when she herself did not?

'Hush,' he said, kissing her mouth again, gentler this time. 'Stop thinking.'

'I'm trying.'

He laughed softly. 'Stop trying.' He kissed her again, his tongue running along the inside of her lower lip, his hands on the swell of her hip, feathering, stroking, soothing and arousing, easing his body from hers, making enough room on the sofa to lay her on to her back. 'The slightest indication,' he whispered, 'and I promise I will stop.'

'Yes. No. Not yet.' Her body was a mass of contrary urges. Every one of her muscles felt taut. *Frisson* after *frisson* of sensation shivered through her as he stroked her breasts, her flank, and his fingers feathered under her petticoats, on to the soft flesh of her thighs. She mustn't think about it, but she couldn't help it, anticipating the rough intrusion.

But it was different. Whatever he was doing caused a coiling sensation to build inside her. And now his tongue, in her mouth, sliding and stroking in the same delightful, delicious rhythm, so that she finally forgot, lost herself in the spiralling pleasure he was giving her. Lost herself so completely that when her climax came it was like falling off a cliff and tumbling towards the ground, only it was not terrifying but freeing, a release. Finally, she understood as she bit down hard on her lip to stop herself from crying out. That was it, a primal visceral release.

Though it did not last long. As the last wave ebbed away, Sophia opened her eyes, aware of her obligation to return what had been given. It was not the same as before, she told herself as she ran her hand over the length of his erection, and it was not, there was no need to disguise her distaste because she felt none. Though she still couldn't prevent herself thinking of it as a task which must be executed as quickly as possible. She briskly undid the fastenings of his breeches and was sliding her hand inside when he caught her wrist.

'What are you doing?'

'Don't you want me to?'

'I would, very much, if you wished to, but you clearly don't.'

'I do.' Her fingertips brushed the silky skin of his shaft. She discovered that she had not lied, though Jean-Luc didn't believe her. Or perhaps she'd misread his meaning. 'Would you prefer…?'

He caught his breath before gently but firmly removing her hand. 'What I'd prefer, Sophia, indeed what I insist on, is that you do nothing out of a misplaced sense of obligation.'

He sat up, pulling her cloak up over her exposed breasts. She had no idea what to think. Suddenly on the verge of tears, she sank down under the cloak, turning her face away. 'I'm sorry.'

'What on earth are you sorry for?'

She had expected him to be angry, but his voice was gentle, his tone genuinely perplexed. 'I don't know what to do. I don't know what you want.'

He sighed. He wrapped his arms around her, dropping his chin on to her head. 'All I wanted was to please you.'

'You did.'

She felt the shudder of his laughter against her back. 'I know, *ma belle*.' He kissed her hair. 'And when you are ready, then we will share our pleasure, but I don't think you are ready yet.'

'I want to be,' she whispered.

He tensed against her. 'What is stopping you, Sophia, what is holding you back?'

Though his back was to her, she could sense his focused attention. She had never tried to articulate her feelings. There had been pain some times, but experience had taught her how to avoid it. She had never believed her protector would harm her, not deliberately. 'Not fear of pain,' she said, her voice so low that she couldn't even be sure that he heard it, 'but of being violated.' The word shocked her, but it was the right word, she knew it as soon as she said it. 'Violated,' she said again. 'Though it was never against my will, it always felt as if it was.'

Jean-Luc swore viciously. His arms tightened painfully around her. He swore again. 'I had no idea.'

And he still had none. A tear trickled down her cheek. She had never allowed herself to pity her situation, knowing that it would be impossible to carry on if she did, and knowing that she had no choice but to continue.

'Do you want to tell me about it?'

'No!' She turned around, burrowing her face in his neck, clutching him tightly to her. 'It's over now, it's all in the past.' She knew it for a lie. The sordid details would stand between them for ever. Her only consolation was that he would never know. It was not too much to ask, surely. She pressed her mouth to his chest. 'I do want you, Jean-Luc.'

'I believe you, Sophia.' He kissed her forehead. 'But there is absolutely no rush.'

It was still very early when they left the *halle aux vins*, though the wharves on the Quai St Bernard were already busy with barges, stevedores working in an ordered chain to unload the casks and barrels. At Sophia's request, they abandoned the carriage and strolled along the quays, past the Île Saint-Louis, where the washerwomen were at work on the banks of the Seine, and on to the Île de la Cité, crossing in front of the majestic cathedral of Nôtre Dame. Once on the Right Bank, the streets became more crowded. Craftsmen and traders carried bundles, pushed carts. Horses pulled drays groaning with produce, heading for the huge food market at *Les Halles* where the crowds became a seething mass.

It was a place where the senses were assaulted, not always in a pleasant manner, though the laborious process of transferring skeletons from the nearby, notorious cemetery of Saints-Innocents to the catacombs, under cover of darkness had, thankfully, finally been completed. The Fontaine du Palmier had also delivered a much-needed fresh water supply to the nearby Place du Châtelet, thanks to Napoleon. But Sophia, Jean-Luc noted with amusement, seemed to relish rather than recoil at the sensory onslaught, her face alight with interest, her arm tucked safely into his, dragging him from one stall to the next with an eagerness that was both endearing and, disconcertingly, arousing. Though that was more likely the residual effect of their early-morning lovemaking.

They were standing at an oyster stall now, and Sophia was discussing the various grades of the shellfish knowledgably, the stall holder quite beguiled, as he offered her a selection of different oysters from Normandy and Brittany in the north, Marennes-Oléron in Aquitaine, and Arcachon near Bordeaux.

There was an unknowing voluptuousness in the way she tipped the shells back to swallow the briny molluscs, accentuating the clean line of her jaw, the length of her neck. The stall holder watched transfixed, colour tinging his swarthy cheeks. 'If she were my wife, *monsieur*, I would have no need for oysters,' he told Jean-Luc with a leering wink, as he handed over the careful selection Sophia wished to take back for the chef's delectation. And Jean-Luc, instead of being offended, permitted himself a smug smile.

They proceeded from stall to stall, with Sophia charming and sampling, the basket he had purchased for her slowly filling with cheeses, sweetmeats, savoury pies, delicate strawberries and juicy raspberries. She seemed utterly at home here among the jostling crowds, exchanging banter with the stall holders, male and female, examining the cages of rabbits and chickens with the experienced eye of a cook, rather than the sentimental one of a lady. He knew, from the dinners which she ordered for him, that she had not been teasing him about her love of food, but it was clear now, that it was a passion, and one she was indulging without restraint.

He remembered the way she had stroked the soft leather of her gloves at the theatre. The way she had luxuriated in the rich silks and damasks of the clothes they had discovered in the attic at the Montendre palace. She was a sensual creature at heart. Yet she struggled to lose herself in that most intimate of sensual experiences.

Violated. Jean-Luc swore vehemently. What kind of man had her husband been to make his wife feel so defiled! The man had not forced her, she claimed, but he struggled to understand why, if this was the case, she felt as if he had. Had his appetites been perverse? To imagine Sophia enduring—*mon Dieu*, no, he would not imagine, he could not bear it. No wonder that she wanted to forget, his beautiful wife.

His wife. Watching her dipping a crust of bread into a dish of Provençal olive oil, he decided that he liked being married. He had enjoyed introducing her to his place of business yesterday, her fascination with his trade, the unfeigned interest in every aspect of it, and her equally unfeigned admiration of his success had flattered his pride. There was a purpose to all his hard work, if it made her happy, if it kept her in comfort, a purpose that had been lacking since his parents died. He had not expected his faux-wife to have any real part in his life, but

Sophia had fitted seamlessly into it, and it made him realise that there had been a gap he'd not even been aware of. He hadn't been lonely, but he would be, when she was gone.

A bottle of olive oil was jammed precariously into the overflowing basket, and Sophia rejoined him. 'I'm having the most wonderful time.'

Jean-Luc laughed, and couldn't resist planting a kiss on her lips, which were slick with olive oil. 'You astonish me.'

'There's only one thing more we need to do, to round off this perfect morning. If you will indulge me.'

'How could I refuse. What is that you desire?'

'A cup of coffee. I'm told the best stall is over there, in the corner with the red awning, and I'm told that the best way to drink coffee at this time in the morning is with a glass of pastis.'

'True, if you have a stomach lined with iron.'

'All one requires is the stomach of a French-woman. I insist.'

'You will regret it.'

'I will if I don't sample it at least once.' She handed him her basket, smiling up at him. 'When one discovers a wonderful new experience, one is compelled to relive it. *Tu comprends?*'

There was a blush on her cheeks, and a glow in her eyes that squeezed his heart and stirred his blood. 'If you are referring to this morning, Sophia, then I both understand and heartily concur.' He tucked her hand into his arm, pulling her close. His wife. There was no need to think about the moment when she would leave. Their wild goose chase would take them weeks yet, more likely months, maybe even longer. Which should be a very worrying thought, but instead was oddly reassuring.

Sophia's evening gown for the soirée comprised white figured gauze layered over a white-satin underdress accessorised with white slippers, long, tightly fitting white gloves and a white spangled scarf. She had been afraid, she told Madeleine, that people would take her for a ghost, but as ever, her dresser was proved correct when, her *toilette* complete, Sophia stood in front of the mirror. The simplicity of the gown accentuated her figure, the neutral colour made her hair seem more golden in contrast, her lips more coral pink, and her eyes a brilliant blue.

She had always been ambiguous about her beauty, for so few cared to look beyond it. Ultimately, it had served its purpose, but she had come to think of it as a mask behind which she could hide her true nature. Tonight should be no different. She was playing Madame Bauduin, it was simply another part, but it didn't feel like it. Sophia and Madame Bauduin had somehow inextricably become the same person, and Madame Bauduin wanted her husband to admire her.

It was clear, from his expression as she joined him in their parlour half an hour before the first guests were expected, that he did.

'*Ma belle.*' He made a sweeping bow, lifting her hand to his lips. 'You look captivating. I will be the envy of every man in Paris.'

Sophia dropped a little curtsy, delighted beyond measure. 'And I shall be the envy of every woman,' she said. 'You look very dashing.' Which wasn't quite true, but she had no words to describe the way his dark, striking looks made her heart skip a beat and her pulses flutter. Like her, Jean-Luc had opted for simplicity, and it made the most of his lean, muscled figure. His tailcoat and breeches were black. His waistcoat was white satin embroidered with silver thread. 'One could be forgiven for thinking we had co-ordinated our attire,' she said, 'we are a perfect match.'

'That is because we are,' Jean-Luc agreed, 'though there is something missing from your own *toilette*, Madame Bauduin.'

He pulled a velvet box from his pocket. Sophia instinctively recoiled. 'No. Thank you, please do not be offended, but I cannot accept a gift. There is really no need.'

His smile faded to a frown. 'Actually, there is. It will be expected that I buy my wife jewellery as a wedding present, and it will be expected that you wear that present on the night of the first party we host together.'

'Of course.' Still Sophia could not bring herself to open the box. 'So it is part of my costume? I will of course return it when I leave.'

He sighed, setting the box down on the table. 'No, it's a present. Not from Monsieur Baudin to Madame Bauduin but from Jean-Luc to Sophia. And regardless of what assumptions you are making, it comes with absolutely no strings attached.'

'I wasn't making any—' But his straight look forced her to cut short the instinctive denial. 'You're right. I'm sorry. I thought—I didn't think, that's the problem.'

'I believe you, Sophia. It is clear that your marriage has tainted your view of the world, but it is very wearing to be constantly judged by another man's standards.'

Guilt made her feel quite sick. '*Mon Dieu*, Jean-Luc I am so sorry.' It was the first time he had complained, the first time he had shown her that her behaviour hurt him. How patient he had been with her. How ungrateful she must have seemed, and selfish too, so concerned about her own feelings that she hadn't considered his. Was this Hopkins's true legacy? No! A thousand times no! 'I am truly sorry,' Sophia said, 'but I owe you more than an apology. I will endeavour to judge you on your own merits from now on, I promise you.'

'Perhaps I ask too much of you, to break such an ingrained habit in such a short period of time.

We have known each other for less than three weeks. though I must admit that I feel as if it has been a great deal longer.'

'So do I.' She caught his hand between hers, pressing a kiss on his knuckles. 'I'm so sorry.'

'Stop apologising. All I ask is that you remember that I only ever have your interests at heart. I simply want to make you happy.'

It was the tenderness in his voice that touched her heart. 'At the risk of sounding pitiful, it has been some time since anyone has aspired to do that.'

'And at the risk of sounding like a domineering husband, I recommend that you choose your company more carefully in future.'

She smiled weakly. 'You are categorically not a domineering husband.'

'Then what kind am I?' His smile was teasing.

'A very caring one. But I hope by the end of tonight to have made you a proud one too,' Sophia said. 'I've never organised a party on quite this scale before.'

'It will be a triumph, Sophia. I have no doubts.'

'Thank you.' The velvet box still sat unopened on the table. If boxes could look reproachful, this one was making a good fist of it. She picked it up. 'May I?'

He shrugged, pretending to consult his watch, but she knew he was watching her. There was, however, no need to simulate her pleasure when she viewed the contents. A large oval turquoise, set with diamonds, hanging from a simple white-gold chain with earrings to match. 'It's perfect,' Sophia said, quite overcome. 'Absolutely perfect.'

'Not quite.' Jean-Luc fastened the necklace around her neck, kissing her nape. 'Nothing could match your eyes. This is the closest I could find.'

'I love it.' She slipped the earrings into place, standing on tiptoe to admire the effect in the mirror. 'You couldn't have picked anything more understatedly beautiful.' Or more of a stark contrast to the ostentatious baubles with which Hopkins had adorned her. Which came at a price, and which had been amongst the first things she had sold. And what was she doing, thinking of Hopkins at a time like this!

Sophia turned around. 'Thank you.' She reached up to kiss him, just as the doorbell rang, making her jump. 'Oh, goodness, our first guests are here already. How do I look?'

'In need of this.' He pulled her back into his arms and kissed her. 'Now,' he said with a wicked smile as he released her, 'you look absolutely perfect.'

'Monsieur and Madame le Foy, may I present to you my wife, Sophia?'

'Madame la Comtesse, may I have the honour of presenting to you my wife, Sophia?'

'Chevalier, may I have the honour…?'

'*Mademoiselle*, it would be an honour…'

For almost two hours Sophia stood by Jean-Luc's side to welcome their guests in person. Every invitation, it seemed, had been accepted, and several hundred had been issued. She knew that, because she had written them out herself. She was relieved to see not one familiar face among the throng. Jean-Luc, on the other hand, not only knew every single guests name, he had that rare knack of making them all feel as if their presence was crucial to the success of the soirée.

He was also extremely adept at whispering just enough background information into her ear as each guest approached. 'Fellow vintner, wife who has just had had their first child.' 'Widow, likes to buy wine, not so keen to pay for it.' 'Very rich, prefers quantity over quality, collects antique maps.' 'Loves cognac, her pug dog and her butler, in that order.' 'Breeds canaries, reputed to be worth her weight in gold. Given her extremely generous proportions that makes her very rich indeed. The man hovering at her side is her nephew, who hopes to inherit. The gold, not the canaries.'

Several times, Sophia had been hard put not to laugh, but Jean-Luc did not once betray himself. She was astounded by the breadth and variety of his acquaintances. As he steered her around the assembled company, she was even more impressed by his effortless charm, his ability to act as a social conduit, introducing merchants to countesses, chevaliers to wine growers.

The rooms were crowded, but a crush was avoided by using the courtyard as an overflow, which Sophia had organised to be lit with strings of lanterns. Slipping from his side to check on preparations in the kitchens, she returned to find Jean-Luc engaged in convivial conversation with a gaggle of their younger guests. If, by some twist of fate, he proved to be the Duc de Montendre, then he would, she thought, fit seamlessly into the role. For a man who had never hosted a soirée before, he was making a most excellent fist of it, effortlessly putting people at their ease.

He was a natural host. Unlike her father, who loved nothing more than the sound of his own voice, Jean-Luc was content to let others hold forth. He had no need to boast and to bluff in order to stamp his authority on a conversation.

'Your husband is a most singular man, Madame Bauduin, if you do not mind me saying so.'

Sophia turned to find herself addressed by the fabulously wealthy canary breeder who, was wearing a white confection that made her look like a galleon in full sail. 'That depends on what you consider to be the source of his singularity, Madame Rochelle,' she replied.

'Ah, a new wife who leaps to the defence of her husband. That bodes well for a long and successful marriage. I merely meant that your husband was a merchant with an aristocratic air. A man whose fortune is matched by his face. It is rare to find such a combination. I should know.'

Madame Rochelle's face creased into a smile. 'Come, Madame Bauduin, there is no need for you to look so politely blank. It is my experience that suitors find my wealth to be very slimming.'

'It is my experience that wealth is in the eye of the beholder,' Sophia said.

'Ha! That is very good, you won't mind if I appropriate it?' Madame Rochelle raised her glass. 'I think you will do very well for our Jean-Luc. We are very fond of him, you know, and of his wine.'

'I am very fond of him myself.'

'An understatement I hope, *ma belle*?' Jean-Luc slipped his arm around her waist. 'I have missed you. Have you persuaded Madame Rochelle to give us a pair of her precious canaries as a wedding present?'

Madame Rochelle tapped him on the arm with her fan. 'Two love birds in this *hôtel* is quite enough. You have done well with your English wife, Jean-Luc. I heartily approve.'

He bowed with a flourish over her outstretched hand. 'I am very grateful for your approval, for you are the very arbiter of taste, *madame*.'

Which remark elicited a trill of laughter. 'You

may not think it to look at me, but it's true,' she said to Sophia. 'It is a little secret which your husband is one of the few privy to, that I have a regular little piece in a certain monthly magazine read by almost every lady present, telling them what to buy and where to buy it. I write under a nom de plume, of course.'

'And may I ask how my husband came to be privy to such information?' Sophia asked, amused.

'Oh, I told him. I hoped that he would manage to source for me a certain wine of rare vintage, and in exchange, I would use my magazine column to advise all of Paris to buy their wine from Bauduin's.'

'I will hazard a guess that he refused the deal.'

'You are quite correct. Though he did, some months later, send me a crate of the wine as a gift. A most generous gesture from a most generous man. I envy you, Madame Bauduin, as does every female here. Now, before I embarrass Jean-Luc any further, I see that your butler is about to announce supper, and if your wonderful canapes are anything to go by, then that is a treat I will not wish to miss.'

* * *

It was very late. The last of the guests had, most reluctantly left, and Jean-Luc had dismissed the servants, telling them to leave the clearing up until the morning. Picking up a bottle of champagne and two glasses, he joined Sophia in the courtyard, where she was sitting on her favourite bench beneath the covered terrace.

'That was a triumph, thanks to you,' he said, pouring Sophia a glass of the cold sparkling wine. 'You charmed the ladies and had the gentlemen eating out of your hands. No one doubted our story, I knew they would not, the moment they set eyes on you. We will be besieged with invitations tomorrow.' He raised his glass to her, unable to resist pressing a soft kiss to her mouth. 'To Madame Bauduin. The most perfect pretend wife a man could ask for.'

She smiled back at him, raising her glass in return. 'To Monsieur Bauduin, the most perfect pretend husband.'

He sat down beside her, sliding his arm around her, quietly pleased when, after only the tiniest hesitation, she let her head rest on his shoulder. Her hair tickled his chin. He could feel the soft rise and fall of her breathing. The night was still, warm for early June, scented with the lilac which was coming into bloom on the parterre. He sipped his wine, enjoying the peace and quiet after the noisy hubbub of the party. 'It is good to have the house to ourselves again, isn't it?'

'Have a care, Jean-Luc, lest you become one of those men who is forever advocating the delights of domesticity. Thus is Paris's most confirmed bachelor fallen from grace.'

'I was never a confirmed bachelor. I simply hadn't met the right woman. Now I have, I will be happy to advocate the delights of domesticity to any man who cares to listen.'

'Our guests have left, Jean-Luc. You may cease your performance.'

He tightened his arm around her. 'It requires surprisingly little effort, don't you find?' He kissed the top of her head. 'I enjoy being your husband.'

She sat up. 'Pretend husband, Jean-Luc. There is a world of difference.' She made a face. 'Perhaps that's why it is so enjoyable.'

'Was it so very terrible, your marriage, Sophia?'

She blanched. 'Jean-Luc.' She cleared her throat, took a sip of her champagne. 'Jean-Luc, I was not...'

It was obvious she was bracing herself to deliver a revelation, and suddenly he found he didn't want to hear it. Not tonight. He shook his head, placing a fingertip over her mouth. 'No. We agreed only hours ago that comparisons are odious. I should not have brought the subject up. Forgive me.'

He could sense her ambivalence and was mightily relieved when finally she shrugged, forced a smile, set her glass down on the paving and took his hand in hers, turning his signet ring over and over, emulating of his own habit. 'Where did you get this? It looks very old.'

'My father gave it to me. I've always assumed it belonged to his father though actually...' He frowned. 'I don't believe he ever said as much. There was an inscription on it once, on the inside, but it has faded too much to make out more than a few letters.'

Sophia ran her fingers over the worn contours of the gold. 'It feels as if there was once a setting, perhaps for a stone.'

'I've never noticed.' He did as she had done, noting the odd little nodules. 'You could be right.'

He poured himself another glass of champagne. Sophia, refusing a refill, snuggled back on to his shoulder. He kissed the top of her head. 'Aren't you tired?'

'Not in the slightest.' She slid an arm across his stomach. 'Look at the stars up there. It's so peaceful, it's difficult to believe we are in the heart of Paris.'

'When I first moved here from Cognac, I couldn't sleep for the constant noise of the city. Which was just as well, since I had to work all hours to establish myself.'

'Do you still have a place of business in Cognac?'

'*Certainement.* It is where the business was founded. I would not dream of closing it. Besides, we buy most of our wine from the Bordeaux region. I visit there at least two or three times a year.'

'It was a portentous day for you then, when your parents became so poor they had to send you out to work.'

He laughed gruffly. 'I've been thinking about that. Why did Maman send me to a school they could not afford, do you think? There was a perfectly good school in Cognac.'

'Not good enough for her son, obviously.'

'She always did want the best for me. Was it as simple as that?' He drained his champagne. 'I can't help thinking there is more to it, Sophia. It is another thing I don't understand, another thing I've never questioned until now, the issue of money. Where did it come from, the money to pay for my schooling almost seven years? I don't know. My parents never worked, they didn't farm, they were not in trade. What did they live on, and why did it dry up? Again, I'm in the dark. In my younger days there was plenty. When I came home from school there was always a celebration. When I returned, there were new clothes and new books. And then there was less food. And less clothes, and no books, and then my clothes were patched and mended. And then there was no school.'

'So whatever their income was, wherever it came from, it dried up?'

'In about 1800. When I first started working,

my parents were very poor.' He set down his empty glass. 'I don't know what I'm trying to say. I don't know that any of this adds up to anything, save my ignorance, their desire, perhaps to cover up some disreputable past, but...'

'You think it is something?'

'It is not nothing,' he said wryly. 'I'm not saying that I am this Duc de Montendre's son, I am still quite sure that I am not, but am I truly the son I think I am? And if not, what does that mean? Does it even matter? I only wish that I had thought to ask some of these questions while my parents were alive, that is all. This damned de Cressy woman, if she had not come along with her silly story, I wouldn't even have thought—but now it is too late, the damage is done. I feel as if I had a picture of my life, and now it has been torn up, and I can't make the fragments fit together into anything I recognise.' He swore softly. 'That sounds ridiculous. I think I have had too much wine.'

'Is there much to be gained by discovering the truth, Jean-Luc? If your parents came to Cognac to escape some sort of scandal, don't you think it would best to let sleeping dogs lie? You might discover something that might taint your memory of them.'

He cupped her face in his hands. 'I doubt very much that there is anything sordid or scandalous in my parents' past. But if there is, I have to know, otherwise I will feel that I am living a lie.'

Living a lie. An hour later, lying wide awake in bed, Sophia realised that was exactly what she was doing, except the lines between their performance as husband and wife and the reality of their relationship as Sophia and Jean-Luc were now so blurred, she could hardly distinguish them. Tonight, when Jean-Luc had placed the turquoise necklace around her neck, she had felt certain she was turning a corner, finally putting her past completely behind her. Standing by his side, telling and retelling the story of their whirlwind romance to their guests, she had almost convinced herself that it was true. It had been so easy to cling lovingly to him, to gaze at him adoringly, to have him kiss her hand and her cheek. She wasn't aware that she was acting. She had always had to try so hard before, to pretend. With Jean-Luc, there was no pretence required.

Save that she maintained not a pretence, but a lie. A monstrous one, that with every passing day grew ever bigger. She curled her hand around the turquoise necklace which she'd been unable to bring herself to take off. A gift, for no other reason than that he wanted to please her. No man had ever bestowed such a gift on her. She had never known any man like Jean-Luc. Who had come to care for her. As she had come to care for him.

She would not be so foolish as to care too much—but how much was too much? He liked her. He trusted her. He thought he knew her. He did not want to live a lie, but she was forcing him to. He thought her married, for heaven's sake. She had to tell him. Before it was too late— though what the devil that meant, she wasn't sure. But she owed him the truth. Their marriage was well established now, she had served her purpose. If he chose to send her away, to tell everyone that her imaginary companion was desperately sick, then it would make no difference.

Sophia's hand curled more tightly around the turquoise stone. 'Please let him allow me to stay. Please let him...' *What? Forgive her? Tell her he understood?* The depths of her own folly struck her forcibly. She knew there could be no more excuses. Tomorrow, she would confess all. And most likely by tomorrow afternoon she would be on her way back to England.

Chapter Ten

'Maxime has just turned up, anxious to speak to me. It had better be important enough to warrant disturbing our breakfast.'

Sophia stood up. 'He will no doubt wish to speak to you in confidence. I will leave you to it.'

'Please sit down and finish your meal. I am happy for you to hear whatever he has to say,' Jean-Luc said firmly. He turned to the servant. 'Have Monsieur Sainte-Juste brought here, and set another place at the table.' He poured a cup of coffee and helped himself to some eggs. 'You are very quiet, Sophia, is something bothering you?'

Something was terrifying her. From dawn, she had been rehearsing her confession in various forms, none of them satisfactory. She couldn't decide whether to be relieved that Maxime's visit would force a postponement or frustrated, as the delay would only add to her anguish. 'I am just a little tired, it was a very late night,' Sophia muttered, realising that Jean-Luc was eyeing her with concern.

'And a very taxing occasion since so much was riding on the soirée being a success. So we will hear what Maxime has to say, and then you will go back to your bed, and I will have your dresser bring you a tisane, and—ah, Maxime, please join us.'

'Would you like coffee, Monsieur Sainte-Juste?' Sophia asked, 'Some breakfast, perhaps? We have eggs, and some very good cheese, and...'

'I thank you Madame Bauduin, coffee will suffice.' The lawyer made his bow, then took a seat beside Jean-Luc. Maxime took a sip of hot coffee. Jean-Luc waited patiently. The lawyer's expression was grave. Sophia's anxiety found a new focus as she watched him finish his coffee and pass his cup over for a refill. *'Merci.'* He took another sip. 'I hear that your soirée went swimmingly last night. I was sorry to miss it.'

Jean-Luc drew his friend a sceptical look. 'No, you weren't, Maxime. You hate parties. And besides, I seem to remember you had another engagement. Dinner, I think you said.'

'Yes. Dinner. With my sister, actually. And—and Mademoiselle de Cressy. The two have become very good friends.'

'Indeed?'

Jean-Luc smiled. It was his *I am waiting patiently* smile, Sophia knew, which preceded his *I'm not going to say anything until you do* ploy. The one that even she found difficult to resist.

Maxime's restraint lasted an unimpressive thirty seconds, by her count, before he spoke. 'I feel obliged to escort them, every now and then,' he said. 'My sister likes to think herself sophisticated, but she is—well, it does no harm, does it, to have a brother around to keep an eye on things?'

'Since I don't have a sister, how am I to answer that?'

Maxime drained his coffee cup for a second time. Sophia filled it for a third. The lawyer took a deep breath. 'Jean-Luc, I have to inform you that Mademoiselle de Cressy is—'

'Very pretty, and I am sure very distracting company, but I presume you did not come here to discuss Mademoiselle de Cressy.'

'You are, for once, quite mistaken. I came here to tell you that we now have incontrovertible proof that she is indeed the daughter of the Comte de Cressy. I am very sorry. I know it is not the news you were hoping to hear.'

'You are absolutely certain?'

'The agent I sent to Switzerland was very thorough, to the extent of bringing back with him one of the staff in service to the Comte and Comtesse de Cressy until Juliette was obliged to let him go, when her papa died.'

If Jean-Luc noticed Maxime's use of the familiar *Juliette*, he made no comment. Her husband's expression, Sophia thought, watching him nervously, was grim.

'So Mademoiselle de Cressy now knows that her story has been verified?' he asked.

Maxime looked affronted. 'Certainly not. I arranged for the servant to identify her without her knowing, but I must say, Jean-Luc, I think it only fair that Juliette—'

'You work for me, Maxime, not *Juliette*, as you

so fondly refer to her. I hope that the time you are spending in her company while chaperoning your sister is not clouding your judgement.'

The lawyer drew himself up. 'Jean-Luc, that was unworthy of you. I am very much aware of where my loyalties lie and my duty too. While you are in dispute with Mademoiselle de Cressy, I cannot possibly be more than a friend to her. As for Juliette, I am sure she has no thoughts save to marry you.'

'My sincere apologies.' Jean-Luc was immediately contrite. 'You did not deserve that. This news has come as a major shock.'

Which admission was a surprise to Sophia. 'But you always knew it was possible that she was telling the truth about herself.'

'I did,' he answered tersely, 'but it appears I hoped more than I realised, that she would turn out to be a fraud.'

He picked up his coffee cup only to find it empty. Sophia got up to pour him a fresh one, earning herself a grateful smile. 'It doesn't necessarily mean that the rest of it is true,' she said, placing her hand on his shoulder.

He caught her hand, pressing a kiss to her fingertips.

Maxime cleared his throat. Embarrassed, Sophia returned to her seat. The lawyer was eyeing her curiously. She had forgotten he was in the room. He was probably worrying that she was taking her role as Jean-Luc's wife too seriously. He might even be concerned that she would be difficult to dislodge when she was no longer required. He knew she was, unlike Juliette, a genuine fraud, so to speak.

'What will we do now?' she asked Jean-Luc, flustered.

'Before you reach any conclusions,' Maxime interrupted, 'I have more news to impart regarding the marriage contract.' He produced a parchment from a document bag and untied the ribbon which bound it. 'One of the signatories is, as you know, Henri Grunot. I have finally been able to gain access to the records at the Conciergerie—that is the prison on the Île de la Cité, Madame Bauduin, where the majority of those arrested were held before they were sent to the guillotine. Prior to their trial and execution they would have been in one of the many prisons scattered throughout Paris. To cut a long story short, the records confirm the story you were told at the Hôtel Montendre. Henri Grunot, occupation listed as valet to the Duc de Montendre, was convicted on the same day as his master, and both were executed that same day. The Duchesse de Montendre's summary trial was held two days later, and she went to the guillotine the following day.'

'*Mon Dieu*,' Sophia said, 'it is barbaric.' She had been in their home. She had walked through the rooms where they had lived. The clothes in the trunks must have belonged to the Duchess. This was no longer a story. It was horribly, tragically real.

'It is a piece of our history which we must be ashamed of for ever,' Maxime said, 'but we cannot deny it happened. The only thing we can do is ensure it never happens again. However…' he gave Sophia another of his thin smiles '…I did not come here to lecture you on the bloodthirsty history of France. The other witness, Jean-Luc, I have been able to trace him to Bordeaux. He is a lawyer, which is very good news for you. Even if he is not alive, his papers will be preserved. It is likely to be a family firm too. What I'm trying to say is, there's a good chance that we have a witness. Or at the very least, someone who is related to the witness.'

'At last. That is excellent work, Maxime. Thank you.'

The lawyer rolled up the marriage contract. 'You will need this, assuming that you intend to go to Bordeaux?'

'As soon as it can be arranged. Since Mademoiselle de Cressy has now been proven to be one party to that cursed marriage contract, it is absolutely imperative that I prove I am not the other.'

Maxime got to his feet. 'And do I have your permission to inform Juliette of the latest turn in events?'

'And how do you think *Juliette* will take the news?' Jean-Luc asked sardonically.

'If you're asking me if it's going to make her more determined to pursue her claim, then all I can say is that she's shown no sign whatsoever of relinquishing it.' Maxime frowned. 'I know you don't want to hear this, but from her point of view, the contract was made in good faith between her father and his closest friend. She feels she has a duty to honour it.'

'Though she might not feel so honour bound were she less poverty stricken.'

Maxime flinched. 'Perhaps not, but she is more or less destitute, Jean-Luc, her situation truly dire. As a gently bred young woman, marriage is her only option.'

'That is as may be, but I am not a viable candidate. I already have a wife.'

'Not in the eyes of the law.'

'But in the eyes of Paris and Mademoiselle de Cressy I do, and that's what matters,' Jean-Luc said firmly.

'Have you considered the possibility—Jean-Luc, what if your trip to Bordeaux proves inconclusive either way?'

'If I cannot prove that I am not the Montendre heir, nor can she prove that I am. As far as I am concerned that will be the end of the matter.'

'What if she does not accept this?'

Jean-Luc shrugged. 'Whether she accepts a settlement as a gesture of goodwill is up to her, but I repeat, her claim would not be enforceable without cast-iron proof. And as my lawyer, I would expect you to persuade her that was the case. In the meantime, I trust you will ensure that Mademoiselle de Cressy continues to honour our agreement by keeping her own counsel? Good. I have no idea how long we will be away, but I will keep you informed of any significant developments.'

He shook Maxime's hand, bidding him good morning. His polite smile faded as soon as the door closed behind him. 'Now we know why Mademoiselle de Cressy was so convincing.'

'So now you must leave Paris on a long trip which, if Maxime is correct, may not even prove to be conclusive.'

'*We* must leave Paris, I'm not going without you. As to Maxime—he is a lawyer, they are trained to be pessimists. But it is as I told him: if, after Bordeaux, we have exhausted all avenues of enquiry, Mademoiselle de Cressy will be forced to accept that no proof is proof enough. I am anxious to be rid of that woman from my life.'

'And this woman too,' Sophia said, forcing a smile.

'Ah, this woman is a very different matter.'

He pulled her into his arms. 'I am not remotely anxious to be rid of you, *ma belle.* You must know that.'

Were any words ever so bittersweet? They warmed her heart, but they terrified her too. She could not afford to let him care too much. One certain way to prevent that would be to confess to her scandalous past as she had planned, but how could she possibly do that now? He needed her by his side while his future was uncertain, and she couldn't bear the thought of being forced to continue to play his wife, when she had destroyed the trust that had blossomed between them.

Sophistry, Sophia? No, she told herself firmly. The contract she had signed with The Procurer obliged her to remain with Jean-Luc until he dismissed her. Until he could rid himself of Juliette de Cressy, he could not dismiss her. Why estrange him, make an endurance test of the time they had together by telling him the sordid truth, when she could instead be a support to him? A wife to him. Why pretend that she didn't care, when she did? Why not make the most of it, exclusive vintages for the celebration of the nuptials. It's a distraction I could well do without, but business is business.'

Though the wine business was the furthest thing on either of their minds as they finally arrived in the bustling port of Bordeaux in the late afternoon five days later. The trip south, made at speed in a private carriage, had been so very different from Sophia's prior experience of the journey, that until she stepped out of the carriage on to the Place Royale, she had not thought of that earlier, tragic procession south. Now, the beauty and symmetry of the square, the buildings extending on either side like welcoming arms as they ran down to the bank of the Garonne River, jolted her memory. Though it had only been an overnight stop, the city had made an favourable impression on her. She had never been back, for her other journeys, including that last return to England, cloaked in such grief she barely registered her surroundings, had been made via Lyon.

Standing on the cobblestones of the huge square, facing out to the wide, sedately flowing river, Sophia closed her eyes, breathing in

for heaven's sake, when it would be over so
enough?

'I don't intend to leave your side any tir
soon.' Smiling up at her husband, Sophia bur
her guilt in the corner of her heart she reserv
for such things. It was becoming a crowded sp

City of Bordeaux

As Jean-Luc had predicted, their triumph
introduction into society had resulted in a r
of invitations to the newlyweds from frie
and business colleagues, delaying their de
ture for almost two weeks. But eventually, t
quit the city, leaving the business in the ch;
of Jean-Luc's secretary and Mademoisell
Cressy seemingly happy under Maxime's (

A scheduled meeting with one of Jean-L
established customers was reorganised to
place in Bordeaux rather than Paris. 'I can'
him off,' he had informed Sophia just be
they boarded the coach, looking harassed. '
getting married, and he wants me to stocl
cellars of his new country estate from cl
pagne to cognac, as well as to supply some

the warm air, which did not quite have the distinctive sweetness of the true south, but was so very different from Paris. Despite the heat, she shivered. Fifteen—no, sixteen months since she had been here. Almost ten now, since…

'Sophia? Our hotel is just a short walk away. The streets are too narrow for the carriage.'

'Would you mind sending the bags on ahead? I'd like to get some fresh air.'

'But of course. I would like to stretch my legs too. We'll walk along the quayside, if you like.' Jean-Luc instructed the coachman, then slipped her hand into his arm.

The quays were relatively quiet, the work of the day done, the warehouses closed up, the ships at anchor creaking in the light breeze. 'A great deal of my time was spent here when I first started in the wine trade,' Jean-Luc informed her. 'Though our offices were in Cognac, all of the wine from the region was shipped from here.'

'Why didn't your employer establish his business here, then, rather than in Cognac?'

'In those days, the main trade was still brandy rather than wine. I have thought often of moving my business premises to this city, but it doesn't feel right. Though it is I who have expanded it into an international concern and given it the Bauduin name, I feel that I owe it to the old man, to keep something of his heritage, you know?'

'And Cognac is also close to your heart too, isn't it?'

'Of course, even if it turns out not to be, as I have always assumed, the place of my birth.' Jean-Luc drew them over to a wooden bench, positioned at the deserted far end of the quays with a view over the river. 'Will you tell me, Sophia, what has made you so maudlin?'

'I'm not...' Catching his eye, she bit back her instinctive denial, shaking her head.

'You know so much about me. This whole journey south, we have talked and talked of my family and the Montendre family, but never of you. I know I have no right to ask, but...'

'It's not that I don't want to tell you, Jean-Luc, it's just that I don't think I can.' Sophia stared out across the river. The tide was changing, making the boats rock rhythmically, the rigging seeming to sigh. There was the faintest tang of salt in the air. She licked her lips and realised she was crying silently. Days had gone by of late when she had not thought of her sister. Now, with the change in air, it all came back to her, and she longed, desperately, to spend one more day, one more hour with her. Ten months. How could it have been ten months?

Jean-Luc handed her a kerchief. She dabbed at her eyes. He did not press her, but there was such tenderness in his expression that something inside her shifted. This man, despite all the turmoil and uncertainty in his own life, cared about her. He understood her as no one else ever had. Not even…

'Felicity,' Sophia said. 'It was because of Felicity that I was here, on my way south. She was my sister. She was resident in the spa at Menton. She was dying of consumption.'

It was as if a dam had burst. Sophia's story tumbled out, an outpouring of tender love, raw grief and aching loss for her beloved sister that touched his heart. Jean-Luc had thought he knew her, thought he understood her, but here was a huge, significant part of her that she had kept completely secret, a wound too painful for her to reveal to anyone. Save that now, she was talking of it to him. He was honoured, but helpless. He wanted to pull her into his arms and tell her, ridiculously, that he would make it better. But he dared not touch her, lest he interrupt the flow.

'She was five years younger than me, and such a lovely, loving child,' Sophia was saying now, her big blue eyes aglow, focused on the distant past. 'When Mama died, Felicity was just turned six. My father dismissed our governess, and so it fell to me to school her while trying to school myself. Despite the fact that he purported to be an advocate for formal schooling for boys...' She blinked, turning her gaze back to Jean-Luc, curling her lip. 'One thing you could say about my father, he was consistent in his hypocrisy.'

'What kind of man was he!' he exclaimed with barely suppressed anger. 'Did he blame your younger sister too, for being the wrong sex in his eyes?'

'It was worse than that. Felicity was never strong and my father—I don't think he ever cared for her. That is a terrible thing to say, I know it is, but it is the truth, though even now, it pains me to admit it. She was often ill, you see, and she was painfully shy, consequently of little value in furthering his career.'

'His career?'

Jean-Luc watched her weigh up whether or not to elaborate. She was the daughter of someone of standing, clearly. He was beginning to wonder if he knew anything about her at all.

'He was a politician, a fairly eminent one, though never as successful as he believed he ought to be. He was too outspoken and opinionated, he alienated many potential allies. And after Mama died, when he lost the funds which had helped cover the cracks in his popularity, when he could no longer sponsor dinners and grease palms—you can imagine.'

'A bitter man with a small mind who blamed everyone but himself for his failures?'

Sophia laughed drily. 'That is him in a nutshell.' Her brittle smile faded. 'And who, when his youngest daughter's health began to fail, claimed that it was nature's way of sorting the chaff from the wheat. I disliked him heartily before that. I hated him then, though no more, I suspect, than he hated himself in the end, when even he was forced to confront his demons. He drank himself to death. After we had paid his debts, there was pretty much nothing left. That was almost four years ago, and by that time Felicity...' Her voice trembled, but when he made to take her hand, she shook her head. 'No, let me finish, if you please. If I stop now, I don't think I'll be able to carry on again.'

She twisted his handkerchief into a knot, her brows drawn fiercely together. 'She needed sunshine and heat. She knew that her lifespan would be limited, the signs of the consumption advancing and ravaging her body could not be ignored. We had heard such good things of the air on the Mediterranean, people with her condition who lived much longer than those who remained in England, so I determined to find the funds to send her to convalesce there.

'My sister—Felicity—she was so stoic, Jean-Luc, not even at the end would she admit to suffering. I don't know how she endured it, knowing that her life would be cut short. She never would admit to it, I suppose that was her secret. Always with her it was tomorrow this, and next month that, and sometimes, she was so very good at it you see, I believed her.'

'She was very brave.'

'Yes. She was very brave.'

'But it must have made it very difficult for you.'

'I didn't think of it, because she did not.' Sophia gazed down at her lap. 'It was a shock when I did lose her, more than a shock. I should have been prepared, but I wasn't. It has been ten months now, and there are still days when I wake up and I've forgotten that she is gone. Though it has helped, coming here to be with you. I have had a purpose again.'

Now she did allow him to take her hand, and to pull her head on to his shoulder. He held her, feeling her gradually relax, and together they watched the river, until finally she sat up. 'I was only here, in this city, for one day. I thought I'd forgotten, but when I stepped out of carriage this afternoon, I remembered it very clearly.'

'You found the means to send her to live in the south then?' Jean-Luc asked.

'Yes.'

Her withdrawal was almost palpable. 'And you found a way to be with her too,' he said gently, 'before the end?'

'Yes.' It seemed he did know her, after all, enough to sense her silent thanks for the change in tack. 'For six months, I stayed with her,' she added.

'And while you were with her, you improved your grasp of my language?'

'Felicity teased me at first, for she was fluent by that time, of course, having been in Menton for about two years, but it turned out that we both had an ear for it. There was a Frenchman, another resident at the spa for the same reason as Felicity, who had taught at one of our English boys' schools, and he helped. Felicity used to say that...'

Jean-Luc listened without interrupting as Sophia spoke, her eyes once again aglow with memories, her soft smile unbearably tender as she confided in him, laughing at this tale, grimacing at that, never once even hinting at whatever sacrifices she must have made, at the silent suffering she must have endured, crediting her sister with the brave heart, not for an instant imagining how much braver hers must have been, for it had to endure the aftermath.

'That is more than enough,' she said, cutting

herself short in the midst of an anecdote. 'Forgive me, I have prattled on.'

'At my request.' He kissed her gloved hand. 'Thank you, Sophia. I am honoured.'

'It is I who should thank you. I have not, as you'll have gathered, spoken of her at all. It has helped enormously.'

'Now I know why you are an excellent listener. And were, I think, a most dutiful sister.'

'I couldn't save her, Jean-Luc. I couldn't do that for her.'

'I suspect you did a great deal more than she ever knew. Two years, I think you said, she was in Menton, before you joined her for the last six months?'

'Yes.' Sophia had got to her feet, shaking out the skirts of her pelisse. 'We must have been sitting here for an age. The hotel will be thinking us lost.'

'So you didn't see her in the interim?'

'Twice I was permitted to visit for a month each year. I made it a—' She broke off, horrified. 'We really should get back before the light fails, Jean-Luc.'

'Condition,' he finished for her. 'Of your marriage, I presume?' For it all made sense now. Horrible sense. Admirable sense. Brave, sacrificial sense. 'Sophia.' Jean-Luc caught her hand between his, struggling with the wealth of emotions coursing through him. '*Ma belle*, what you did, what you sacrificed—' But seeing her face, he broke off, cursing under his breath. 'You cannot possibly be ashamed. It was a noble thing to do.'

'You think I married for Felicity's sake, don't you? But I didn't.'

'Sophia, you know there is nothing you can tell me that would make me think ill of you?'

She gazed at him for a long, painful moment. 'I believe that is what you think,' she said, finally, 'but you deserve better than me.' She turned away. 'We must get back. I have the headache. You will have to excuse me from dinner.'

Chapter Eleven

Jean-Luc had secured the most luxurious suite
in the hotel for their stay, the two bedchambers
separated by a drawing room and a small dining room. Conscious of his far-too-perceptive
gaze, Sophia drew on her vast experience of af-
fecting indifference, keeping her face blank, her
smile bland, as the housekeeper showed them
round their accommodation. She turned down
the offer of a lady's maid, closing the door of
her bedchamber firmly on Jean-Luc as soon as
they were alone. And then she stood rooted to
the spot in a maelstrom of regret and uncertainty
and guilt. She had done the one thing she had
promised herself she would not do, and spoilt
things with her impulsive confession.

In despair, Sophia tugged off her hat and cast

off her pelisse, only then noticing that a bath had been prepared, the steam rising from behind the screen. Jean-Luc must have ordered it. He knew how much she enjoyed the luxury of bathing after a day's travel. She did not deserve such an attentive, kind, thoughtful husband. He did not deserve such a lying, deceitful, ungrateful, tarnished wife. So it was just as well she was not actually his wife. Even if she wished she could be.

No! Sophia stopped in the act of unlacing her gown. 'No, no, no, no, no,' she whispered viciously, 'you must not be so stupid, so reckless.' Her fingers shaking, she continued to undress. She wasn't stupid, she was simply over-emotional. An understandable response to talking about Felicity, Jean-Luc being so understanding, the relief of finally confiding details of her personal life in him. Yes, that was it.

She wriggled out of her corset, casting her remaining undergarments on to the bed. Stepping into the deliciously hot, scented water, sinking down into the bath, she closed her eyes as the water began to soothe her tense limbs, and clear her fogged brain.

You think I married for Felicity's sake, don't you? But I didn't.

Meaning that she had not gone through with marriage to Frederick. She'd thought it obvious, but it was actually quite ambiguous.

You think I married for Felicity's sake, don't you? But I didn't.

Meaning that she *had* married, but for quite another reason. Sophia sat up, reaching for the soap. Was it wrong of her to hope that this was the interpretation Jean-Luc had put upon her words? Another lie. Though she hadn't actually lied. And she would have gone through with it for Felicity's sake if Frederick had kept his promise.

Sophia shuddered. Thank the stars he had not kept his promise! To be married to Frederick, to *still* be married to Frederick without even the comfort of knowing she was supporting Felicity, did not bear thinking about. How very different it would have been, compared to marriage to Jean-Luc. Not that she was married to Jean-Luc, she reminded herself once again as she stepped out of the bath, wrapping a large towel around herself. Though it felt like marriage. Or what marriage ought to be. Perhaps because it was not marriage!

Her husband was on the other side of that door, most likely having his customary glass of madeira before dinner. Tomorrow, she would accompany him to a lawyer's office in the next stage of their quest to find the lost Duc de Montendre. He had been adamant, on the journey down, of the impossibility of he and the Duke being one and the same, but less and less certain of who he was. It was difficult to watch him struggling to reconcile the love he knew his mother had for him, with the possibility that she had been lying to him all his life.

These last few nights Sophia had been so exhausted after each leg of the journey that she had been fit for little more than to bolt down her dinner and fall into bed. Now, on the eve of what could be a momentous day, she could not in all conscience simply abandon Jean-Luc and leave him to fret in solitude. He, who had listened to her outpouring of grief and love, regardless of his own concerns. He had comforted her. And though he had leapt to the wrong conclusion, he had understood what drove her to do it.

You cannot possibly be ashamed, he had said.

Sophia gazed at herself in the mirror. She was not ashamed of her motives. She had not lied, when she told Jean-Luc she would have done more if required. She had succeeded in what she had set out to do, and she had freed herself at the end of it. Was she ashamed? Yes, of what she had endured in the interlude, forced herself to do, but of what had compelled her to do it? 'No,' she said firmly to her reflection. 'No, not any more.'

It would make no difference to the world. She would be judged by her actions, not her motives. Let them judge! She was not returning to that world. And Jean-Luc? Sophia sat on the edge of the bed, wrapping her arms around herself. Jean-Luc was a very different matter. He was a respectable, honourable man, with an impeccable reputation and a business which prospered in no small part due to the integrity which she so admired in him. She didn't just admire him, she liked him. A great deal too much to burden him with the truth. There could be no future for her with Jean-Luc, but it was her duty to support him in whatever way necessary while he uncovered his past.

Smiling, Sophia set about dressing in fresh underclothes, selecting a muslin gown of rose-pink with three-quarter sleeves which was loose enough not to require a corset. Some times, doing one's duty was astonishingly pleasant.

Jean-Luc was in their drawing room, gazing out at the busy street in front of the hotel. Like her he had bathed and changed, exchanging his buckskin breeches and travelling coat for a pair of knitted fawn pantaloons that clung to his muscled legs, and a black tailcoat that emphasised the breadth of his shoulders. He turned as Sophia closed her bedchamber door behind her, a surprised smile lighting up his face. 'Your headache has receded?'

'I didn't have a headache.' Sophia took the madeira he poured for her, touching the rim of the delicate crystal glass to his. 'Thank you for ordering my bath.'

'Your nightly pleasure, and my nightly torture, imagining you soaping yourself in it.'

'You do not!'

He kissed her softly on the lips. 'Oh, but I do. And now you have a complexion to match your gown. You blush so very charmingly it is a delight to tease you.'

She set her glass down beside his, on a side table. 'Are you teasing me?'

'Would you prefer me to lie to spare your blushes? Or would you prefer me to tell you the truth?' He pulled her into his arms. 'Which is that I picture you lying naked, the water lapping around you,' he whispered in her ear, 'your skin flushed with the heat, your hair streaming down your back like a river of gold, and your eyes closed in bliss.'

He kissed the pulse behind her ear. His hands were resting lightly on her arms, barely touching. There was still a gap between their bodies, yet Sophia was sure she could feel heat emanating from him. Though perhaps it was from her. She reached up to touch him, smoothing her hand on his freshly shaved cheek. 'I do close my eyes,' she said, pressing a brief kiss to the corner of his mouth. 'I do find it blissful.'

Jean-Luc groaned. 'Now I think it is you who are teasing me.'

She stepped closer, twining her arms around his neck. 'Do you like it?'

He slid his hands around her waist. 'Very much.'

She closed the last few inches between them, pressing herself against him, feeling the unmistakable ridge of his arousal, for the first time in her life, pleased to discover this proof of his desire. He wanted her. She caught her breath. She wanted him. She smiled up at him, a smile she hadn't known she possessed, that let him see just how much she wanted him. She kissed him, not a fluttering kiss but a real kiss, shaping her mouth to his, touching her tongue to his, arching her body against his. A kiss which could leave him in no doubt of what she wanted. How far she had come, she thought hazily, in learning the unspoken language of kissing. How naive she had been, thinking kisses the most innocent of endearments, when they were actually the most intimate act of all.

But when she angled her mouth to deepen it still further, Jean-Luc dragged his mouth away from hers, his breathing ragged. 'Sophia, if you are still teasing me...'

'No.' She kissed him again. 'I promise you, I am entirely serious.'

'Then I should tell you, *ma belle*, that so too am I. More serious than I have ever been in my life.'

He gave her no time to ponder his meaning, but when he kissed her, it was different, though she could not have said how. She very quickly ceased to care as his kisses woke the fire in her belly and heated her blood, welcoming the building tension inside her that she now knew for her own arousal. As before, there were kisses trailing paths from her mouth, down her neck to her breasts, but now she followed his lead, pushing aside his coat, tugging his shirt free from his pantaloons, wanting to touch flesh, skin, no barrier between them.

They sank down on to the thick rug in front of the fireplace, where a huge bouquet of roses filled the hearth, kneeling face to face, kissing and touching and stroking. His coat was quickly discarded along with his waistcoat. She pulled his cravat free, burying her face in the warm skin at his throat, pressing feverish kisses that made him groan, made his breathing quicken like her own, left her in no doubt of the effect she was having on him, of how much he wanted her.

There had been no doubts with Hopkins either. He had never attempted to rein in his passion. Experience had taught her the little tricks which would bring him quickly to a conclusion. It was her only satisfaction, knowing she could play him like an instrument, make him dance to her tune.

'Sophia?' Jean-Luc's eyes were heavy-lidded, his cheeks flushed, his breathing ragged, but his expression was one of concern. 'You were miles away. Do you want me to stop?'

'No.' His asking the question encapsulated the difference, which was vast. She was his lover, not his mistress. He wanted to make love with her, not to her. 'I'm fine, I promise. Don't stop. I don't want you to stop.'

'Sophia.' Her name was a caress. He kissed her. 'Sophia,' he said again, softly, '*mon amour*, I want you so much.'

He untied the sash of her gown, then the laces at the back, easing the muslin over her shoulders, down her arms, until it pooled on the rug where they knelt. Her chemise was next, his sharp intake of breath as he gazed at her naked breasts stilling any embarrassment. Then his mouth on her nipple, his hands cupping and stroking, making her forget everything save his touch and the mounting excitement building inside her.

Fighting it, wanting to prolong the ecstasy, she tugged at his shirt, watching with another new-found pleasure as he pulled it over his head, drinking in the sleek, muscled strength of him, her hands following her eyes, relishing the contrast of the rough hair on his chest with the smoother skin of his belly. And then her lips followed her hands, adding taste to touch and to sight, as she pressed a kiss to the dip in his chest, then dared further, to lick where she had kissed, making him moan, a feral sound that set her heart racing. He wrapped his arms around her, easing her on to her back.

'You test my resolve to its limits,' he said, kissing her.

She twined her arms around him, lost in the sensation of his chest against her breasts, of his mouth clinging to hers, and now the urgent clamour inside her for release. He sensed it, helping her to wriggle free of her gown, her chemise, her pantalettes. his hand cupping the heat between her legs.

She bit back a moan. He said her name. A question. 'Yes,' she answered, wanting, desperately wanting, afraid it would stop if she thought about it. He touched her, sliding inside her so easily, so delightfully that this time she barely managed to stifle her moan. And then his mouth covered hers, his tongue sliding into her mouth and his fingers sliding between her legs, and she struggled to cling on because she didn't want it to stop, suddenly afraid that the memories of all those other encounters would pollute this one. But then he said her name again, and she opened her eyes and met his gaze, saw passion mixed with tenderness.

'Jean-Luc.'

'Sophia, *ma belle*.'

'I want you so much.'

'No more than I want you.'

And then she was lost as he kissed her again, and she kissed him back, and he stroked her to a shuddering climax, and this time she surrendered to her instincts, pressing herself against him urgently, caught up in a primal need to be part of him, to meld with him in a way that she had never before even imagined possible.

It was nothing like before. He slid inside her so easily, so carefully, each push making her muscles clench around him, and each clench making her shiver with delight. Higher, and more, his breathing harsh, his arms braced at her side, his eyes locked on hers. Time froze, and then he moved inside her, and this time Sophia couldn't bite back her guttural moan of pleasure. And then he moved again, and she moved with him, and his mouth covered hers, and he thrust higher inside her, and she wrapped her legs around his waist, and he thrust higher, and she cried out as her climax reached a second wave, lost and yet not alone, clinging to him, mouths locked, bodies conjoined, as he thrust again and again and again, each thrust a shivering delight which she never wanted to end, tightening around him, until he cried out, tearing himself away from her as he came, spilling on to her belly with a hoarse, guttural cry that echoed her own.

'I am sorry,' Jean-Luc said, dabbing at her stomach with his kerchief, 'I was not expecting to make love to my wife for the first time on the floor of a hotel-suite drawing room. Your bed-chamber is ten steps away, but it was ten steps too many. It is your own fault for being so irre-sistible.'

She threw her arms around him, burrowing her face into his chest. 'You are so lovely.'

He laughed, smoothing his hand over her hair. 'I think that is my line.'

She pressed a kiss over his heartbeat. 'I mean what you did, at the end, to take such care…'

'No man worthy of the name would do less.'

She could think of one man not worthy of the name, but he had no place here. She shook her head to banish the unwelcome intrusion on what they had just shared. 'I feel—different some-how,' she said kissing him. 'In the most delight-ful way.'

He pulled her tightly against him, rolling on to his back to take her with him. 'Different, in the most delightful way. Strangely, that is exactly how I am feeling.'

Astonishingly she could feel his shaft stirring between her legs. Even more astonishingly, So-phia felt herself stirring in response. She wriggled and he stiffened. 'Jean-Luc, how you are feeling is not at all like a man who has just been delighted.'

'Sophia, I am feeling like a man who hopes to be delighted again.'

She laughed. 'What a good thing it is then, that I am a woman who feels exactly the same way.'

'What did you order for dinner?' Sophia, dressed only in a navy-blue silk wrap embroidered with improbably large sky-blue roses, was curled up on the sofa in their drawing room.

'You said earlier you didn't want dinner.' Jean-Luc, wearing his shirt and pantaloons, sat down beside her, planting a kiss on her mouth.

'That was before I ravished you. Now I am ravenous.'

'Then it is as well that I ignored you and ordered *entrecote* bordelaise with *boulangère* potatoes, haricots verts, asparagus and peas. Does that meet with *madame*'s approval?'

'Very much. I should get dressed before it arrives.'

'Wait in here until they have served it in the dining room, then there is no need.'

'I can't eat my dinner in my dressing gown.'

'I can think of nothing more delightful. Save you eating dinner wearing nothing at all, of course, though I would starve, not being able to concentrate on the food.'

'Then perhaps it would be better if I got properly dressed. I would not want to spoil your appetite.'

'Talking of appetites, I should warn you that I plan to undress you again, straight after dinner.'

Her eyes widened. 'You do?'

'With your permission.'

She looked charmingly flustered. 'In that case, perhaps it would be best if I spared us both the effort and kept on my wrap after all.'

'I think that is a very good idea. Then I can have the pleasure of unwrapping you.'

He kissed her again, and only a sharp rap on the main door of their suite prevented him kissing her yet again. 'Dinner is served,' Jean-Luc said.

Later, much later, with both culinary and carnal appetites totally sated, they lay with their limbs tangled together in Sophia's bed. 'Are you worried about tomorrow?' she asked him, turning on to her side to face him.

He pushed himself upright against the pillows. 'My greatest concern is that the outcome is not definitive. Until Mademoiselle de Cressy came along, I had no reason to question my history, but since her arrival, I really do feel that I know nothing at all about myself, and I feel so—so stupid, for never having asked the many questions now rattling around in my head when my parents were still alive.'

'Are you starting to think the unthinkable,' Sophia asked tentatively, 'that they are not your real parents?'

'In all honesty, I don't know.' He pulled her against his chest, resting his head on the silky softness of her hair. 'Perhaps tomorrow, this lawyer will produce some incontrovertible proof that the lost Duc de Montendre and myself cannot possibly be one and the same person, and then I can get on with my life.'

'And I with mine.'

Which thought was even less palatable than speculating about what revelations lay in store for him at the lawyer's office tomorrow, Jean-

Luc discovered. 'When you first arrived in Paris, you told me that you didn't know what your plans were.'

It was a tiny movement, but he felt it all the same, a slight tensing of her body against his. 'That's true. I still have no fixed ideas as yet.'

'But you are still set on living an independent life? I thought you enjoyed being married to me as much as I enjoy being married to you. Does that not give you pause for thought about being committed to a solitary existence.'

'No, because this is not real, it's fantasy.' She freed herself from his embrace. 'We have your future to settle before I can even think about mine. That should be our focus, not indulging ourselves in fanciful conjecture.'

He laughed wryly. 'We have just indulged ourselves rather delightfully in another way. I hope you don't view that as an unwelcome distraction.'

She plucked at the sheet. 'Very far from unwelcome but a distraction we can't afford, Jean-Luc. Not at the moment.'

'As always, you are quite right. We both need a good night's sleep.' One step at a time, he thought, getting out of her bed. Time enough to worry about the future when the doubts he had about his past were resolved. Grabbing his shirt and pantaloons, he leaned over to kiss her softly on the lips. '*Bonne nuit*, Sophia. Sleep well.'

Sophia had taught herself how to fall sleep at an early age. How to lie perfectly still, empty her mind of thoughts, and to force her body to relax, from her toes to her calves, fingertips to shoulders, focusing only on this until she fell into oblivion. It almost always worked. An argument with her father, a long day spent nursing Felicity, a night spent enduring Hopkins's attentions, all could be obliterated by forced unconsciousness. There were a few exceptions. The first night with Hopkins. Her only night with Frederick. The last nights of Felicity's life and Sophia's first nights without her.

Tonight was another exception. Hardly surprising, she thought as she watched the sun rise over the Bordeaux rooftops. Jean-Luc was exceptional in almost every way. The first man she had kissed. Not the first man she had shared a bed with, but tonight, it had felt like the first time. The first time she had relied upon her instincts, and not the instructions she had been given or the lessons she had been taught. Not one person exacting his pleasure from another, but two people pleasuring each other. Uniting, to become one. Astonishingly, it really had felt as if that was what had happened. As if they were made for each other, shaped to perfectly fit each other.

It would be easy for her to tell herself it was so very different from her other experiences because those other men had cared only for themselves, but she wouldn't lie to herself. Yes, Jean-Luc was a generous, attentive and thoughtful lover. But it was because he was Jean-Luc that made their lovemaking just that. Making love.

Her heart sank like a stone, and she saw herself for a fool. A stupid, stupid fool. She loved him. She had fallen in love with her husband. Who could never, ever be her real husband, though just for a moment, she allowed herself to imagine it, the blissful idyll of their time in Paris, only with no end.

But if they were really married, then things

would be different, wouldn't they? Real marriage would require her to bend her will to his, it would mean she was no longer Sophia, but someone else's property. That's what she'd always thought. Independence, that's why she was here, wasn't it? To imagine herself as a wife, that was to go against everything she was working towards.

But she was Jean-Luc's wife, and she liked being Jean-Luc's wife, not because it wasn't a real marriage, but because it was marriage to Jean-Luc. It wouldn't change, he wouldn't change, just because they made their vows in front of the Mayor.

As if that could ever happen! He might excuse her Frederick, but Hopkins—no. Even in the most sympathetic light, her dealings with him had been wholly mercenary. The plain truth was that she had prostituted herself. The body which she had shared so freely and so pleasurably with Jean-Luc, had been for two years the instrument which sated another man's appetites, bought and paid for to do with as he saw fit. It mattered not that she had loathed every second, that every encounter was a violation. She had served him willingly. Jean-Luc would be revolted. For such a truly honourable man to marry such a dishonoured woman as she, was unthinkable.

So she had better stop wasting time contemplating it, and turn her mind to more important matters. A tap on the door preceded the maid with her hot water and morning coffee. From her sister, Sophia had learned how to live in the moment, and to make the best of what she had. What she had, she reminded herself, was a great deal more now than she could have imagined, the day The Procurer came calling. She could never be more than a temporary wife to Jean-Luc, but when this faux marriage was over, she would have the means to her independence. She would be free to live, if not free to love. She was much more fortunate than most women.

Chapter Twelve

'Monsieur and Madame Bauduin, it is indeed a pleasure. Welcome to our humble premises. Please, step into my office, make yourselves comfortable. I must say, *monsieur*, your letter was something of a bolt from the blue.'

It was immediately apparent to Sophia as she sat down in front of the desk beside Jean-Luc that the rotund, luxuriantly moustached Monsieur Fallon facing them was far too young to have been the co-signatory on the marriage contract.

And equally apparent to Jean-Luc. 'Your father is not able to join us?' he hazarded.

'That would require a miracle of Lazarus-like proportions, *monsieur*. I'm afraid my father stands before a very different jury these days. But I indulge myself in lawyerly verbosity. In a nutshell, to summarise, he is dead, sir. His case was dismissed in March of last year, so to speak, with no prospect of an appeal.'

Sophia sought Jean-Luc's hand, an instinctive gesture of comfort, knowing how disappointed he must be. He cast a fleeting smile in her direction, as if it was she and not he who needed reassuring.

'So it falls to me to discharge my late father's obligations, which I will endeavour to do both humbly and with due diligence,' Monsieur Fallon said earnestly, stroking his moustache. 'I take it you have your copy of the marriage contract with you?'

'There is more than one?' Jean-Luc produced the document, placing it on the desk.

'Three copies were made. I have one in my possession, as you see.' A second, red-ribboned scroll was produced. 'You have one which I think your letter indicated was held by the Comte de Cressy? And the third, naturally, would have been held by the Duc de Montendre.'

The lawyer busied himself with comparing the two scrolls. It did not take him long. 'As you see, both are signed by my father. The contract was drawn up in this office a year after the birth of the Duke's son, as was the Montendre tradition. Our family law firm served the Montendre family for generations, so this was not the first such contract executed here. My father often lamented the fact that it was likely to be the last, however. He was much affected by the tragic death of the Duke and Duchess.'

'Were any provisions made for the maintenance of the estates?'

Monsieur Fallon pursed his lips. 'Were the circumstances not so extraordinary, Monsieur Bauduin, I would tell you that I cannot discuss such matters. As it is—well, you will see for yourself if you visit them. The château itself still stands, but it is a shell. There was a fire, the result of looting, I am afraid to say. When it became common knowledge that the Duke and Duchess were dead—alas, so it was with many other such estates. All the family papers, every remaining portrait, all destroyed. Of course the lands are still there, and the vineyards, and many of the farms are still cultivated, but there has been no one to collect the rents since the Duke's man of business fled. I was too young myself to remember those times very clearly, but from what my father told me—not pleasant, Monsieur Bauduin, not pleasant at all. You know, I can't quite believe this is happening. When I received your letter—if only my father had been here.'

'Unfortunately he is not,' Jean-Luc said crisply. 'In fact, I would much rather circumstances had not brought me here at all—with all due respect to yourself—but as it is, you will understand my eagerness to hear if you have any information which can be of assistance.'

'As to that.' With an air of repressed excitement that gave Sophia a horrible sinking feeling, Monsieur Fallon produced a leather book and pushed it towards Jean-Luc. 'As you can see, it is a statement of account. A lump-sum deposit was entrusted to my father by the Duc de Montendre. Here you see the record of withdrawals over a number of years. And then the closing statement in...'

'1800,' Jean-Luc said. 'The year I was taken out of school.' He looked, Sophia thought, as if he had been punched in the stomach. 'But who was the recipient of these payments?'

'Ah, now that is a mystery my father never

fully resolved.' Monsieur Fallon settled himself more comfortably in his chair. 'Once a year, a fixed sum of money was to be withdrawn from the safe and transported to the church of Saint-Pierre in the little hamlet of Archiac—do you know it, Monsieur Bauduin? It is about two or three days on horseback from Bordeaux.'

'And about half a day from Cognac, where I was raised,' Jean-Luc said.

Monsieur Fallon's brows shot up. 'We always assumed that Angoulême was the money's final destination. It is the largest town, and also less than a day's ride from Archiac.'

'Forgive me, *monsieur*,' Jean-Luc said, 'but I am afraid I'm not privy to your assumptions yet.'

His clipped tone made the lawyer sit up. 'I can see this has come as a shock to you. I understand your wine business, Monsieur Bauduin, is based in Cognac? Yes, I see, it is beginning to make sense.'

'Not to me.'

'No.' Monsieur Fallon shook his head several times. 'Well, the story is quickly told, albeit the cloak-and-dagger nature of it offends my lawyerly sensibilities. The money was deposited in a leather purse, on the same day every year, in the same place, hidden behind the altar of the church. We had no idea who collected it and, as I said, my father assumed that whoever it was resided in Angoulême.'

'But I note that the amounts diminish significantly in the later years.'

'I applaud your observational skills, sir. The lump sum was sufficient for the payments to be made for five years from the initiation of the fund in 1790, with a little contingency built in. A prudent suggestion of my father's, I believe. He taught me to consider all eventualities. Advice that has stood me in good stead. In 1790 you were, Monsieur Bauduin, two years old, I think?'

Waiting only for a nod from Jean-Luc the lawyer continued. 'The Duke and Duchess died in 1794, as you know, but they were, like almost everyone else, trapped in Paris from the previous year, when The Terror began. If they tried to communicate with my father, word never reached him. As you can see, after 1794 he reduced the sum each year in an effort to eke it out, but by 1800 there was nothing left.'

'The Duke's financial arrangements are obviously fascinating, but what do you think this account has to do with my visit here and the marriage contract?'

Monsieur Fallon spread his hands. 'My father's view was that the only explanation which made sense was that the money was payment for the care of the Duke's son. The boy was being raised in the château, as all the Montendre children always were. In the autumn of 1790 the Duke and Duchess returned to Paris, to protect their palace in the turmoil of the Revolution. They let it be known that they were taking their son with him. This account was opened by the Duke before he left, as you can see. Only my father guessed the reason, and only then when he had word from a connection in Paris that the boy was not, as everyone believed, with his parents.'

'So your father surmised that the Duke had placed his son into hiding as a precaution, given that members of the aristocracy were starting to be executed? Yet when your father heard the Duke himself had fallen victim to the guillotine, he made no attempt to recover the child?'

'My father was sworn to secrecy by the Duke,

Monsieur Bauduin. He made a solemn vow never to speak of this fund, never to make any attempt to trace the recipient, under any circumstances whatsoever. It was imperative that the boy's identity remained a secret, for his own safety. That vow gave my father many sleepless nights after the Duke's death, he told me, but there was nothing to be done. This little account book seemed set to be a mystery never to be resolved.' Monsieur Fallon's eyes brightened. 'Until I received your letter. I cannot help but think from your expression, that this document means something to you.'

'It proves that the money paid for the upbringing of the Duke's son dried up at exactly the same time as my parents' finances dried up. But that is all it proves. It certainly is not evidence enough to conclude that I am the lost heir of the Duc de Montendre.'

'Not on its own, of course not. But a most persuasive case can be made when all the other circumstantial evidence is taken into account. The marriage contract. Mademoiselle de Cressy's family tale which makes a direct link between your name and the Montendre one. This little account book here, which ties in with the changes in your own youthful circumstances. And the fact that you have been able to find no trace of your birth—or more correctly I should say the birth of Jean-Luc Bauduin.' Monsieur Fallon pursed his lips. 'That is a great accumulation of evidence. You are, Monsieur Bauduin, in my legal opinion, in a very strong position to press a claim to be the rightful heir to the Montendre title. If I may say so you look much less excited than I would be, in your shoes.'

Jean-Luc got to his feet. 'That is because I am not yet certain in whose shoes I am standing. I would be very much obliged if you would keep the content of this meeting confidential, for the time being.'

'But there is so much to do if you wish to reclaim your title. The château, the Paris house…'

'A shell and a ruin,' Jean-Luc said, sardonically. 'You get ahead of yourself, *monsieur*, nothing is yet proved irrefutably.' He got to his feet, holding his hand out for Sophia. 'I need time to assimilate all you have told me. I will be in touch when I have decided what, if anything I wish to do. In the meantime, I rely on your discretion, and bid you good day.'

Jean-Luc hired a carriage to take them to the Château Montendre, which was an hour's drive south-west of Bordeaux on the Garonne River. The majestic ruin looked to have its origins in mediaeval times, judging by the huge keep, which had formed the original structure. The main building, four storeys high and now roofless, was built between two other, smaller towers whose steeply pitched roofs, perched like witches' hats, had survived the fire. Ivy covered all the south-facing façade. The carriageway and formal gardens were almost entirely overgrown, though the crumbling walls of the kitchen garden still stood on three of the four sides, small, hard fruit from the peach and apricot trees which had once been espaliered, rotting in the tall grass.

It was a melancholy place, Sophia thought as they followed the remains of a path into a cluster of outbuildings built around a courtyard. A row of broken barrels sat outside one of them. This must have been where the estate wine was produced, though on the slopes which surrounded them, the endless rows of vines looked dead. The hot, arid air of the summer afternoon was permeated by the sweet scent of decay.

Jean-Luc had said almost nothing since leaving the lawyer's office, shaking his head in answer to her anxious enquiries, lost deep in thought on the drive, a heavy frown drawing his brows together.

Standing now, shading the sun from his eyes with his hand, for he had abandoned his hat and coat in the carriage, he sighed heavily. 'Absolutely none of this is familiar. Nothing strikes a chord, not a single thing. Perhaps if the interior had not been destroyed...' He grimaced. 'But like everything else in my history, it no longer exists. I have no idea who I am, never mind who I am not.'

'You are the person you have always been.'

'I most sincerely doubt it.' Sweat trickled down his temples. He mopped it with his kerchief. 'I forget how hot it gets here. Come, let us see if we can find some shade.'

There was a stone bench on the north-facing wall of the kitchen garden. Sophia removed her pelisse, fanning her face with her bonnet. 'You think it is true, then?'

'Fallon was right. Taking all the circumstances together, it's simply too much of a coincidence. My parents are not my parents. My name is not even my name. I can't take it in. Why didn't Maman say anything? Why couldn't she have explained…?'

A pulse beat in his cheek as he fought for control, but he sat so rigidly, Sophia was afraid if she tried to touch him he would break. 'Monsieur Fallon's father was sworn to secrecy. Your parents probably were too. The Duke…' The Duke! Jean-Luc's father. She was finding it almost as impossible to believe as he.

'I know,' Jean-Luc said, with a poor attempt at a smile, as if he had read her thoughts, 'it's preposterous.

And dreadful. If she'd thought any future with Jean-Luc Bauduin, wine merchant was impossible, how much more preposterous would it be to imagine herself the wife of a duke? Sophia's stomach lurched. Not that she had imagined herself as Jean-Luc's wife, she reminded herself. In fact she'd cautioned herself against imagining just that this morning. Was it only this morning? It seemed like a lifetime ago. And if she felt that, what must Jean-Luc be feeling?

She risked taking his hand. To her relief, his fingers curled tightly around hers. 'You were only two years old. They must have loved you a great deal, Jean-Luc, to send you away for safe-keeping, as they did. It must have been an agony for them to part with you.'

'You think so? They abandoned me.'

'To a woman who loved you as her own. Perhaps she was your nurse.'

'I'll never know now. One of the many things I'll never know. I don't even have any idea what my real parents looked like. Do I resemble them?' He thumped his free hand on his thigh. 'What the hell do you think they were playing at, Sophia? What did they imagine would happen to me?'

It was an agony to see him, normally so certain and confident, now so vulnerable, and to be able to do so little to help. 'You heard what Monsieur Fallon said. The Duke left enough funds to support you for five years, with a little more besides. It was 1790, long before the Terror. He would not have imagined that he and the duchess would be trapped so long in Paris, and it would have been beyond his wildest imaginings at that point, thinking that they would be executed, else they would have escaped, don't you think?'

'I don't know.'

'Perhaps they tried to get a message to Cognac, but it didn't make it.'

'Or perhaps it did,' Jean-Luc said heavily, 'and the instructions were to keep me in the dark for ever.'

'I don't believe that.' Sophia gave his arm a shake. 'To have gone to such lengths to protect you as the Duke and Duchess did proves how much they cared. And as for your *maman*—'

'Who was not my mother,' he interjected bitterly.

'No, but she was the next best thing. She loved you. She tried to do the best she could for you, under very difficult circumstances, making sacrifices, never complaining.'

'As you did, for your sister?'

'It's not the same.'

'No. At least my—my father made some provision for me. What you did for your sister, Sophia, it was beyond admirable. I hope she appreciated it.'

'She never knew.'

Jean-Luc's brows shot up. 'She did not know you were married?'

Sophia's mind went blank for a horrible few seconds. 'Don't change the subject. What I'm trying to tell you, Jean-Luc, is that you were loved. Not by one set of parents, but by two.'

If he noticed it was she and not he who changed the subject, he made no comment. 'Now I understand why my father—my adopted father—resented me a little.'

'No doubt he too thought that situation was temporary. It must have been a terrible strain for him, when the money began to dry up. And he'd have known, don't you think, that the Duke and Duchess were executed?'

'I suppose so.'

'You said he was proud of you in the end, Jean-Luc. Don't forget that.'

'I should be grateful to him. It was he who found me work at the vintner's. As the son of a duke, I would have been permitted to drink any amount of the wine I sell, but trade in it—no!'

He nodded at the château. 'They would have been appalled.'

'Or perhaps they too would have been proud,' Sophia countered. 'Not of the way that you earned your living, but the reasons for it. You worked hard so that your parents—adoptive parents—could live comfortably, didn't you? And as I believe I have informed you on several occasions,' she added softly, 'you are the most honourable man I have ever met. I think they would be proud of you.'

He kissed her hand. 'Thank you, you are a very loyal wife, but… What is it, Sophia?'

'Juliette,' she exclaimed, horrified. 'The contract. Her claim is valid. You are legally obliged to marry her.' She clutched at her heart, which seemed to be intent on lurching out of her chest.

'No!' Jean-Luc leapt to his feet. 'Under no circumstances!'

'You gave her your word of honour that you would inform her of the outcome of our investigations.'

'There is no definitive outcome yet! There is not yet irrefutable evidence…'

'And yet your own instincts tell you otherwise.'

'No!' He swore, kicking a stone, sending it flying high into the ruined succession house where it shattered one of the few remaining panes of glass. 'There goes one of the last pieces of my heritage,' he said sardonically, but the action seemed to calm him. 'It is too soon to be making decisions about anything. I need time to become accustomed, to consider my options.'

'Of course you do.' Sophia tucked her arm into his. 'To say that today has been momentous is one of the great understatements.'

They made their way back round to the front of the château, where Jean-Luc had left the carriage in the shade of what had once been an alley of lime trees, but which was now a veritable forest. Tying the ribbons of her bonnet, Sophia wandered up the shallow flight of steps to the main door, a massive affair of oak and iron, which lay off its hinges at a crazy angle. 'There is a crest above the door,' she said over her shoulder to Jean-Luc, who was pulling on his coat. 'It's Latin, I think. *Ab Ordine Libertas.* Something about freedom?'

'From order comes freedom.' Jean-Luc said. 'I may have left school prematurely, but while I was there, I was a most attentive pupil.' He rolled his eyes. 'A monastery boarding school to learn Latin and Greek! Why the devil didn't I question that!' He held out his hand. 'Enough. If we don't leave now, we'll miss our dinner. I've ordered a seafood extravaganza for you.'

'Then let us make haste,' Sophia said, taking his hand. Her fingers encountered his heavy gold signet ring. 'Jean-Luc.'

'What is it?'

'This. You said it was given to you by your father—Monsieur Bauduin, I mean—but do you remember, we thought there had once been a stone set in it. And on the back...'

'The inscription.' He twisted the ring off, frowning down at it. 'I always assumed it was two words, a name.'

'A... R... D... N... L... B... S...' Sophia said, tracing the faint outline of the few remaining letters. 'Do you think...?'

Jean-Luc's gaze was fixed on the Montendre family motto above the door. '*Ab Ordine Libertas*. From order comes freedom.' He turned back to her, his eyes stormy. 'The irrefutable proof I was referring to. My family motto lauds freedom. That is appropriate, because I do not intend to surrender mine.'

Although Jean-Luc took dinner with her, he was present in body only throughout the lavish meal, eating little, saying less, and staring often, distractedly, at the engraving on the back of his signet ring. He excused himself immediately after, telling her rather unnecessarily that he was not fit company for her, and that he needed time to think. Though Sophia desperately wanted to help him, she understood his need to be alone. Waking in the night, she heard him pacing in the drawing room of their suite, but forced herself not to go to him, trusting that he would come to her when he was ready.

He arrived while she was finishing her breakfast the next morning, freshly shaved, only the dark shadows under his eyes testament to his sleepless night, but she was relieved to see he seemed in good spirits, that his smile was not forced when he leaned over to kiss her. 'I'm perfectly well, I promise.'

'I heard you pacing in the night. I confess, I was very tempted to join you, but I didn't think you would welcome my presence.'

'Just this once, you were right. I needed to be alone, to try to accustom myself to the situation.'

'Your world has just been turned upside down, I imagine it will take more than a day for you to accustom yourself to this particular situation, which is almost unprecedented.'

He took a cup of coffee from her, draining it in one gulp, pulling out a chair to sit down beside her. 'Yesterday was a shock, a huge shock, but it was being faced with the evidence, rather than the outcome itself. You know, because I've told you, that I've been questioning, doubting my own history—the history that I thought was mine,' he added wryly. 'None of it made sense, and now it does. I couldn't prove who I thought I was because I wasn't who I thought I was.'

'So you believe you are the Duc de Montendre?'

He laughed, shaking his head. 'That will take a great deal of getting used to. I believe that I am the lost heir. At least now I can start to uncover my history. There are people here who knew my family, some who may even remember me as a child, servants, estate workers. I called on Monsieur Fallon first thing this morning to ask him to find some of them for me to talk to, and to set my claim in motion. I've also asked him to liaise with Maxime in order to obtain a sworn statement from Mademoiselle de Cressy. Her testimony, ironically, is vital, since it establishes the link between the Bauduin and the Montendre names.'

'She will be very happy to help, I am sure.'

'Don't give me that forced smile, *ma belle*, I can see right through it.'

'She's the perfect wife for you. It was your father's dearest wish…'

'No.' He took her hand, pressing a kiss to her palm. 'Throughout all this, from the very beginning, I have been certain of one thing. I am not going to marry Juliette de Cressy. And as time has passed, I have become even more certain. Now, it is as you say, my world has been turned upside down, but even were I to be sent to live on the moon, and even if she was the only woman there, I wouldn't marry her.'

'But...'

'No.' He got to his feet. 'I have far more important matters to talk to you about. I have plans I want to share with you.'

'Ah.' Sophia stood up. 'You have a plan. That explains why you look more like yourself, Jean-Luc.' She stood on her tiptoes to kiss his cheek. 'Or should I call you...?'

'My name is Jean-Luc. I have a very long list of other names too, but I have no intentions of assuming any of them. Now, I have something to show you.'

'What?'

'Patience, Sophia. Go and get your hat.'

'I remembered last night.' They were in the courtyard which had once been the centre of the Château Montendre's wine-making business. Jean-Luc closed his eyes, trying to recall the image which had popped into his head. 'I think it is this one.'

He led the way to the largest of the buildings. The fire had not reached here, but the looters had. Empty bottles and shattered glass covered the floor. On one long wooden bench, the heavy iron lever which was used for corking the bottles was still fixed in place, a box of crumbling corks by its side. Crates, on which the Montendre name could still be read, stood stacked but empty. 'Yes, it is here,' Jean-Luc said, examining the floor, kicking the dust away to reveal the outline of a trapdoor. 'See?'

'The cellars?' Sophia asked.

'Yes. That is what I remembered. I must have escaped from my nurse. I remember running, chasing something, I think it was a cat. Anyway, it came in here, and I ran in after it and this hatch must have been open and I fell, head first down the stairs.'

Sophia gasped in horror. 'You could have been killed.'

Jean-Luc shrugged. 'I don't even have a scar.'

'Then you must have borrowed one of the cat's lives. The cellars here are probably built into rock.' Sophia looked around the bottling store, shaking her head. 'They must have produced thousands of gallons of wine here.'

'It was quite an enterprise, according to Monsieur Fallon. They didn't just grow it to stock their own cellars.'

'How odd, don't you think, that you happen to be a wine merchant? Perhaps it wasn't a co-incidence after all. I think wine must be in your blood.'

'I hadn't thought of that,' Jean-Luc said, much struck by the notion.

'So you see, you did not escape your heritage after all. In fact, by selling wine, you could say you were continuing the family business that was based here.'

He laughed. 'I don't think my father—my father the Duke, that is—would see my trade in quite such a light, but we are, as ever, thinking along the same lines.'

'Are we?'

'It will take years. The vines will have to be completely replaced, and you can see for your-self that all of this will need to be rebuilt, but I'm thinking of extending my business empire to include wine produced from my own vine-yards. What do you think?'

Sophia clasped her hands together, her eyes

shining. 'I think it's a wonderful idea. It's perfect. It is so—so perfectly you.'

Which was exactly what he'd felt when he'd had the idea in the middle of the night, but somehow her saying so made it even more perfect. He picked her up, whirling her around, making her laugh, clutching at his shoulders.

'Put me down. You're making me dizzy.'

He did as she asked, though he kept his arms around her waist. She was making him dizzy. Looking into her eyes, he felt as if his heart was being squeezed, as if the ground was once again shifting under him, as it had done yesterday. Only this time, he was not overwhelmed by uncertainty. Quite the opposite, for he saw clearly, for the first time ever, that he belonged here. And that she belonged here with him. He had fallen deeply and irrevocably in love.

'Jean-Luc?' She reached up, pushing a lock of damp hair from his brow. 'Are you feeling quite well? There is a flask of water in the carriage, shall I fetch it for you?'

Dazed, he nodded, watching her as she walked with that floating, graceful sway despite the rooted-up cobblestones and the wine-making detritus covering the courtyard. He loved her. It seemed so obvious now, explained so much. The way she had fitted so seamlessly into his life, his desire to talk to her, to consult her, to please her, to be with her. And that feeling he'd been ignoring, when they made love, of it being somehow right, a feeling of harmony that he'd never felt with any other woman. It was because he loved her.

He drank from the flask she passed him, watching as she took delicate sips after him, her lips touching the rim where his had been. Such an intimate gesture. And arousing. He dragged his eyes from her. He loved her. The need to tell her was almost irresistible. But as she recapped the flask, Jean-Luc forced himself to bite his tongue. It was too sudden. There were too many matters unresolved, not least of which was Sophia's oft-stated desire for freedom. She had not said she wouldn't ever marry again, but she had made it clear it was not one of her ambitions. And then there was the small matter of Juliette de Cressy, the bride his father, the Duc de Montendre had selected for him, though she hadn't even been born until after he died.

No! He would fulfil his duty to the Montendre name by restoring his heritage. *From Order Comes Freedom.* The *ancien régime* was over now. He was the new order. Yes, there were a good many things for him to sort out before he asked Sophia to be his duchess, but—*sacré bleu*, look at her, was there ever a more perfect duchess?

'What are you smiling at?' Sophia asked him.

He took her hand, leading her out into the courtyard. 'All this. Not just the winery, but the château, it's beautiful, isn't it?'

'Very. Are you thinking of restoring the château too?'

'I could not make wine here, and live in Paris.'

'But you love Paris.'

'I do, but I've just discovered something. You know what they say, a home is where the heart is?'

'Your heart is here?'

He pulled her into his arms and kissed her lingeringly. 'It is right now,' he said. Once again, the urge to tell her was almost too much to ignore, but there was too much at stake for him to be precipitate. So instead, he took the map which

Monsieur Fallon had miraculously obtained for him. 'Château Montendre and the estate,' he informed Sophia. 'Let's set about making some plans and then we'll have some lunch.'

'Lunch? We're in a ruined château miles from the nearest hotel.'

'I think you'll find that I have prepared for every eventuality.'

Chapter Thirteen

They ate the sumptuous picnic the hotel had assembled on his instruction in the shade of what had been, in the château's heyday, the impressive lime-tree walk. Poached eggs in aspic gleamed with little emerald jewels of parsley and chives. A fish terrine comprised of layers of trout and turbot smooth as silk, separated by spears of white asparagus. The *rémoulade* of celeriac was tart, the *rillettes* of duck rich and creamy. *Cabecous*, the little discs of goat's cheese from nearby Périgord, spread on Sophia's favourite country bread made her close her eyes in bliss, and the wine, a young red from a château just a few miles down the river, was served, to her surprise, chilled.

'That was one of the best meals I've ever had,'

she said, accepting a quartered apricot from Jean-Luc.

He laughed. 'You say that after every meal.'

'At the risk of sounding extremely unpatriotic, French food is undoubtedly the best in the world.'

'It would be extremely unpatriotic of me to disagree, but Portuguese cuisine is responsible for the world's greatest pastry—Pastéis de Nata. I always make a point of sampling some when I am in Lisbon.'

Sophia finished her apricot, and gave in to the temptation to relax, lying on her side, her head resting on her hand. 'What kind of pastry is it?'

'A custard tart.' He lay down beside her. 'But not just any custard tart. Pastéis de Nata are made with sugared pastry, rolled very thin and cut so that you can see all the little spirals on the base, like a snail's shell.'

He had removed his coat, waistcoat and cravat. His shirt was damp, clinging to his chest, the dark shadow of hair clearly visible through the white cambric. He smelt of sweat and dust and soap. A trickle of perspiration ran down Sophia's back. 'And the custard?'

'Flavoured with vanilla, cinnamon and lemon.' He trailed his fingers down her bare arm. 'Sweet.' He licked into the corner of her mouth. 'And yet tart.' His hand travelled back up her arm, brushing the side of her breast.

She shuddered. 'Jean-Luc, are you trying to seduce me with recipe ingredients?'

'Yes. Is it working?' His fingers drifted over her breast, unerringly finding her nipple, which immediately peaked in response.

'Yes.' Sophia said. 'Dear heavens, yes.'

Taking him by surprise, she pushed him on to his back, leaning over him to claim his mouth with a slow, sensual kiss. He tasted of wine and sunshine. She loved him so much. He could never be hers, she would never see this beautiful château brought back to life, but she could claim this perfect day for her own. She kissed him again, aroused by the way her kiss made his eyes darken, made his breath quicken. He might not love her as she loved him, but she could be in no doubt about the depth of his desire.

He pulled her on top of him and their kisses changed from languorous to passionate. His hands roamed down her back to cup her bottom.

She could feel him, hard between her legs, and the driving need to have him inside her made her forget all about their surroundings. She whispered his name, arching against him.

Desire took over, hot and fierce as the summer sun which dappled through the leaves as they touched and kissed, tearing impatiently at their clothes, his boots and his breeches, her shoes and her undergarments, cast heedlessly aside as their bodies strove for that most intimate connection. And then, as he lay on his back beneath her, she caught her breath, wanting, suddenly, just to touch him, curling her fingers around the sleek, thick length of him. The tension of her own arousal tightened inside her as he pulsed in response, as he watched her, as she watched him responding to her touch, taking her cue from his response, for the first time in her life relishing what she did, not thinking about what she did, wanting only to please, confident that she did.

His chest heaved. The muscles of his belly rippled. She could see, in his eyes, and in his mouth, that she was testing him, taking him to the brink of his self-control, and it was exciting, very, very exciting, but she wanted more from him. She wanted all of him. So she leaned over to kiss him on the mouth, and as she did, she slid up his body and took him inside her.

He bucked under her. The movement sent her right to the edge of her own climax. Not yet, she thought, forcing herself to slow down, to lift herself then thrust slowly, and then again, eliciting a deep groan from him as he slid his hand beneath her gown and touched her. She lost control then, in a wild, frenzied drive to completion that made her cry out in astonished delight, her own climax triggering his, his self-control better than hers as he lifted her away from him only seconds before he came.

But afterwards he pulled her tightly against him, as if he wanted to meld them together, and she burrowed her face into his chest, listening to the pounding of his heart and wishing she could stay like this for ever. *I love you*, she thought, sealing the thought with a kiss. *I love you so much.*

The silence was broken by the distinct, rhythmic, sawing sound of a cicada. She stirred, but

Jean-Luc's arms tightened around her. 'I don't want to move. Not yet.'

'Nor I.' She kissed him softly. 'Not yet.'

Scowling, Jean-Luc picked up the visiting card which the maid proffered on the tray as she arrived to clear breakfast away the next day. 'I can't believe I forgot I had arranged this meeting. You remember,' he said to Sophia, 'the customer who is getting married. He is waiting in the foyer.'

'The one who wants to buy a whole warehouse-worth of wine? You had better not keep him waiting. Business is business.' She got to her feet. 'I will leave you to it. 'I can go for a stroll, call on Monsieur Fallon if you like, and postpone our appointment with him till later?'

'There's no need. I'll have the hotel porter deliver a message to him. Why don't you stay here, meet my client? I had Maxime make arrangements for a tasting at a premises down near the docks, you'll enjoy that. I have the details in my bedchamber. You go through to the drawing room. I will have him sent up and will join you both momentarily. I just need to take a quick look through my notes. I hate to be unprepared. I'm so sorry.'

'It's absolutely fine. As you said, business is business, especially if it allows you to keep me in the manner to which I have become accustomed,' Sophia teased.

Though she had better not become too accustomed, she reminded herself firmly, wandering through to the drawing room, where she checked her appearance in the mirror. Fortunately, she had dressed for the visit to Monsieur Fallon, in a walking dress of white muslin designed to be worn with a mint-green half-pelisse. The sleeves were long, the neckline high, perfectly suitable attire for her to receive morning callers.

A polite tap and the door was opened to reveal the maid and a tall, well-dressed gentleman. A tall, well-dressed and horribly familiar gentleman.

For a terrible moment, time stood still. Sophia had the distinct impression that the ground was opening up beneath her. There was a rushing sound in her ears. The room appeared to spin before her eyes.

'Sir Richard Hopkins, Madame Bauduin,' the maid announced.

The man who had been her protector for two years stood on the threshold. 'Sophia! In the name of all that's sacred, what are you doing here?'

She stood rooted to the spot, utterly appalled, sick to the pit of her stomach. It was unmistakably him. Handsome in a swarthy way. Immaculately garbed. Suave, sophisticated and utterly vile. 'Get out,' she hissed. 'Get out right now.'

'Since when do I do as you tell me, Sophia? Don't you recollect that it was always the other way around, when you were my—'

'I was never yours.' A gust of anger coursed through her. 'You merely rented my body for a period.'

'Describe our arrangement how you will. I came to meet my vintner, not call on damaged goods.' Collecting himself, Hopkins closed the door and strode towards her. He caught her hands. 'So, you are now plying your trade in France. You look very well, at any rate. A deal better than when I last saw you.'

She snatched her hands away. 'Four weeks

after my sister died! You called not to offer your condolences, but to make me an offer you thought I could not refuse.'

'Yet you did refuse it.'

'Yes, I damn well did.' Resentment rose like bile in her throat. 'The bargain we made was complete, I no longer needed to subject myself to your ministrations.'

'I do not recall that you found me repulsive.'

He spoke in that cold, clipped tone that she remembered so well, and which she had always appeased with compliance, if necessary with feigned affection. But she no longer needed to appease him. 'Our contract required me to please you. What I actually felt about you was another matter entirely.'

He took a step towards her, then halted. 'Women of your sort, Sophia, cannot afford the luxury of feelings.'

'We can certainly not afford to show them.'

'You entered into our liaison of your own free will. You knew exactly what my terms were, I made them perfectly clear.'

'And then duly breached them out of spite.'

'What do you mean?'

'When I refused to resume our arrangement after my sister had died, no longer having a pressing need for your bribes, you blackened my name. Do no deny it, sir, it is the only explanation for the plethora of other offers of protection I then subsequently received from your friends. You promised you would not talk, and you did.'

'Not while you were mine.'

'I was never yours.'

'Sophia, come back to me. Perhaps I was hasty. I will make you a proper settlement.' Hopkins grabbed her around the waist. 'An annuity as well as a quarterly sum.'

'Let me go.'

'Sir Richard! What the devil are you doing?' Jean-Luc threw down the bundle of papers he was holding. 'Take your hands off my wife.'

'Your wife?' Hopkins drew Sophia a baffled glance then stepped hastily away, holding his hands in the air. 'Monsieur Bauduin. There has been a grave misunderstanding.'

'Get out,' Jean-Luc said, his hands curling of their own accord into fists.

But though Hopkins put some distance between himself and Sophia, he made no move to leave. 'Let us not be too hasty, Monsieur Bauduin. I swear that I had no idea this lady was your wife, otherwise—in any event I have travelled all the way from England in the expectation of placing laying before you an extremely large order...'

Jean-Luc took a step towards him. 'Get out before you need wine for your funeral rather than your nuptials.'

Sir Richard turned tail. The door slammed behind him, and Sophia's knees buckled. She sank on to a sofa.

Jean-Luc was at her side in an instant. 'Forgive me. I would never have left you alone with him for an instant if I had thought—but he always appeared to me to be a perfect gentleman. I am so very sorry.'

'It's not your fault.' She couldn't resist clinging to him for a moment, burrowing her face into his shoulder.

'But it is my fault, I should not have left you alone, though I did not imagine—*mon Dieu*, that he could think for a second that placing an order for wine entitled him to molest my wife!'

Sophia lifted her head. She freed herself from

his embrace for the last time, for he would not want to touch her after what she was about to tell him. 'Jean-Luc, it's not what you think. Sir Richard and I, we are already acquainted.'

'You know him? But that makes it even worse, why would he…?'

'I *know* him.' Something in her voice alerted him. He went very still. Her throat was dry, but she no longer felt sick, only a dull, aching sense of loss. It was over. She met his gaze without flinching. 'I was his mistress.'

He must have surely have misheard, Jean-Luc thought, but the expression on Sophia's face gave him pause. She was ashen, but there were no traces of tears, and she continued to hold his gaze. 'His mistress? I don't understand.'

'You will, in a moment. I know it is early, but I think we are both going to need a stiff drink,' she said, getting up to pour them both a cognac.

He took his, setting it down on the table by the sofa. When Sophia downed hers in one swallow, his heart sank. When she sat down opposite him, he knew that whatever she was about to tell him, he didn't want to hear.

'I convinced myself it was for the best, not to tell you the truth,' she said. 'I knew you would be appalled and disgusted, and who could blame you? I knew you would hate me, and I couldn't bear that.'

'Sophia! I could never, ever hate you. If you only knew...'

He reached for her, but she shrank away from him. 'Don't. You won't want to touch me, not after you hear what I have to say.'

She wrapped her arms around herself, obviously girding her loins. Jean-Luc reached for his cognac, bracing himself.

'When my father died,' Sophia began, 'he left us penniless. I think I told you that? And Felicity, I told you that too, didn't I, that the only way to extend her life was to send her here, to a reputable spa. I tried to persuade my father to provide the funds. He made a series of empty promises, but he never made good on any of them. His money was earmarked for more important things, such as advancing his political career. He never did believe that Felicity's life was worth preserving.'

'While it was his own which was not,' Jean-Luc said viciously.

'Well, he made a good job of destroying it in the end, and as a result he left us with almost nothing.'

'Had you no relatives who could help? Your mother's family?'

'My father estranged all of them. To be fair, Mama's sister did offer to take us in, but she lives in Yorkshire, and my sister needed a better climate, not a wetter and colder one.'

'And so you married? Or have I got that wrong? I thought you said you were Hopkin's mistress?'

'I told you I was not an innocent, and you assumed that meant I must have been married. I didn't contradict you. In fact I did try to marry. Like Juliette, I had no dowry, I had nothing to offer save my looks and my bloodline.'

'I've just realised that I still don't even know your surname,' Jean-Luc said.

'No. I have always been Simply Sophia to you.' For the first time, her voice wavered. It took a Herculean effort not to wrap his arms around her. 'My name is Lady Sophia Acton. My father was Lord Jasper Acton. He served in various positions in both the Duke of Portland's government and that of Spencer Perceval.'

'*Sacré bleu!* I knew you must be gently born, but I had no idea...'

She shrugged contemptuously. 'Being gently born, Jean-Luc, is the equivalent of being born to be useless, if one is a female. I was not exactly a prize catch. I had no dowry, and I had my sister to care for. If it were not for her I would never have considered such a marriage—but then my story would not end with my sitting here, telling you all this. I would not have met you.' She stared down at her lap, lacing and unlacing her fingers. 'I'm sorry, this is turning into a very convoluted tale.'

'Take all the time you want.' Jean-Luc poured them both another glass of cognac. He was no longer apprehensive but angry. Whatever she had done, it was clear her motives were utterly altruistic. He hated, loathed that she should have suffered, but what was the point in telling her so. All he could do was listen, and once he understood, try to make it better.

Sophia took a small sip of her brandy, but set the glass to one side, taking a deep breath. 'To cut a long story short, Frederick, my second cousin, offered for my hand. I was honest with him, I thought he'd value that. I did not pretend to return the love he claimed to have for me, but I promised to make him the best wife I could, provided he agreed to send Felicity to Menton and pay for her treatment.'

'And how did this Frederick take your candidness?'

'I thought he appreciated it,' Sophia said, with a mocking smile. 'You are thinking that was naïve of me, I can tell.'

'I suspect he would have preferred to go to the altar under the illusion that you had chosen him for the same reasons he had chosen you,' Jean-Luc said drily. 'I presume that this love he avowed for you preceded the death of your father? That the proposal he made to you was not his first?'

'That is very astute of you.'

'No, Sophia, it is very obvious. He knew he was not worthy of you. He took advantage of your circumstances. You were honest with him, but he chose to delude himself.'

She sighed. 'He deceived me too. The date

of our marriage drew nearer, and still he had not set up the trust fund for Felicity's convalescence. When I pressed him, he told me that he was concerned that when the fund was put in place I would renege on my promise to marry him. I was shocked that he'd even consider me capable of such dishonesty, but none of my protestations swayed him. He demanded tangible proof of my intentions.'

Jean-Luc set his cognac glass down, afraid it would shatter in his hand, he was gripping it so tightly. 'He wanted you to pre-empt your wedding vows as some sort of obscene test of good faith,' he said, striving to keep his tone even.

Sophia nodded.

Let her have broken the engagement, he thought. But her face told him the truth. 'You agreed.'

She nodded again. 'For Felicity's sake. I felt I had no option. And then, afterwards, he told me...'

'That there were no funds for your sister. But because he had seduced you, you would still have to go through with the marriage.'

'He didn't seduce me,' Sophia said scrupulously. 'I acceded to his request.'

'He lied to you.' The suppressed rage in his voice made her shrink. 'I am sorry, I did not mean to frighten you. I am so—it is so—I want to eradicate the whole ghastly episode, make it so that it never happened.'

'But it did, and one thing you have learned of late, Jean-Luc is that there is no escaping the past.'

'But it is done now, Sophia. Your husband is dead, no?'

'No. I never married him, you see.' She lifted her eyes from her hands, her expression defiant. 'Are you shocked?'

He laughed gruffly. 'I am surprised, though I should not be. You told me, didn't you, over dinner that first night in Paris.' He searched his memory for her words. 'Lies offered in exchange for promises, I think you said. No marriage could flourish under such conditions. I thought you spoke from experience. I thought that your marriage had been a bitter one.'

'When in fact it was simply non-existent, despite Frederick's best efforts. He begged and he cajoled and he threatened. I called his bluff. He called mine, and broadcast my deflowering to anyone who would listen.'

'*Salaud!*'

'My thoughts precisely. I had lost my one asset, and my sister's days were numbered. And then Sir Richard Hopkins came calling.'

And now Jean-Luc felt sick again, but across from him Sophia's expression almost broke his heart. Such shame mingled with defiance. He wanted to hug her. He wished he had thrown Sir Richard head first down the stairs, breaking his aristocratic neck. He didn't need to know the tawdry details, he understood her meaning completely, but he could see that she needed to confess, and he hoped that doing so would be cathartic. 'Go on.'

'He offered to act as my protector and establish me as his mistress. He knew that I had no experience, but he was willing to teach me.'

He could not disguise his revulsion. Such a dilettante, with Sophia in his clutches. His beautiful, innocent, selfless Sophia. Now, he was finally beginning to understand the enigma that she was.

'Whatever else he was,' she said, 'he was very generous, Felicity was able to live in comfort, and I was permitted to visit her once a year.'

'At a cost, I suspect,' Jean-Luc said grimly, for another piece of the puzzle had fallen into tragic place. 'There is no such thing as a free gift, no?'

'I thought so, until I met you.'

Which remark should have warmed his heart, but instead made him even more furious. Sophia was heroic, but so far her life had been a tragedy. 'So for two years you were his...' Victim, was the word which sprang to mind.

'Mistress,' Sophia said. 'His own little bird of paradise, he called me, which was apt enough, I suppose, for he kept me in a gilded cage, in the form of an apartment on Half Moon Street. He would visit me there. It suited me,' she added hastily, noting his exclamation of disgust. 'I told Felicity that I had married Frederick. The fewer people who knew that I had sold myself, the better.'

'Do not talk of yourself in that way.'

'What other way is there to describe it?' she demanded harshly. 'I could not claim that Hopkins seduced me. He paid me. I gave myself to him.'

'And every time, it felt like a violation, that is what you said. He callously took advantage not just of you, but your desperate situation.'

'I know, and I despise him for it,' Sophia said bitterly, 'but I hate him even more for breaking his promise.'

'What promise?'

'To keep his mouth shut.' Sophia jumped to her feet. 'I terminated our arrangement when I went to Menton to share Felicity's last months with her. When I returned to London, he offered to take me back into his bed. I had completely mis- judged the costs of everything associated with my sister's demise. I was in dire straits, but not that dire. I refused. He took it very badly. His punishment was to broadcast my activities and laud my accomplished technique. This gener- ated many offers of varying degrees of disgust- ingness which I rejected out of hand. And then, out of the blue, The Procurer arrived with your offer. So there you have it. The sad and sorry tale of my fall from grace.'

She picked up her cognac, draining the glass. Jean-Luc ran his fingers through his hair. The extent of her bravery, her endurance, her determination to do her best by her beloved sister could not be quantified. The treatment meted out to her, the sheer injustice of it, and her stoicism in the face of it, there was nothing and no one to compare with her. All of this he would explain to her, he would force her to see how wonderful she was, but at this moment he could think of only one thing to say.

He removed the cognac glass from her hand. He put his arms around her. 'I love you so much.'

'What did you say?'

'I love you, Sophia.'

'You can't.' She struggled free of his embrace, using the sofa to create a barrier between them.

'I know you want your freedom, I understand that. *Mon Dieu*, who could not understand that, after all you have been through. I did not mean to speak yet...'

'Please, I beg you, don't speak at all. You can't possibly love me, Jean-Luc, I'm not fit to be loved by you. Weren't you listening to me? I know what I've done. I know that it's shameful and disgusting. It *was* shameful and disgusting, but I would do it again if I had to.'

'You will never have to. Sophia, I love you.

I want to marry you, to marry you for real, I mean. I did not intend to declare myself, not until I have dismissed this claim of Mademoiselle de Cressy's but…'

'Ironically, Juliette is the perfect wife for you.'

'No. The real irony is that my pretend wife is the perfect wife for me.'

'I couldn't be less perfect, and when you reflect on it, you will see that I am right. I would bring such dishonour to your noble family name, a name you have only just reclaimed for yourself.'

'Sophia…'

'No, listen to me,' she interrupted desperately. 'You have to listen to me. You would be ruined by association with me, which is bad enough, but it is not the worst aspect of it. No matter what you think you feel for me now, it won't last. Every time we make love, you will be thinking, did she do this with him, did she do that, and I couldn't bear that, not after it has been so perfect.'

'Sophia, when you make love with me, do you think of my other lovers?'

'Of course not, but it's not the same. They were your lovers. I was Hopkins's courtesan.'

'Not any more. You are my lover.'

She flinched. 'It is over. My past will fester in your mind, eroding all that is precious between us. It will taint everything it touches. You would come to find me revolting, and then you would resent me, and eventually you would hate me. When you have had a chance to think through all I have told you, you will thank me for refusing to let me ruin your life, I know you will. Please, don't say any more, I beg you.'

'I am saying what is in my heart, Sophia.'

'Tomorrow, you will know in your heart that it was a mistake.' He made to protest, but she shook her head violently. 'Please, no more. It's bad enough that I have spoiled things between us. Regardless, I will continue to assist in whatever way I can. We will maintain the charade of our marriage until such times as you judge it appropriate for me to take my leave.'

He wanted to sweep her into his arms, to tell her over and over and over until she believed him how much he loved her, but she looked so fragile, and she was in the right of it too, in a sense. His mind was reeling. Though he was certain of his love for her, he was not at all certain he could persuade her, and he was beginning to doubt the strength of her feelings for him.

'You are right,' he said. 'We both need time to reflect.'

'Thank you. I will leave you alone with your thoughts. You will come to see that I am right.'

She turned away, shoulders slumped. The door closed behind her, and Jean-Luc picked up his notes from the floor, tearing every single page of his very lucrative wine order for Sir Richard Hopkins into tiny pieces. It did not make him feel better, but as he dropped the pieces into the grate and watched them burn, the one thing Sophia had not said struck him.

I don't love you. Those words would have put an end to his declaration once and for all, but she had not said them. The world, which had seemed so bleak, was once again a blaze of southern sunshine. If Sophia loved him, he would find a way for them to be together. All he needed was a plan.

But first he had unfinished business with a certain English aristocrat.

Chapter Fourteen

'This is where Louis VII married Eleanor of Aquitaine,' Jean-Luc informed Sophia the following morning, as they entered the huge Gothic Cathédrale Saint-André. 'More importantly, as far as I am concerned at least, it is where my parents were married.'

The cathedral had that familiar smell of ancient stone, candle wax and incense, but unlike churches in England, there was a mellow warmth to this one, a welcome sense of sanctuary and peace, an intimacy at odds with the austere, massively vaulted interior. Sophia felt some of the tension generated by yesterday's traumatic revelations and her long sleepless night, begin to ease as she walked up the huge central aisle at Jean-Luc's side. She loved him, of that she was utterly certain, and though it was her heart's desire to be by his side for ever, she loved him far too much to ruin his life by being selfish.

Did he love her? The question had tormented her throughout the long, lonely hours of darkness. It mattered not, she'd told herself time and time again, but she could not bring herself to believe the lie. If he loved her even a fraction as much as she loved him, how happy she could be. If he loved her, if he truly loved her, then surely nothing else mattered? If he loved her...

And on it went, until she returned full circle. His love would wither and die when the full price he must pay for it became apparent. He would not want to touch her. She was tainted, damaged goods, a social pariah. And from that, nothing but misery could spring. No, she could not inflict herself on him. Better to cling to the notion that he did not love her, than torment herself in the future over what might have been.

Jean-Luc would be glad that she had rejected his declaration yesterday. Though what he was actually feeling right now, she had not the remotest idea, Despite studying him covertly over breakfast and on the short stroll to the cathedral, she could not discern his mood at all. Her confession did not seem to have disgusted him. So far. As for her rejection—far from being angry or even depressed, he bore an air of suppressed excitement.

Which, when he led her to one of the side chapels, where a huge tome had been set on a table, she thought she finally understood.

'Monsieur Fallon organised this,' Jean-Luc said, pulling what Sophia surmised must be the Parish Register towards him. 'Monsieur Fallon, I am rapidly discovering, despite being both verbose and pedantic, is a man capable of pulling strings in this city. I look forward to doing a good deal more business with him.'

He rapidly flicked through the ledger until he reached the appropriate year, and then began to turn the pages more slowly, running his finger down the columns, coming to a halt at one particular entry. 'See here, Sophia.'

'"Baptism, 2 July 1788",' Sophia read. '"Nicolas Frances Henri Maximillian, Marquis de Montendre, son of Nicolas Charles Frances Claude, Duc de Montendre, Born 2 June 1788." My goodness, that is you.'

'Finally, a tangible fragment of my true history.' Smiling, Jean-Luc ran his hand over the copperplate writing. 'It doesn't change who I am, I see that now. You were right about that, I am, exactly as you said, the man I have always been. But knowing where I have come from makes a huge difference to my future.'

'I know.' She covered his hand with hers. 'I understand.'

'No.' He closed the register and turned to her. There was a light in his eyes that seemed to contradict what she was sure he was about to tell her. 'You don't understand at all, Sophia. You are thinking that you were right yesterday, when you told me that you could not be part of that future, are you not?'

'You are the Duc de Montendre.'

'I am also Jean-Luc. The man who loves you more than all the stars in the heavens.'

'You can't. It's impossible.'

'I can. And with you by my side, anything is possible.' He shook his head when she made to speak. 'I know what you think, *ma belle*, and I understand why you think it, but you're wrong. You put forward your case yesterday, let me put mine now, but not here in this sacred place. Let us go somewhere more appropriate, where we can talk freely.'

Bordeaux's public garden was a ten-minute walk away. Bordered by town houses, it was a pleasant, open space, consisting of parterres bounded by paths, and a small boating pond where two little boys were sailing their toy yachts.

They sat down together on a wooden bench in a shady, secluded spot. 'First of all,' Jean-Luc said, 'I want to assure you that I speak from the heart, but also from the head. I have thought long and hard about all the terrible things you told me yesterday, and I do not dismiss any of them lightly. But I want to try to show you that your thinking is muddled.'

'You won't ever persuade me that I'm worthy of you. I wish that I could wipe the slate clean, but I can't.'

He took her hand, his fingers twining tightly around hers. 'If we are to talk of worthiness, it is I who am not worthy of you. As for the past, we both know, in our own ways, that it cannot be undone. I hate what you have been forced to endure. If I could have spared you a second of suffering at the hands of that vile cabal of men, your father, your fiancé, and that other abomination of a man, then I would, but I cannot. We can't alter the past, Sophia but we can make a much better, brighter future together.'

Her heart was an agony of longing, but her resolve was made of sterner stuff. 'I would not make you happy, Jean-Luc. My past would haunt you.'

'No, it haunts you, not me. It is time to lay the ghosts to rest.' He let go of her hand to pull off his hat, mopping the sweat from his brow. 'You think that you will be judged for your actions. Perhaps so, by those who do not know you or those who are eager to judge others rather than themselves, but why should you care what such people think? I do not give a damn about them.'

'You do business with at least one of them.'

His lip curled. 'Not any more. I had a subsequent meeting with that man not worthy to be called a gentleman, and made it very clear that my wine will not be sullied by residing in his cellars. I have also made it clear,' he added, his hand curling into a fist, 'that he will be well advised not to mention your name or his recent encounter with you to anyone. Ever.'

'But how can you prevent him?'

'You need not concern yourself with the particulars. Content yourself with the knowledge that I have considerably more influence in high places than he. Something else which he now understands.' He unfurled his fist, flexing his fingers. '*En effet*, he is gone from your life for ever.'

Ruthless, Sophia thought, was the perfect word to describe Jean-Luc at this moment. His cool eyes, his satisfied smile, his utter assuredness. It was a side of him she had not seen before. What had he said to Hopkins? She could not imagine, but she could easily imagine Hopkins's reaction. He liked to think of himself as all-powerful. She would have liked to have witnessed that encounter. It was wrong of her, but she found this iron-fisted side of Jean-Luc more than a little alluring.

'He is not a man who reacts well to being bested,' she said, making no attempt to hide her pleasure.

Jean-Luc shrugged. 'We have wasted enough time on him. Let us concern ourselves with the future.' He gathered her hands between his again. 'Our future.'

Oh, but it was so tempting to be swayed by his certainty. When he looked at her like that, it was easy to believe that love shone in his eyes. 'We have no future,' Sophia said, the words sounding strangled as she forced herself to utter them. 'Even if you are indifferent to the gossip, the fact that I will be shunned by society, and you too by association...'

He laughed at that, shaking his head. 'You think yourself so worldly, but you are such an innocent in many ways. For a start, this is France, not England. We have been through a Revolution, Sophia. The *ancien régime* is dead.'

'You forget that you are now a member of the ruling class.'

'Yes, one who intends to create a new order. Not only do you overestimate the impact of what you view as your fall from grace, you underestimate my influence. The guests who attended our soirée adored you, Sophia. Did you not feel welcomed into the heart of Paris society?'

'Of course, but they didn't know the truth.'

He shook his head. 'And they will remain in blissful ignorance, unless you feel obliged to wear your shame like a—a badge of dishonour. Can't you see, Sophia, this is all in your head? It is time you realised you have nothing to be ashamed of.'

'Nothing!'

'Absolutely nothing. At every step in your life, you have put others first, even that domineering fool of a father of yours. Your love for your sister was pure and deep and utterly unselfish. You sacrificed yourself for her, and you did all you could to ensure that she never knew the cost.' His hands tightened around hers. 'It makes me want to weep, thinking of your suffering, but when I think of your reasons, my heart swells with pride. How can you talk of dishonouring me by becoming my wife, when it is I who would be privileged and honoured to call myself your husband?'

A lump rose in her throat. 'That is the nicest thing anyone has ever said to me.'

'It is what anyone would say, who really knew you. You are the most beautiful woman I have ever met, but your inner beauty shines even more brightly than this ravishing exterior. I love you.'

She could no longer doubt it. For a moment she allowed herself to bask in his love, but only for a moment. 'Unfortunately, it doesn't alter the facts. You are the Duc de Montendre, for goodness sake.'

'Yes, I've thought of that too. If I decided not to claim the title, I wondered, would Sophia be more likely to marry me?'

'No!'

'That is what I concluded. You see, I know you almost better than you know yourself, and you understand me too, in a way that no-one else does. You understand that I owe it to my heritage to restore the lands and to restore the livelihoods of those who lost them during the Terror.'

'You wish to make the Montendre name great again?'

He laughed. 'I'll settle for making Château Montendre wine the finest in France. I can't do any of those things until I claim the lands, and to do that, I must claim the title. I've set Monsieur Fallon on the case, and asked him to do all he can to expedite the hearing. He seems to think that by presenting me as a philanthropic duke, the courts will be sympathetic.'

'And will you like being a duke?'

'Only if you will be my duchess.'

'Juliette expects to be your duchess, Jean-Luc. In fact, she has a legal right to be.'

'I wondered how long it would take you to bring her into it.' Once again, he released her, frowning down at his hands. 'From the very first, I have been determined not to marry her. It has been the one constant, through these last tumultuous months. At first, it was because I thought she was a charlatan, but from the moment you walked into my life, I could not help comparing my faux wife with the woman who, it now turns out, was the wife my family arranged for me.'

He angled himself towards her again. 'I do not take any account of that. I am prepared to sacrifice a great deal to restore my family heritage, but I won't sacrifice my happiness. I don't love Juliette de Cressy, I love you, Sophia, and I know in my heart that I will never, ever love another woman in the same way. No matter what happens, I'm not marrying Juliette de Cressy.'

'But what about the contract? You gave her your word of honour that you would tell her the truth, and the truth is that you are the Duc de Montendre.'

'I will do as I promised. It has always sat ill with you to lie to her, I know. To be honest, it has of late sat very ill with me too. She is desperate, as you said. You see in her parallels with your own situation.'

'She has no other resources. She has been bred to make a good marriage and is equipped to do nothing else.'

'If you had not had to support your sister, would you have agreed to marry this Frederick person?'

'No, but I am more resilient than Juliette.'

'Because experience has forced you to be. It has made you the woman you are. The woman I love with all my heart, and the only woman I want to marry, which is what I intend to tell Mademoiselle de Cressy when I see her. I will tell her the unvarnished truth, that we deceived her, that we are not married, but I will make it clear I don't give a fig for her claim. It changes nothing.'

'What if she threatens legal action?'

'I will inform her that I am prepared to fight it all the way to the highest court in the land. She can then either accept a generous settlement from me made in good faith, or decline it, but I will make no offer for her hand and that is the end of the matter, *tu comprends*?'

Sophia was beginning to understand, and she was beginning to hope. In fact, she was finding it very difficult now, to rein in her hopes. Had she been nurturing her shame? She had most certainly been allowing others to judge her, or to imagine that they would. Did she care? Yes, she did, though for Jean-Luc's sake much more than herself. 'I may sympathise with Juliette's predicament, but I confess I find the prospect of you marrying her distressing,' she conceded.

His smile was tender. Her defences were crumbling rapidly. 'Which brings me to the most important point. After all you have suffered and all the sacrifices you have made, you deserve to be happy, my love. If I can make you happy then I will spend the rest of my life doing so. But if I can't, if what you want is your freedom, then I will let you go, for the same reason that I dare to hope you have been so determined to let me go, because I love you, Sophia.'

She could not restrain herself any longer. 'And I love you Jean-Luc, more than I can ever put into words.'

He caught her to him, wrapping his arms tightly around her. 'My beautiful Sophia, you will try to put it into words, yes?'

She beamed. 'I will, and there's no time like the present. I love you, Jean-Luc.'

'I know how much your freedom means to you,' he said fervently. 'I want you to share every aspect of my life, but I don't want to smother you. I want you to feel free to live as you choose.'

'What I choose is to want to live by your side. I know you would never smother me. I *know* you. I trust you.'

'I want you to accept the fee you have earned from our contract...'

'I can't take that.'

'It is yours, Sophia, you have earned it. Stash it away somewhere, use it as you see fit, but have the security of knowing it is there.'

'Thank you, that means a great deal to me.'

'It is nothing compared to what you deserve.'

He let her go, only to drop to his knee in front of her, her hand in his. 'I do not deserve you, Sophia, but I dare to ask you all the same if you will make me the happiest man on earth. Be my duchess and my wife.'

Her heart was making a very determined attempt to leap out of her breast. She thought she might burst with happiness. Was the sun shining brighter above them? It felt as if it was. 'You could not be happier than I, *mon amour.* Yes,' Sophia said, kissing his hand fervently. 'Yes, please.'

He gave a shout of joy, leaping to his feet and pulling her into his arms, and kissing her. And kissing her. And kissing her. Until they were both breathing raggedly.

'You told me once that public parks were designed expressly for the purpose of kissing, but I don't think you meant this kind of kissing,' Sophia said.

'You are quite right.' His smile was wicked. 'This kind of kissing requires some privacy.'

'Should we return to our hotel? Then, I can not only tell you how much I love you, but show you.'

He shook his head. 'An excellent plan but I think we can improve on the location.'

The light was fading when they reached Château Montendre, having postponed the drive until the worst heat of the day had subsided. Jean-Luc led her to a terrace built between the two protective arms of the towers, with a prospect overlooking the slopes of the vineyards. The tent was pitched on the old cobblestones, secured to the façade of the building. 'How on earth did you manage to organise this?' Sophia said, eyeing the billowing canvas in astonishment.

'As I said, Monsieur Fallon is a man who can pull many strings. And I am a man in love,' Jean-Luc said, pulling her to him for a long, tender kiss. 'We have to return to Paris tomorrow, but I wanted us to have this special night here first. It marks the beginning of our new life together.'

'Home is where the heart is, you said.'

'Which means that my home is wherever you are, my love. Though I hope that we can be happy here.'

Sophia looked around her in wonder. The sky

was turning from azure to indigo, the stars tiny pinpoints of light high above. The air was humid after the heat of the day, heady with the scent of the verdant green all around them. The dusky light masked the worst effects of the destructive fire, turning the overgrown gardens into a magical wilderness, giving her a breathtaking glimpse of how beautiful Château Montendre would be, restored to its former glory. 'I could be happy anywhere with you,' she said, 'but here— it feels like home, don't you think?'

'I do,' Jean-Luc said, 'but the time for thinking is over.'

He swept her up into his arms, shouldering aside the layers of gauze which formed the doorway of the tent to set her down inside. A table was set for two, silverware glinting, crystal glasses gleaming, candelabra ready to be lit. Red wine had already been decanted. Champagne was cooling on ice. An array of covered salvers were set out on a long, low table. 'You have gone to an enormous amount of effort to arrange all this. Did it ever occur to you that I might turn you down?' Sophia asked.

'I could not allow myself to imagine such a

disaster. You could have told me that you didn't love me, you see, and you never did. I clung to that and hoped. And prayed. And now my prayers have been answered. Would you like to eat now? I have ordered...'

'Jean-Luc, for once, I'm not remotely interested in food. What I'd like...' She could feel herself blushing, but she was determined to do as he bid her, and put her past behind her. 'What I'd like more than anything,' Sophia said, twining her arms around his neck, 'is for us to make love. I have promised to be your duchess, and I can't wait to be your wife, but what I want above all is to be your lover.'

She kissed him then, letting her lips and her tongue show him what was in her heart, and when he returned her kiss, the last tiny shreds of doubt disappeared. He loved her. Gazing into his eyes, she saw her love reflected there, and knew that he thought only of her. Both their pasts had been settled, laid to rest. There was now only a glittering future to look forward to. Though first, there was the small matter of the here and now to be savoured.

She kissed him again, murmuring over and

over, in the space between kisses, that she loved him, she loved him, she loved him, and her kisses were returned, tenderly, lovingly, and then ardently. There was a bed, discreetly set behind a veil of curtains at the rear of the tent. This time there was no need to rush as they shed their clothing item by item, kissing every inch of skin revealed, sinking on to the piles of soft blankets, lost in a haze of passion and love.

Jean-Luc's mouth was on her breasts, her nipples. The sweet, dragging ache of desire began building inside her as he kissed his way down her belly, then the top of her thighs, untying her garters, kissing the back of her knee, her calf, her ankle, as he removed her stockings. He set her on fire with his kisses, making her writhe and moan under him, until his mouth claimed that most intimate kiss of all, and she cried out in astonishment and delight.

Honey, she thought, as his tongue licked over her sex, her veins felt as if they were sweet with honey, fizzing like an icy cold champagne. She had never experienced such sensations, longing for surrender but desperate not to give in, for she wanted this to go on for ever. These kisses took her to a place she had never been before, where passion soared to new heights, where she floated, like a billowing cloud, until somehow, the sensation changed, deepened, and she was rushing mindlessly, desperately, towards completion.

She cried out her pleasure when her climax came, unrestrained, wanting to unleash the same passion in Jean-Luc. She tugged at his shoulders, arching herself shamelessly against him. His eyes met hers, drugged and dazed with desire. And then he thrust into her, and she was lost again, clinging, thrusting with him, in a wild, feral rhythm that was not hers or his but theirs. Harder, faster, deeper, he drove until he cried out too, and she held him fast as he spilled inside her, and finally Sophia knew what it felt like for two people to truly be as one.

Epilogue

Paris—three months later

An invitation to the soirée to be held later that evening to celebrate the nuptials of the Duc and Duchesse de Montendre was the most sought-after card in the social calendar. When Jean-Luc Bauduin had been officially declared as the long-lost heir to the Montendre duchy, the news had caused a sensation.

No one more befitting the title could have emerged, Paris raved, for not only did the former Monsieur Bauduin epitomise the looks, demeanour and stature of such a distinguished noble, he had the financial wherewithal required to restore the Montendre estates and châteaux to their former grandeur.

When it became clear that the new Duke was

very much his own man, choosing to expand his business empire rather than retire from the trade for a life of leisure, tongues wagged, but the weight of opinion was very much in the new Duke's favour. This was France, after all—unlike England, a country which had freed itself from the stifling conventions of the past. Could England boast such a fine example of a thoroughly modern duke? *Certainement pas!*

Unfortunately for the matchmakers, this perfect example of a duke was already married, but Paris agreed that no more perfect duchess could be found than the beautiful Madame Bauduin, and no couple could be more obviously in love than the Duke and his Duchess.

To be invited to attend the wedding ceremony taking place this morning would have been a coup, but it was understandable, since the Duke and Duchess had already been married in England, that they wished this second ceremony to be conducted in private.

As the much-anticipated day arrived, those fortunate enough to be in possession of the coveted invitations busied themselves with their preparations for the soirée. The Duc and Duchesse of Montendre were already renowned for their fabulous dinner parties. Madame la Duchesse's menus were so incomparable one would think she had been born a Frenchwoman. As for Monsieur le Duc's selection of wine to accompany tonight's feast—rumour had it that he had somehow managed to source a select few cases of the very last burgundy produced at his father's estate, secreted away from looters deep in the cellars of Château Montendre.

Much discussion and speculation was taking place over breakfast coffee and croissants in the various Paris *hôtels particuliers* as to whether or not the rumour was true that the happy couple would be quitting Paris for Bordeaux within the month. If so, the continued restoration of the Hôtel Montendre surely guaranteed their residence in the city for a portion of the year at least.

But all that was for the future, the ladies of Paris informed their husbands dismissively. For them, the subject of most interest right now was what the new Duchesse de Montendre's wedding gown would look like.

Sophia and Jean-Luc were due at the Mairie for the civil ceremony in half an hour, with the church service scheduled to take place an hour later. Sophia stood in front of the mirror as Madeleine put the final touches to her *toilette*. She was not nervous as such, but she was in something of a daze. So much had happened these last three months, her life had been quite utterly transformed, and she still could not quite believe it. She had laid the ghosts of her past to rest. Jean-Luc had been right about that, they had resided in her head and not his. She was no longer ashamed, but accepted what she had done, and put it behind her, embracing every day of this bright new life, and the man who loved her.

'*Magnifique,*' her dresser declared, stepping back with justified pride, for she had played a key role in the design of the gown. 'Never has there been a more beautiful duchess, *madame.*'

For once, Sophia was inclined to agree. A simple underdress of silver-grey silk which clung to her slim figure was transformed by the overdress of silver gauze and lace. The sleeves were elaborately gathered at the shoulders, then tightly fitted to the wrist where a fall of lace covered her hands. The skirt of the overdress was made of the same gauze, the hem trimmed with the same lace, the material shimmering with a myriad of tiny diamonds, like stars in the twilight sky. The décolleté was an elaborate leaf design formed of silver lace, seed pearls and larger diamonds. The largest diamond of all, a wedding present from Jean-Luc, was suspended on a delicate chain around Sophia's neck. He had urged her, when the date of the wedding was set, to dress like a duchess. His Duchess. Turning around to hug a tearful Madeleine, Sophia hoped she had done him justice, that he would be proud of her.

Jean-Luc was waiting for her in their private parlour. Dressed in his customary black, his cravat more elaborately tied, his silver waistcoat, embroidered with the Montendre coat of arms, adding a touch of ducal splendour. But he needed no badge to proclaim who he was, Sophia thought, making her curtsy. He was as he had always been, his own man, and in her view, the perfect man.

'Well? Am I fit to be your Duchess?'

'You are fit to be my Queen,' Jean-Luc said. 'How long is it since I told you that I love you?'

'At least three hours.'

'I have been remiss. That is two hours and fifty-nine minutes too long. I love you, Sophia.'

'And I love you, Jean-Luc. Even more than I did when I told you this morning after we made love.' She stood on her tiptoes to kiss his mouth. 'What's more, I think I can safely promise you that I will love you even more when we make love again tonight as man and wife.'

He groaned, pulling her carefully towards him for another, deeper kiss. 'Our wedding night.'

'Patience, or you will crush my gown. Besides, our witnesses, Juliette and Maxime will be here any minute.'

'The only couple in Paris almost as much in love as we are,' Jean-Luc said, smiling. 'Maxime told me that they are waiting only until our nuptials are formalised before they announce their own.'

'I am so happy for them. How poor Maxime must have suffered, forced to stifle his feelings for Juliette in those weeks when your true identity was unclear. What an agony he must have been in that day when you told them both that you really were the Duke.'

'Unbeknown to me, it was not only Maxime's hopes I was shattering, but Juliette's too,' Jean-Luc said ruefully. 'I'm not sure which revelation was the biggest shock to her. The fact that I was the Duke, or the fact that we were not married. My best friend thought that I was honour bound to marry the woman he was secretly in love with, and she thought she was going to have to honour the loveless contract she had come all the way to Paris to enforce, and forgo the man she had, most inconveniently, fallen in love with. When I confounded them both by announcing that, notwithstanding the two facts, I had no intention of marrying her under any circumstances, Juliette was quite unable to disguise her relief. And as for Maxime, he almost punched the air in delight. He did not fall on his knees before her, but he made his feelings clear enough. Which came as a very welcome surprise to Juliette, sparing me the need to persuade her my mind could not be changed.'

Sophia chuckled. 'And now they are to be married, and I gather from Juliette, sooner rather than later.'

'Maxime doesn't like her being in any way beholden to me. He won't accept the dowry I offered.'

'No, but we will find a way to give them a wedding present he cannot refuse. Talking of which,' Sophia said, producing a small leather box from the reticule she carried, 'I have a wedding gift for you.'

'You are the only gift I want or need.'

'My love, you have showered me with gifts, including this latest,' Sophia replied, touching the diamond at her throat. 'I wanted to give you something to remember the day by. Open it.'

She watched as he did, his eyes widening as he took out the signet ring, in which a large, finely cut emerald had been set. 'Of course it's not the original stone,' she said. 'As you surmised, that was most likely sold by Monsieur Bauduin to keep the family solvent when the trust fund began to dry up, but we know from the various tenants you've spoken to since, that it was an emerald, for several of them commented on the fact that your father was never without it, so I thought—do you like it?'

Jean-Luc turned the ring over, to find the engraving newly etched. '*Ab Ordine Libertas.* You told me you were having this cleaned, not restored. This must have cost a small fortune. I can guess where the money came from.'

'From Order Comes Freedom. Our new world order, Jean-Luc, is what's provided me with my freedom. I don't need all that money you insisted on giving me. I don't need an insurance policy or financial security. All I need is you.'

His throat worked with emotion. His eyes were alight with love as he crushed her to him and she wrapped her arms tightly around him, the pair of them quite heedless of her wedding gown. 'I love you so much, Sophia. You too are everything I need.' He kissed her softly, then let her go, holding out his arm for her. 'My most perfect, beautiful, admirable Duchess. Our wedding party, and the rest of our life, awaits.'

* * * * *

Historical Note

As you may have gathered from reading this book—if the dedication didn't give it away— I have a long-standing love affair with Paris. I spent much of the time writing this story sighing nostalgically over maps and photographs and longing to jump on a plane and travel there. *Again!*

Of course the city in which Jean-Luc and Sophia fall in love bears little resemblance to Baron Haussmann's radically transformed version of today, with its wide boulevards, parks and, perhaps most critically, modern sewage and water supplies. In 1818, Paris was, frankly, a very smelly place. But this is a romance, and when it comes to that city I'm a hopeless romantic, so I glossed over a few of the gritty realities.

If you would like to know more about Paris at the time, though, then I can recommend either Alistair Horne's *Seven Ages of Paris*, or Andrew Hussey's *Paris, the Secret History*—both of which are highly readable and guaranteed to make you want to go there to explore all the history for yourself.

Napoleon was the first to encourage those who fled France during the Revolution to return home, and they came flooding back after the Bourbon Restoration in 1814, when Louis XVIII, brother of guillotined Louis XVI, came to the throne. In case you're wondering what happened to Louis XVII, he was the Dauphin, Louis XVI's son, and uncrowned King during the two years between his father's death and his own.

Claims by purported relatives to titles were not exactly common, but they did happen. My thanks to Dr Jonathon Spangler for drawing my attention to the case of the Prince of Lambesc, who tried to establish his post-Revolution claim to property using feudal documents. He failed. In an effort to make Jean-Luc's claim less complex, I turned to two English *causes célèbres* instead. The Tichborne Claimant and the Douglas Cause. Thank you yet again to Alison Lyndsay for these. Both relied heavily on circumstantial evidence, identification of the claimant by servants, et cetera.

Would Jean-Luc have been forced to renounce Sophia in favour of Juliette had they really been married? The jury is out on that one, but it is likely either that Jean-Luc would have bought his way out of the problem, or that Juliette's countercase would have been conveniently 'lost' in the system if Jean-Luc was prepared to cough up the bribe money! Thanks to Dr Spengler again for this information.

As ever, there's a ton of other reading and history in this book—and, as ever, I'm running out of space to cover it all. If you want to know more about the Revolution and The Terror, Christopher Hibbert's *The French Revolution* is an excellent place to start. If you want to see more of the fabulous Flying Vengarovs in action, then you can read my story *The Officer's Tempta-*

tion in the fun duet I wrote with Bronwyn Scott: *Scandal at the Midsummer Ball.*

And if you want to talk books or history or, for that matter, food or sewing, or any number of other things, then please do join me on Twitter or Facebook.

LET'S TALK

Romance

For exclusive extracts, competitions
and special offers, find us online:

f facebook.com/millsandboon

◯ @millsandboonuk

✈ @millsandboon

Or get in touch on 0844 844 1351*

For all the latest titles coming soon,
visit millsandboon.co.uk/nextmonth

Want even more
ROMANCE?

Join our bookclub today!